LOVE OR DUTY

Rosie Harris

severn House

This first world edition published 2014
in Great Britain and the USA by
SEVERN HOUSE PUBLISHERS LTD of
19 Cedar Road, Sutton, Surrey, England, SM2 5DA.

Trade paperback edition first published
in Great Britain and the USA 2014 by
SEVERN HOUSE PUBLISHERS LTD.

British Library Cataloguing in Publication Data

Harris, Rosie, 1925- author.
Love or duty.
  1. Poor children–England–Liverpool–Fiction.
  2. Caregivers–Fiction. 3. Great Britain–History–
  George V, 1910-1936–Fiction.
  I. Title
  823.9'14-dc23

ISBN-13: 978-0-7278-8361-2 (cased)
ISBN-13: 978-1-84751-503-2 (trade paper)

All Severn House titles are printed on acid-free paper.

Severn House Publishers support the Forest Stewardship Council™ [FSC™],
the leading international forest certification organisation. All our titles that
are printed on FSC certified paper carry the FSC logo.

Typeset by Palimpsest Book Production Ltd.,
Falkirk, Stirlingshire, Scotland.
Printed and bound in Great Britain by
TJ International, Padstow, Cornwall.

To Roger and Jenny Harris

Acknowledgements

With many thanks to Edwin Buckhalter, Kate Lyall-Grant and the wonderful team at Severn House. Also to my agent Caroline Sheldon and to Robert Harris for continuing to maintain my Web.

One

'I can't stop to talk about it now, Mother, or I will be late and you know how Arnold hates to be kept waiting,' Penny Forshaw protested as she tilted her white straw hat to an attractive angle.

Penny was a slim and pretty young woman with neatly bobbed fair hair and light blue eyes, She was wearing a knee-length apple-green dress that emphasized her trim figure and shapely legs. As she fastened the single button of the white linen jacket she was wearing over it and pulled on her white gloves she took a satisfied look at her reflection in the full-length mirror fixed on the inside of the hall cupboard door.

'Very well, Penelope, but we must fix the date as soon as possible,' her mother went on. 'There's an awful lot involved in planning a wedding, especially one that is going to be as important as yours will be.

'As well as our own family and friends there's Arnold's family to be considered. They may want to invite some of their important contacts in shipping circles. You and Arnold will want to invite your friends from the tennis club and the Amateur Dramatic Society as well as some of your other friends too. I need to prepare a list of names as soon as possible.'

'Yes, Mother.' Penny smiled patiently, knowing how much all this meant to her mother. 'On our way back I'll try and finalize the date with Arnold so that we can tell you at lunchtime,' she promised.

If her mother had her way their wedding next year was going to be the most momentous occasion of 1925. Apart from deciding on when and possibly where it was to take place it seemed to Penny that she and her fiancé Arnold Watson were going to have very little say in any of the other arrangements.

When she'd mentioned this fact to Arnold a couple of weeks ago he had dismissed it as being of no great importance. 'Simply think of it as delegating responsibility,' he'd told her breezily. 'It's something I do all the time.'

When she'd pointed out that that was when he was at the office and dealing with business matters but their wedding was a much more personal event he'd simply dismissed the problem with a shrug.

'Well, run along then and drive carefully,' her mother said, her voice cutting through her thoughts. 'Do remember, Penelope, that you are driving your father's Humber and that it is twice the size of your little Baby Austin and far more powerful,' she reminded her.

Penny nodded but didn't answer because she knew that in the next breath her mother would remind her of how lucky she was to have an Austin Seven motor car of her very own and to have been taught to drive at her age. Instead, she picked up the keys to her father's car from the hallstand and left before her mother could once again protest about her driving it and say she should have asked his permission before doing so.

It was a lovely warm summer's day and as she gingerly edged the big Humber car out of the driveway of their large detached house in Penkett Road and into the tree-lined road she found herself squinting in the bright sunlight.

She took a quick peek at her watch and was alarmed to see that it was almost twenty minutes past twelve. The *Royal Daffodil* ferry boat bringing Arnold across to Wallasey from his office in Liverpool's Old Hall Street, was due to dock at Seacombe Ferry promptly at twelve thirty. Arnold hated to be kept waiting even for a few minutes. Well now he would probably have to wait for much longer than that, she thought worriedly as she turned into Manor Road and joined the busy Saturday morning traffic.

As she reached King Street, the main road that would take her to Seacombe Ferry, she saw there was a hold-up. Cars and trams were all stationary while a stocky young man unloaded churns of milk from a horse-drawn float outside Webster's Dairy.

Biting her lip in frustration Penny decided to turn left down one of the side streets that led down to the Mersey. Going that way it might take her a little longer to reach the ferry but there would be far less traffic than there was in King Street so she would be able to put her foot down and make up for lost time.

As she drove along the promenade road, which ran parallel with the River Mersey, she could see the *Royal Daffodil* ferry boat was already churning its way through the grey water and would be pulling up at the landing stage at Seacombe at any minute.

Long before she reached there passengers began disembarking from the boat and making their way up the floating roadway. As well as office workers who had finished work early because it was a Saturday there were day trippers, eager to enjoy the summer sunshine. Some were boarding the waiting trams while others were walking along the promenade towards Egremont and New Brighton.

Suddenly Penny was aware of a ball bouncing across the road in front of her and almost hitting the windscreen of the Humber. Her heart raced as she applied the footbrake and simultaneously pulled on the handbrake in an effort to stop quickly. The next moment she felt a slight bump followed by a piercing scream that made her heart pound. Someone must have run out into the road after the ball, she thought in horror. Surely she hadn't hit them.

As she breathed in deeply trying to quell the upsurge of panic that was making her feel nauseous she saw people were beginning to cluster around a small figure lying prone on the ground directly in front of her car and howling with pain.

By the time she had opened the car door and stepped out she found herself facing a crowd of irate day trippers. Several of them began shouting at her and accusing her of driving too fast and not looking where she was going; others were saying that women shouldn't be allowed to drive.

A man who was bending over the child looked up and said that she was badly injured and needed to go to hospital. Penny felt numb as the crowd hassled her. She didn't know what to do; she had never felt so helpless or so scared in her life. Someone pointed towards the newly installed red telephone box and told her to use it to call an ambulance. While she fumbled in her handbag to find some coins so that she could do so, others called out instructions about how to use the newfangled invention.

Penny was relieved when a uniformed policeman arrived on the scene and things immediately became calmer as he took control.

In a complete daze and full of remorse about what had happened Penny did her best to answer all the questions the policeman fired at her. She couldn't take her eyes away from the tiny scrawny figure with matted jet-black hair lying on the ground in front of her car and still screaming with pain.

When the ambulance arrived the child was gently lifted on to a stretcher and covered over with a blanket. Penny turned up the collar of her linen jacket to try and control her own shivering as the child was then put into the ambulance.

As the attendant slammed shut the ambulance doors ready to leave she managed to move forward and grab at his arm. 'Do you know the name of the little girl you're taking to hospital?'

'No!' He shook her hand away. 'Ask the policeman he'll probably be able to tell you.'

'Can you tell me the little girl's name?' Penny asked, turning back to the policeman who had been interrogating her.

'Yes, miss. The child's name is Kelly Murphy and she's six years old and –' he paused and flicked back a page in his notebook – 'I'm told she lives with her mother Ellen Murphy in Cannon Court which is off Scotland Road in Liverpool.'

'Is there no one here with her, she's so small to be so far from home all on her own.'

'She was on a day out with a party of older kids as far as I can understand.'

'Have any of them gone to the hospital with her? Has her mother been told about what has happened?' Penny asked worriedly.

The policeman frowned and then snapped shut his notebook. 'It's all in hand, miss,' he told her stolidly.

'Yes, of course. Such a terrible thing to happen; she must have darted out after the ball . . .' Penny's voice trailed off guiltily as she saw the impassive look on his face.

'Can I go now,' she asked quickly. 'I was supposed to be meeting my fiancé, Arnold Watson, at Seacombe Ferry terminal at half past twelve and he hates to be kept waiting so he will be wondering where I am. You have my name and address so you can contact me if you need any more information.'

'It's not as simple as that, miss,' the policeman told her, reopening his notebook, licking the stub of his pencil and then recording what she had said.

'By rights I have to take you straight to the Police HQ in

Manor Road so that you can make a full statement about what happened and sign it.'

'Oh dear!' Penny looked crestfallen. 'Do you have to do that? Can't I go there after I've collected Mr Watson from Seacombe?'

The officer shook his head. 'I really ought to take you along there myself, miss.' He hesitated as he looked at his notes and read her details again.

'I see you live in Penkett Road, so is Captain Marcus Forshaw your father, miss?' he asked deferentially.

'Yes, that's right. He's a magistrate as I'm sure you know,' Penny affirmed.

'Well, in that case, if you report to the duty sergeant at Manor Road just as soon as you have picked up Mr Watson, I suppose it will be all right,' he agreed reluctantly.

'Yes, of course I'll do that,' Penny promised.

As she made to get back into the driving seat of the Humber, several bystanders who had witnessed what had happened pushed forward angrily as if to try and stop her leaving but the policeman waved them back.

Arnold Watson looking very much the successful young businessman in his well-tailored dark grey suit, pristine white shirt and grey and black striped tie was impatiently striding up and down outside the terminal. As Penny pulled up alongside him he made a point of consulting his gold pocket watch with a deep frown on his handsome face.

The moment he had seated himself in the car Penny explained to him about the accident and everything that had happened since. Doing so brought everything back and all her fears about how badly the child may have been injured flooded her mind. Within seconds she burst into tears.

'Oh, Arnold, it was terrible; you should have seen the poor little mite lying there in the road screaming with pain. She looked all twisted and no one seemed to know how badly hurt she was. I was so frightened because the crowd that gathered were so hostile,' she added choking back the deep sobs that seemed to shake her from head to toe.

'Well, it's all over now,' he told her briskly as he patted her on the shoulder.

'Do you really think so?' She gave him a pleading look, her blue eyes still awash with tears. More than anything she wanted him to take her in his arms and comfort her but she knew that wasn't Arnold's style; not in a public place where everyone could see what was happening.

'A couple of weeks in hospital and she'll probably be quite all right and home again chasing round the back streets of Liverpool as if nothing had ever happened to her,' he commented brusquely.

Penny bit down on her lower lip. 'I do hope you're right.'

'Come on, we'd better make a move; your parents are expecting us for lunch and we're late already,' he said crisply. Once again he took out his pocket watch and frowned when he saw the time.

'Oh dear! I've been told to report to Manor Road police station on my way home in order to sign a statement. I promised the policeman that I would do it the minute I'd picked you up so we'd better stop there on the way and do that. It should only take a few minutes; I gave the policeman all the relevant details,' she added with a watery smile.

'If the accident was that serious and they think you are in some way to blame for what happened then should you be driving?' Arnold said, frowning.

'If I don't then how are we going to get home?' Penny questioned. 'We could take a tram I suppose,' she added hesitantly, 'but I can't simply abandon the Humber; father would be furious if I left it here.'

'Then you'd better let me drive. Furthermore we'd better go back to your home first and explain the situation to your father before you go to Manor Road police station,' he told her decisively.

'Do you really think so? I was hoping not to say anything about the accident when we got home; well, at least not yet, not until I know how seriously hurt the little girl is.'

Arnold shrugged. 'We're wasting time, Penny. You'd better move over into the passenger seat and let me take the wheel,' he said firmly.

'I'm not sure if I should let you drive,' she protested hesitantly. 'You've never driven this car before.'

'Don't be so naive, Penny. If you are caught behind the wheel after such a serious accident they could charge you with dangerous driving and you might be detained for hours or even arrested.'

'I don't think you can be right about that, Arnold,' Penny protested.

'Oh yes I am, which is why we are going straight back to your place before you go to Manor Road police station.'

'But I promised . . .' She wanted to argue with him and reminded him that the policeman had seen her get in the car and he had not said she couldn't drive. Yet Arnold was usually so right in these matters that she said nothing.

'The best thing you can do is to explain the whole situation to your father before you do anything else,' Arnold insisted. 'Remember it is his car that was involved and since he is a magistrate he won't want that fact to be divulged to the local newspapers, now will he.'

'Oh dear, I hadn't thought of that!'

'If you talk to him first it will give him the opportunity of finding a solicitor to represent you before you are charged. He might also want to have a word with the chief constable; after all, they are old friends and in the same lodge.'

They drove in silence, Arnold concentrating all his attention on the road. Several times Penny started to say something but she noticed the way Arnold's shoulders immediately tightened when she began to speak, so she remained silent.

'The whole thing gets worse by the minute,' Penny murmured, her voice quivering as they pulled into the driveway at Penkett Road. 'I really don't know how I am going to tell my parents about what's happened. They will be so upset.'

'Yes, I'm sure they will be,' Arnold agreed grimly. 'This is only the start of it all,' he muttered as he turned to face her. 'My own parents aren't going to be any too pleased by all the adverse publicity your accident will engender.'

'The accident wasn't my fault, Arnold, truly it wasn't,' Penny defended unhappily, her face clouded by misery.

'Then whose fault was it? You were the one driving the car!'

'Yes, I know, but I was momentarily distracted by the ball. The little girl must have dashed out into the road after it and she was such a tiny little thing I simply didn't see her.'

Arnold shook his head as if he didn't accept her explanation.

'Anyway, what on earth were you doing driving your father's Humber? Why weren't you in your own car?'

'I had a flat tyre,' Penny told him. 'I know how you hate to be kept waiting, so I asked if I could borrow the Humber.'

She stretched out her hand to take Arnold's but he completely ignored it. At that moment more than anything she needed him to take her in his arms and tell her that he understood and assure her that given time everything would be all right.

She waited in vain; Arnold remained stern-faced and elusive. It was almost as if he didn't want anything to do with what had happened.

With an exasperated sigh he reached for the briefcase that he'd tossed on to the back seat and then opened the car door and walked towards the house leaving Penny to follow.

Two

'Where the devil have you two been until now?' Captain Forshaw demanded gruffly, his thick bushy eyebrows drawn together in a frown, as Penny and Arnold walked into the dining room.

'It's really too bad of you to keep us waiting like this, Penny. You know we always like to start our lunch promptly at one o'clock and it's now almost gone two; our meal is probably spoiled,' Leonora Forshaw added in a petulant voice.

'I'm sorry we're late, Mother, but it was quite unavoidable,' Penny told her as she bent to kiss her mother's rouged cheek.

'Unavoidable? What do you mean? Was the boat delayed or something?' Leonora asked tetchily as she patted her marcelled hair to make sure that Penny hadn't ruffled it.

'No, nothing like that; I was involved in . . . in a sort of accident,' Penny explained tentatively.

'You had a prang!' Captain Forshaw exploded, the colour deepening in his florid face. 'I hope my Humber's not damaged in any way.'

'Oh dear . . . I . . . I don't really know. I didn't check it,' Penny stuttered, looking helplessly towards Arnold who avoided her eyes and merely shrugged his shoulders in a non-committal way.

Muttering to himself, Marcus Forshaw put down the glass of sherry he'd been drinking and headed for the door.

'Not now, please, Marcus. Lunch is late enough as it is. Surely you can leave it until later to see if there are any marks or dents on your precious car,' his wife pleaded.

Marcus Forshaw hesitated then, scowling, he picked up his drink again.

'Very well, come along then, let's all sit down. Ring for Mrs Davies and ask her to send Mary in with the first course providing it isn't already ruined by being kept waiting for so long.'

'Arnold, you sit over here,' Leonora beamed, indicating the chair beside her.

'I'm sorry, Mother, Penny interrupted, 'but we can't stay for lunch you see . . .'

'You can't stay for lunch!' Leonora Forshaw's voice rose to a crescendo. 'Of course you must; we have waited all this time for you to join us. Now sit down and stop being so silly.'

'Mother, we can't. I have to report to Manor Road police station. I shouldn't even have come straight home because I promised the policeman who was at the accident that I would go there as soon as I had picked up Arnold. We only came home because we thought you might be worried when we were so late and . . .'

'I thought it might be advisable if Penny came home and discussed the matter with you before reporting to Manor Road, sir,' Arnold interrupted, looking directly at Captain Forshaw. 'I thought that you might not want it generally known that it was your car that was involved in the accident.'

'What the hell are you both on about? What sort of accident was it that you were in? Was it serious?' Marcus Forshaw demanded.

'It happened about an hour ago,' Arnold explained. 'A young child was involved. She was knocked down and had to be taken to hospital—'

'Good God! This gets worse by the minute,' Marcus Forshaw exclaimed exasperatedly. 'How were you involved, Arnold? Surely you weren't driving my car?' he asked fiercely.

'No, Father, I was the one driving it,' Penny admitted, her face scarlet and her eyes brimming with tears.

'*You* were!' He seemed to become even more angry as he waited for the details.

'I was driving along the promenade towards Seacombe and suddenly a ball bounced into the road in front of the car and then this child must have run out into the road after it. I'm afraid I didn't see her because she was so small and the next thing I knew she was lying in the road in front of the car screaming. A crowd had gathered round and—'

'Do I take it that the police were involved?' interrupted Marcus Forshaw.

'Yes. A policeman came and then an ambulance and the child was taken to hospital. I told the policeman what had happened and he said I must report to Manor Road HQ right away and sign a statement about what had taken place. I promised him that I would do so as soon as I'd picked Arnold up from Seacombe,' Penny told him breathlessly.

'Have you been there and done that?'

'No. Not yet. Like Arnold has told you we decided that we ought to come home first and let you know what had happened.'

'Also, I thought you would be very worried because we were so late,' Arnold added addressing Leonora Forshaw.

'Dear Arnold, how very thoughtful of you,' she beamed.

'I also thought that you might wish to have a word with the chief constable first before Penny went along to the police station since he is very well known to you,' Arnold said looking directly at Marcus. 'You might even wish to arrange for your solicitor to accompany Penny to Manor Road police station.'

Marcus Forshaw nodded his head thoughtfully. 'Very sensible,' he agreed. 'My God, what a mess, and for it to happen while you were driving my Humber, Penny, makes things so much worse. Are you quite sure that my car isn't damaged? Or that you aren't hurt in any way,' he added as an afterthought.

'You're not hurt are you, Penny?' her mother repeated anxiously, looking her up and down.

'No, I'm not hurt but I am rather shaken up by what has happened.'

'I'm sure you must be, darling.' Her mother shuddered.

'A glass of wine and some food will soon steady your nerves,' Arnold stated.

'Yes, you are quite right, Arnold. Now can we forget about all this until after we've had our lunch?' Leonora Forshaw pleaded as Mary, their little maid of all work, came into the room carrying a tray loaded with plates and dishes.

'Yes, yes, very well,' Captain Forshaw agreed as he took his place at the head of the table. 'Sit down and let's eat. We certainly need to talk the matter through and decide what is the most appropriate procedure,' he muttered.

'What about my promise that I would go straight to Manor Road police station on my way home?' Penny asked in a subdued voice.

'We'll deal with that the moment we've finished lunch,' her father decided. 'In fact, I'll set our minds at rest on that point right away,' he said, putting his napkin down on to the table and standing up.

'Where are you going now?' Leonora asked, frowning.

'I'll only be a minute. I'm going to telephone James Robertson, the chief constable, and see if he thinks it really is necessary for Penny to report to Manor Road police station. In all probability it will suffice if my solicitor goes along and acts on her behalf,' he added as he left the room.

Penny and her mother were listening intently to Arnold expressing his opinion about what ought to be done when her father returned to the table. Marcus Forshaw quickly took charge again and told them that he had successfully negotiated exactly how they were to proceed.

Although it was imperative that Penny did go along to the police HQ as soon as possible she ought to talk to a solicitor first of all. The solicitor should then accompany her to the police headquarters and speak on her behalf so that there would be no fear of her saying anything in her statement that might later appear to be in any way incriminating.

'I have telephoned Sidney Porter and given him all the relevant details, so he is checking them out before he comes along here to accompany Penny to the police station.'

'Now that is all arranged let's hope we are going to have time to finish our lunch before Sidney Porter arrives,' Leonora murmured irritably,

'We'll have plenty of time, my dear,' Captain Forshaw assured her as he filled his wine glass and looked round the table to see if anyone else wanted their glass topping up.

Leonora sighed dramatically. 'I do hope Marcus that you can manage to keep all this out of the local newspapers.'

'I very much doubt if that will be possible,' he told her gloomily.

'Oh dear you must try! I can't bear to think of all the repercussions it will have if you can't!' Leonora wailed, dabbing at her eyes with a lace-edged handkerchief.

'What sort of repercussions are you talking about, Mother?' Penny asked in a puzzled voice.

'All the charities we support and the committees that we are both on, of course, not to mention our many friends. We are so well known in Wallasey that we don't want our name besmirched and our position in local society to be tainted forever. However could you become embroiled in something like this, Penny.'

'I'm sorry, Mother but it was an accident,' Penny said, struggling to keep back her tears.

'Yes, my dear, so you keep telling us,' her mother sighed.

'From what you say it was obviously the child's fault if it ran out into the road,' Marcus Forshaw said consolingly as he picked up his knife and fork and resumed eating.

'Nevertheless,' he added thoughtfully, 'we will have to make sure that the matter is handled extremely carefully.'

'What do you mean?' Arnold asked, looking at him questioningly.

'I'm thinking that if the child involved comes from a very poor Liverpool family then those sort of people can be very cunning indeed,' Marcus Forshaw stated ominously.

'You mean they may try to make themselves some money out of a situation like this?' Arnold mused thoughtfully.

'Yes, that is precisely what I mean. I'm quite sure that is what they will try and do.'

'Surely, as you have already said, the child was at fault if she ran out into the roadway after a ball,' Arnold pointed out.

'We know that but if the case goes to court and they can put the blame for the accident on Penny then they may well be hoping for a handsome sum in compensation.'

Penny remained silent; she felt too choked to speak. She could still hear the child's agonized screams ringing in her ears. In that moment she knew that the memory of the scrawny little figure with matted jet-black hair lying in the roadway in front of the car would haunt her forever.

Penny spent a sleepless night, tossing and turning and pondering whether, despite what had been said at lunch, she ought to visit the child and find out how badly hurt she was.

When she had suggested that to Arnold as they had parted the previous evening he had been very scornful of the idea. He'd told her not to be such an idiot and to stay well clear of them. He reminded her what her father had said about them trying to make money by asking for excessive compensation when the case went to court.

It was much the same advice as her father's solicitor, Mr Porter, had given her. He had in fact been quite adamant on that point when she had suggested contacting the hospital to enquire after the child.

Her mother had refused to talk about any of it saying that it made her feel quite unwell to do so. Nevertheless Penny felt she had a duty to try and find out how badly hurt the child was and if there was anything she could do to help.

She worried about it all the next day but there wasn't very much she could do on a Sunday without either her parents or Arnold discovering what she was up to.

Penny spent another restless night and then on Monday morning knowing that her father and Arnold would both be at work and her mother was attending one of her numerous committee meetings she decided to take matters into her own hands.

She resolved she would go over to Liverpool and see what she could find out.

Three

Penny Forshaw paused at the entrance to Cannon Court and held her breath wondering if she had the nerve to go any further.

She had never visited the Scotland Road area of Liverpool before but she had heard about it. Now that she was here she was appalled not only by all the dirt and dreadful smells but also by the abject poverty that she could see all around her.

She stopped by the house marked number five, trying to pluck up the courage to go through with her mission.

For a minute she wondered if perhaps she should have listened to her family's advice after all.

As she stood there debating whether to go up the steps to the scabby front door or down to the equally battered looking door in the basement, a woman carrying a baby wrapped in a shawl came along the road. She stopped by the stone steps where Penny was standing. 'You looking for someone, luv?' she asked, hitching the baby higher in her arms, almost as if it was a bundle of washing she was carrying.

'Yes, as a matter of fact I am. I'm looking for the Murphy's house.'

'In that case then you've found it. I'm Ellen Murphy.' Her sharp dark eyes narrowed as she stared in a hostile way at Penny. 'If you've come asking about why our Kelly hasn't been to school then I can explain,' she added in a hard voice.

'No, no, it's nothing like that at all,' Penny said quickly.

The two women stared at each other in silence for a moment; one smartly dressed in a crisp green and white outfit, the other slatternly and drab in a black skirt and stained dark red blouse.

'Was you the woman that was driving that motor car that knocked our Kelly down?' Ellen Murphy rasped in an accusing voice.

Penny bit her lip and then nodded her head. She felt unable to admit it out loud for fear of how the woman might react.

'My Kelly's in a bad way,' Mrs Murphy stated aggressively.

'As well as having a broken leg she has cuts and bruises all over her.'

'I'm so sorry,' Penny said quickly. 'She ran out into the road after her ball, you know. I didn't have a chance to stop in time. There was no way I could avoid hitting her,' she added defensively.

Ellen Murphy sniffed disbelievingly and hitched the baby into a more comfortable position.

'Is she still in hospital?' Penny asked.

'Course she bloody well isn't. They turfed her out the very next day and insisted that I should take her home and look after her there. Her leg's in a sodding great splint and what's more she can't walk.'

'Oh, I am so sorry,' Penny murmured. 'It must be very worrying for you.'

'Bloody nuisance since she has to share a bed with two of my other kids. We had a real night of it last night, I can tell you. They woke up screaming when Kelly kicked them with that great splint and then she woke up crying because one of them was lying on her bad leg. It's bloody hell for all of us, I can tell you.'

'I'm so sorry to hear all this, Mrs Murphy,' Penny said apologetically. 'If she is at home then can I come in and see her?'

Ellen Murphy stared at Penny for a long moment. 'Yes,' she agreed finally, with a shrug of her shoulders. 'I suppose you can; that's if you're not afraid of dirtying your fine clothes.'

Penny bit her lip and said nothing. She felt dreadfully uncomfortable. She could sense the anger and frustration bubbling up inside Ellen Murphy. Whether it was against her, blaming her for Kelly's accident, or whether it was against the whole world she wasn't sure.

'Come on then, I can't stand out here in the street jangling all day,' Ellen said ungraciously as she turned and led the way down the cracked and jagged stone steps to the basement area.

'Watch how you go,' she called over her shoulder as she kicked a screwed-up piece of greasy newspaper, that looked as though it had once held fish and chips, out of the way.

As Ellen Murphy pushed open the battered black door and led the way into a dark and dingy passage, Penny almost choked on the putrid smell that assailed her nostrils. It seemed to be a mixture of sick, urine and stale cooking all rolled into one.

She could hear a child crying; a thin, plaintiff whining cry that went right through her head.

'That's young Kelly moaning,' Ellen Murphy told her. 'She's in bed down here,' she added leading the way along the passage.

Penny took out her handkerchief and held it over her nose as she followed Ellen Murphy. She shuddered as something soft and furry brushed against her ankle, hoping it was a cat and not a rat.

The room Ellen Murphy led her into was airless; the small window looked out on to a brick wall and was so streaked with dirt that it let in very little light. Penny wondered if it had ever been opened.

There were two beds crammed into the room; one was a single and the other a three-quarter bed that was jammed tight up against the wall at one side.

The space between the two beds was so narrow that Penny had to edge along sideways to reach Kelly who was lying in a midst of rumpled bedclothes in the larger bed. Her small face was streaked with tears. She looked so thin and unkempt that Penny's heart went out to her.

As she saw the grazes and deep lacerations on the child's face and arms Penny wanted to gather her up, smooth the greasy hair back from her little elfin face and try and comfort her.

As Penny approached the bed Kelly pulled the grubby sheet up over her face so that only her eyes were visible.

'What you grizzling about now?' Ellen asked as she leaned forward and pulled back the sheet. 'Come on, sit up and show the lady your bad leg.'

Kelly tugged hard at the sheet and cowered back down, sneaking a sideways glance at Penny as if not at all sure who she was and half afraid that she might be in some sort of trouble.

Ellen pulled it back, completely exposing the child who was wearing only a dirty vest that was wrinkled halfway up her body.

Penny gasped and her heart beat faster as she saw the heavy plaster cast on the child's leg.

Kelly looked fearfully from her mother to Penny and back again and then tried to lift her leg in the air but the weight of the plaster made it impossible for her to do so and her sobs became louder.

'You can see for yourself that she's pretty badly hurt,' Ellen Murphy stated with a triumphant note in her voice.

Penny nodded, too overcome to speak. She wanted to comfort the child but she knew that she must not do so. Her father's warning words about the possibility of the family suing for damages when the case came to court rang in her head.

'Time you were up,' Ellen told Kelly harshly. 'I can't keep running backwards and forwards waiting on you all day.' Come along.' Catching hold of Kelly's arm Ellen hauled the child off the bed and on to her feet.

Kelly swayed and then clutched wildly at the bed frame as she tried to balance. As she put her weight on her injured leg she let out a yelp of pain the moment her foot touched the ground. Tears rolled down her cheeks but she brushed them away with the back of her hand.

'Come on, I haven't the time to stand here all day,' Ellen muttered, hitching the baby higher in her arms and grabbing hold of Kelly by one shoulder and half lifting, half dragging her. 'Into the kitchen with you and I'll find you a crust. You'd better come along as well and I'll make us both a cuppa and we can have a talk,' she added looking over her shoulder at Penny.

The kitchen was at the far end of the passage. It was a narrow room with an oblong table in the centre of it. On one side of it, under the window that looked out on to a yard that was cluttered with a miscellany of junk, there was a wooden bench seat. On the other side were three wooden chairs. The centre slat was missing in the back of one of the chairs and the seats of the other two were stained with spilled food and drink.

A tousled-haired little girl who looked about two years old was tied into a rickety high chair. She was picking up food with her fingers from an enamel bowl that was on the tray in front of her. Another child, a boy who appeared to be a couple of years younger than Kelly, was sitting on the floor pushing a battered tin car backwards and forwards and making zooming noises as he did so.

Ellen Murphy pushed Kelly towards the bench and left her to struggle on to it. She dumped the baby she was carrying into a dilapidated wicker clothes basket on the floor. Then, delving into the pocket of her skirt, she brought out a dummy and jammed it into the baby's mouth. Picking up a box of matches she lighted the gas ring that was standing on top of a low wooden cupboard and put a tin kettle on top of it to boil.

Kelly was whimpering in a high-pitched whine and the small girl banged her metal dish on the tray to try and attract attention.

'Shut up the lot of yer,' Ellen Murphy yelled at them. 'Let's be having a bit of quiet while I talk to this lady. Sit yourself down,' she ordered, wiping crumbs from the seat of one of the chairs with her skirt before pushing it towards Penny.

Penny hesitated for a moment because there was still a greasy patch on the seat of the chair but decided that there was nothing she could do about it so smiled politely and accepted.

'So you were the one who knocked our Kelly down, were you,' Ellen Murphy stated triumphantly. 'As you can see her leg's broken and they says at the hospital that she won't be able to walk properly for a month or more. She's hurt her arm and shoulder as well and she's bruises all over. How the hell I'm going to manage to look after her for that length of time I don't know. Brian's a little terror and I needs to be keeping my eye on him most of the day as well as Lily who's into everything unless I keep her tied into the high chair,' she rattled on as she banged a couple of chipped cups down on to the table in front of Penny.

'Takes me all my time looking after the new baby so I count on Kelly to keep an eye on Lily and young Brian. Now, the state she's in she won't be able to do so will she? Not that you'd understand what it's like to be tied with four young kids; not you, a well-to-do young lady who's dressed up and drives round in a big motor car all day.'

Penny felt the hot blood creeping into her cheeks. Although Ellen Murphy hadn't added 'and knocks children down' it was implied by the tone of her voice.

'I do understand you have problems, Mrs Murphy,' Penny told her. 'I'm a school teacher, so I do know how demanding young children can be, especially if they are not kept entertained or occupied.'

'Entertained? What's that when it's at home?' Ellen asked with

a shrill laugh. 'If you mean being taken to the park, playing ball
games or going to the flicks well that's all very well if you have
the money to do all those sorts of things. My lot have to make
do with playing out in the road. Takes me all my time to find
enough bread and scrape to fill their little bellies, especially our
Paddy's. He's me older boy, and he's growing so fast that he's
hungry all the time.'

'Yes, I can see you have your hands full,' Penny murmured
uncomfortably.

'Humph!' Ellen Murphy made a scathing noise as she turned
to make the tea. In silence she filled the cracked brown teapot
and put down the kettle. 'So you are a school teacher are you,
miss. Then in that case you'll be on holiday for the next few
weeks. In fact, practically all the time my Kelly will have that
great heavy plaster on her leg. Maybe the court would think
more kindly about what you did if you was to look after Kelly
while you are on holiday.'

'Court? What are you talking about?' Penny blustered. She
could feel her heart thumping and she knew her voice was
pitched higher than normal. She wished she had not told Mrs
Murphy that she was a school teacher and once again her father's
words about them being sued for compensation rang inside her
head like a warning bell, but it was too late now to do anything
about it.

'As I was saying,' Ellen continued as she poured tea into the
two chipped cups and pushed one of them towards Penny, 'when
we goes to court about poor little Kelly's accident the judge
would probably be a lot less harsh on you if I was to be able to
tell him as how you helped me to look after her.'

Penny looked down into the pool of dark brown liquid in
front of her desperately trying to marshal her thoughts. Her father
had been so right. If he ever found out that she had been here
he would be absolutely furious and so would Arnold. That was
unless she was able to persuade Ellen Murphy not to make any
charges about the accident, she thought hopefully.

'Here, help yourself.' Ellen pushed a tin jug of milk and a jam
jar half full of sugar towards her.

'Thank you.'

'If you's a school teacher like you said, miss then as I was saying, you'll be doing nothing for the next few weeks. That means you could look after young Kelly, then,' Ellen Murphy persisted.

'And if I did as you asked and looked after her does that mean you wouldn't be going to court about her being knocked down?'

'I'm not so sure about that!' Ellen stirred her tea noisily and shook her head doubtfully. 'I'd have to wait and see what my Shamus thought about it all. He's away at sea at the minute.'

'Shamus? Is he your husband? He's Kelly's father is he?'

'Of course he's Kelly's dad and the father of all my children,' Ellen Murphy answered sharply.

'So he doesn't know anything about Kelly's accident yet?'

'No, not yet. I've told Father O'Flynn all about it though and he said he would write a letter to him but it may be days or weeks before Shamus gets it. Wonderful man Father O'Flynn. He's promised that if Shamus isn't home from his trip then he'll help me to sort things out and come with me when I has to go to court. I could tell him to put in a good word for you and he'd be sure to do so if he knew you'd been helping out with Kelly,' she added craftily.

Penny took a sip of her tea. It was so strong that she shuddered. As she looked across at Kelly, who was watching and listening to what was being said, Penny wondered if she could do a deal with Ellen Murphy to stop her going to court at all.

Perhaps if she did agree to look after Kelly then Ellen would drop all charges so that no one outside her immediate family need know about the accident, Penny mused. There would be no adverse publicity; nothing in the newspapers, so Arnold's name would not be dragged into it and her family's reputation would remain unsullied. Her mother and father would not be incriminated, so they'd both be able to hold their heads high as pillars of the local society.

It would mean her own life would be badly disrupted though, she reminded herself. If she had to look after Kelly then she would probably have to forgo all the exciting outings, picnics and countless other activities that she had arranged and which she and her many girlfriends had been looking forward to enjoying during the summer holidays.

There was also the very important question of how Arnold

would react if she took on the responsibility of looking after Kelly. She had been planning to partner him in several tournaments at the tennis club as well as competing in some swimming events at Guinea Gap Baths.

She cast a quick glance at Kelly and suppressed a shudder; she was so pitifully scrawny and unkempt that she seemed half wild. She couldn't see Arnold agreeing to letting her take Kelly with them on any of their outings.

She knew that Ellen Murphy was waiting for her answer so she took another sip of the strong bitter tasting tea in order to give herself time to think.

If she did agree to take Kelly home with her then would her parents understand that she was doing it to save their reputation? Or would they think she was stupid to let herself be pressurized into such a compromise. Whichever decision she made she knew that her father would upbraid her for visiting the Murphys in the first place.

As Penny put down her cup, Kelly stretched out a grubby hand and caught hold of her arm. 'I'd be real good, miss, I promise.'

'I'm sure you would be,' Penny said quickly, a lump rising in her throat at the pleading in Kelly's voice. 'It's just that I have to think about it; I'm not sure where you would sleep.'

As her voice trailed off uncertainly, Kelly gave her a wide grin. 'I can always sleep with you in your bed. I don't take up much room. I sleep with Lily and Brian so I'm used to sharing a bed.'

'The lady wouldn't want to have someone like you in her bed,' her mother cut in with a contemptuous laugh, 'You could always put down a mattress for her on the floor,' Ellen Murphy added quickly.

'I don't think that would be very comfortable, not with her leg in a plaster.'

'Be better for her than having to share a bed with our Brian and little Lily.'

Penny shook her head. 'I don't think it would be a very good idea,' she prevaricated.

'Father O'Flynn says that if you saves a person's life then you should care for them for the rest of their lives because from then on they're your responsibility,' Ellen Murphy mused.

'I didn't save Kelly's life,' Penny said quickly. She felt utterly bewildered by the way the argument was going. She could understand that Ellen resented the added burden of Kelly being a semi-invalid during the school holidays. Even so, it seemed unnatural that she was so willing to let her go and live with a complete stranger.

'No, you nearly took it from her, though, so in my eyes it amounts to the same thing. You should be the one looking after her at least until she can walk again,' Ellen Murphy declared heatedly.

Penny remained silent. She didn't agree with what had been said but she was so consumed by guilt about what had happened that she felt helpless.

Four

'You've been where and you've promised to do what? Oh Penny, how could you. I warned you not to have anything at all to do with those people. What a preposterous idea,' her father exclaimed angrily.'

'You must be out of your mind, Penny, to go there and then to agree to look after her. I really can't believe that you've even contemplated the idea of bringing some little street urchin here. As for expecting us to welcome her into our home, well, that is beyond belief,' Leonora Forshaw exclaimed almost hysterically.

'What about all the outings you'd planned with your friends during August and, most important of all, what about me and all the holiday plans we've made?' Arnold exclaimed tetchily. 'I've certainly no intention of having a slum kid accompany us.'

Tears stung Penny's eyes as their chorus of disapproval rang in her ears on Monday night and she saw the angry faces all around her.

She had been afraid that her father wouldn't approve of what she had done but she had hoped that perhaps her mother would understand that she had done it for the best. She had certainly expected Arnold to give her his support. Judging from their reactions this was far from being so; she had been wrong on all counts since none of them approved of her action.

'How could you act in such a stupid manner, Penelope?' Captain Forshaw exploded, his face puce with anger, as he paced up and down the room. 'It would appear that you didn't listen to a word I said when I warned you not to go anywhere near the child's family or have anything to do with them because they were bound to be trouble.'

'It was because of what you said that I went to see the Murphys,' Penny defended. 'I was afraid that if they did take the matter to court your name would be besmirched and I was trying to stop that happening. I thought that if I went to see the little girl's family and explained exactly how the accident had happened and

told them how sorry I was about it, then they would accept my
apology and let the matter drop.'

'What utter rubbish, you silly child! They're far more likely to
press charges and want compensation now that you have admitted
your guilt than they would have done otherwise,' her father told
her in a scathing voice.

'Don't you understand, that's the whole point of my promising
to care for Kelly while her leg is in plaster and she is unable to
get around,' Penny argued. 'Mrs Murphy has promised that if I
take care of Kelly until her leg is better then she will let the
matter drop and she won't go to court about the accident.'

'And you believed her!'

The scorn in her father's voice brought fresh tears to Penny's
eyes.

'Even so, Penny, to say you would have the child here is
preposterous,' Mrs Forshaw intervened. 'It's quite out of the question.
You've already admitted that the child is dirty and unkempt, and
by the sound of things she'll have no table manners at all.'

'Why not simply put her in a home of some kind until her
leg is better and pay for her to be looked after,' Arnold suggested.

'I promised Mrs Murphy that I would take care of Kelly myself,'
Penny said stubbornly.

'Putting her in a nursing home would be taking care of her,'
Arnold insisted. 'Furthermore, it would ensure that she would
have proper treatment for her leg and she would be taught how
to walk again after the splint is taken off,' he added.

'No!' Penny shook her head vehemently. 'Caring for her until
she is able to walk again is my responsibility and that is what I
have promised to do.'

'A very selfish promise,' Mrs Forshaw protested. 'You didn't
stop to think how it was going to affect your family or dear
Arnold. Having the child here will disrupt all our lives. Where
on earth is she going to sleep? I certainly don't intend putting
her in the guest room.'

'She can sleep in my room.'

'What utter nonsense, Penny! You've no idea what you are
talking about, my dear. She's probably got fleas and possibly head
lice as well. The next thing we know we'll all have them.'

'Mother, she's one small sick little girl who is in a great deal

of pain and can hardly walk more than a couple of steps unless
someone helps her.'

'That's how she is at the moment, my dear. Give it a couple
of weeks and she'll be as active as anything. She's probably used
to playing out in the street with all the other children so she
won't be content to stay indoors on her own all the time. She'll
be into everything; she'll run wild and break things and cause
absolute mayhem.'

'She won't have to stay indoors. I intend buying a pushchair
and taking her out and about and she will be able to play in the
garden.'

'Furthermore,' Mrs Forshaw went on, completely ignoring what
Penny had said, 'she'll be missing her mother and her brothers
and sisters and probably be crying most of the time.'

'Well, now that you've said all the bad things possible about
my idea perhaps you should stop and consider what might happen
if I go back and tell Mrs Murphy that I've changed my mind
about taking care of Kelly,' Penny pointed out.

'If Mrs Murphy goes ahead and takes me to court then I might
end up in prison and it will all be reported in the *Liverpool Post*
and the *Liverpool Echo* and you know how they like to build
things up.'

'Really, Penny, this is outrageous,' Leonora Forshaw said wearily,
pressing a hand to her brow.

'Very likely they will mention your name, Mother, and all the
committees you are on,' Penny went on relentlessly. 'They will
most certainly mention father's name, his business and all the
committees he's on. Possibly they will also mention Arnold . . .'

'Which is why I said that you should put the child into a
private nursing home and not become involved any further,'
Arnold interrupted testily.

They argued endlessly about what was the right thing to do
but Penny stuck to her guns. She had made a promise to Mrs
Murphy and she had no intention of breaking it. She had agreed
to look after Kelly and that was what she was going to do.

When Penny arrived at Cannon Court the next morning Ellen
Murphy seemed to be surprised to see her. Penny also found that
Ellen Murphy was even more astonished than even her own

family had been that she intended to redeem her promise to look after Kelly.

'I said I would look after her until she is able to walk again if you were prepared to drop the case against me,' Penny reminded her firmly.

'Well, miss, I don't know what to do for the best,' Ellen said hesitantly. 'Perhaps I should ask Father O'Flynn what he thinks about it all.'

'I'm sure you want to do what's best not only for Kelly but for your other children as well, Mrs Murphy. You have already said you are finding it hard work to look after them as well as Kelly since she is unable to get about,' Penny reminded her.

'Well, sure now that's true enough,' Ellen Murphy agreed.

'Right. Well, while you pack Kelly's clothes I'll go and see if I can buy a pushchair,' Penny told her. 'Perhaps you can tell me the best place to shop for one.'

'There's nothing much to pack; just a spare vest and a pair of knickers,' Ellen told her. 'Everything else is what's on her back. I rinses her dress out at night if it's grubby and she puts it on again next morning.'

'What about her night clothes?'

Ellen Murphy gave a harsh laugh. 'She don't have none of those, miss. She sleeps in her vest the same as the rest of my kids do.'

'Right, then in that case she's more or less ready. You have told her that she is coming to stay with me and explained that she won't be seeing you or her brothers or sisters for quite a long time?'

'She knows all about it and she's looking forward to living with you. I've threatened to scalp her if she doesn't behave herself.'

'So it's simply a matter of getting hold of a pushchair. Do you know anyone who would loan me one or who has one for sale?'

Ellen Murphy looked puzzled. 'What do you need a pushchair for when you have a motor car? She can ride in that can't she?'

'I'm afraid not. My father has forbidden me to drive it since the accident,' Penny said unhappily. A vision of her Austin Seven, her very own Baby Austin with its bright blue bodywork and black roof filled her mind, She loved it so much and treated it as a friend and always referred to it as 'Bluebell'. She knew she was the envy of so many people, especially those of her own age, to have her very own motor car when she was still so young.

'Since Kelly isn't going to be able to walk any distance for quite a while, I shall need a pushchair to take her out in,' she explained to Ellen Murphy, bringing her thoughts back to the present.

'You might be able to get one at the pawnbrokers or at one of the second-hand shops in Scotland Road,' Ellen suggested. 'Make sure you haggle with them though or else they're bound to diddle you when they see how posh you are,' she warned as she appraised Penny's crisp pink cotton dress and matching straw hat. 'Would you like me to go and see if I can get one for you?'

'That would be very helpful, Mrs Murphy. I'll wait here with Kelly.'

'I'll take the baby along with me and leave the other two with you as well as Kelly then,' Ellen Murphy told her as she pulled a heavy black shawl around her shoulders even though the sun was beating down outside. 'How much do you want to pay for it?' she asked holding out a grubby hand for some money.

'I've no idea what they cost,' Penny said hesitantly. 'Can I leave that to you. Mrs Murphy,' she added trustingly as she handed her a crisp five-pound note. 'Make sure its a nice one and big enough for Kelly to be comfortable in.'

Ellen Murphy was away such a long time that Penny became worried and wondered if she was ever coming back. Kelly was whimpering with pain and frustration and the two smaller children were sitting on the floor with their thumbs in their mouths simply staring at her.

Penny tried talking to them but they didn't seem to understand what she was saying and she felt completely out of her depth. When she asked if they would like to play a game together all three of them completely ignored her question.

She breathed a sigh of relief when she heard Ellen in the hallway. The two children seemed to come to life and rushed out to see what she had bought. Even Kelly stopped whimpering and stared with interest as Ellen manoeuvred the pushchair into the room.

Penny studied the cumbersome contraption dubiously. 'That certainly looks very sturdy, Mrs Murphy,' she said with a forced smile.

'It ought to be – it cost enough. The pawnbroker wanted three quid for it but I managed to beat him down to two pounds and ten shillings,' she said triumphantly as she handed Penny the change.

'Well then, if Kelly is ready we'll get going. Can you help me to settle her into it.'

Kelly made no protest other than to let out a whimper when her mother tried to bend Kelly's leg so that her foot could be on the footrest and then jammed her crutches in at her side.

'If that is hurting then you may be more comfortable if you keep your leg out straight,' Penny suggested. 'Perhaps we can find a cushion or something to support it,' she added looking around the room hopefully.

'Cushion! We've no cushions in this place,' Ellen told her sourly. 'There's an old cardboard box the other kids play with; you might be able to use that.'

'No, I don't think so,' Penny demurred.

'Then what about sticking that paper bag with her vest and stuff in it under her bad leg and letting her hold her crutches on her lap.'

Penny felt very conspicuous as she began to walk from Cannon Court to Scotland Road after Ellen had helped her to get the pushchair up the steps from the basement. Try as she might, she found it difficult to steer it in a straight line.

It was a long walk to the Pier Head and by the time she reached the top of Water Street Penny was already feeling exhausted. At least I'll be able to sit down and have a rest once we are on the ferry boat, she told herself. At the other end, though, there would be a long walk home along the promenade from Seacombe to Penkett Road.

Although she kept talking to Kelly and asking her if she was all right, especially when she jolted her rather violently when negotiating the pushchair up and down the kerbs, Kelly remained silent.

Penny wondered if she was already missing her mother and the rest of her family but was afraid to mention the fact out loud in case Kelly dissolved into tears.

By the time they reached the ferry and she was negotiating the pushchair up the ramp on to the *Royal Daffodil* Penny realized that the reason Kelly was so silent was because she was so over-awed by what was happening to her.

'Where are you taking me, miss?' she gasped fearfully staring at the dark swirling waters of the Mersey.

'Over to Wallasey; it's where I live,' Penny told her lamely.

'You mean you are taking me to your house?'

'That's right. I thought your mother explained to you that I am going to look after you until your leg is better and you can walk again?'

Kelly regarded her solemnly, her deep blue eyes filling with tears. She nodded her head, her teeth biting down on her lower lip. 'Yes, I know that, but I thought you meant you were coming to live at our place and look after me there,' she gulped in a small voice.

Before Penny could answer there was the noise of the boat grinding against the landing stage and a shuddering as it began to slowly move out into the open river. Kelly let out a scream and clutched at Penny's hand, her eyes wide with fright.

'It's all right; it means we are on our way. In ten minutes' time we will be at Seacombe landing stage. There's nothing to worry about.'

'I'm frightened – I don't like it,' Kelly sobbed, tears running down her cheeks.

'You've been on a ferry boat before. You must have done because it was over on the other side in Wallasey that you ran out into the road after a ball right in front of my motor car. That was how you came to be knocked down,' Penny reminded her.

Kelly looked at her blankly. 'I can't remember nothing about what happened,' she muttered. 'I know my mam said that I could go to New Brighton with some older kids for the day. The next thing I knew was that I woke up in hospital and my leg was hurting.'

She was still clutching tightly at Penny's hand when they reached the other side of the Mersey. She wouldn't let go even when the *Royal Daffodil* was manoeuvred alongside the landing stage at Seacombe Ferry and the gangplank was lowered into place so that passengers could go ashore.

Because the school holidays had started, there were a great many young families on board. All the children were excited and eager to disembark. Penny waited until they had done so before she made her way off the boat with Kelly in the pushchair.

It was now almost midday and the sun was burning hot and Penny found it was hard work pushing Kelly. She longed to stop and sit down but the thought of reaching home and enjoying a refreshing glass of cold lemonade kept her going.

At least she was managing to control the pushchair much better, she thought with some satisfaction half an hour later as she wheeled it into her own driveway without mishap.

She sighed nervously as she saw a curtain at the front room window twitch. Then, taking a deep breath, she braced her shoulders in preparation for her family's reaction to little Kelly.

Five

Penny felt it was better that Kelly met her parents separately so that she wasn't too overwhelmed. She was pleased that she had arrived back at Penkett Road when only her mother was at home. She knew her father would probably be arriving home for lunch but that would not be for another hour.

'Kelly, this is my mother, Mrs Forshaw. Are you going to say "Hello" to her?'

Kelly held her head down so that strands of her greasy dark hair fell over her eyes like a curtain.

'She is finding it all rather overpowering,' Penny said lamely as she saw her mother's thin lips tighten when Kelly refused to speak. 'She probably needs a drink. I know I'm gasping for a glass of lemonade,' she hurried on. 'It's absolutely baking hot out of doors and it was such a long walk all the way from Seacombe Ferry.'

'I had no idea you had gone to Liverpool; utter madness on such a hot day,' Mrs Forshaw said sharply. 'Well, if it's a drink you both need then take the child through to the morning room and have it in there in case she spills it over the carpet.'

Her mother's tone and the wave of her hand were so dismissive that Penny was made to feel uneasy, but she merely nodded in agreement.

She wheeled the pushchair along to the morning room and left Kelly sitting there while she went to the kitchen for two glasses of lemonade.

As she returned with them she noticed Kelly was looking around wide-eyed and could understand how frightened she must be feeling. The house was so bright and large and so very different from her own squalid surroundings. Even so, if her mother's greeting had been warmer and more welcoming then she was sure Kelly would have responded.

Kelly gulped down her lemonade as if she was indeed very thirsty. She managed a smile as she wiped the back of her hand across her mouth when she'd finished.

'Did you enjoy that?' Penny asked as she took the empty glass from her.

'It was lovely,' Kelly breathed. 'Can I have some more?'

'Not at the moment because it is almost lunchtime and if you drink any more lemonade you won't have room left for anything else,' Penny said with a smile.

'What's lunch?' Kelly's small brow creased into a frown of bewilderment. 'Do you mean we're going to have some grub?'

'That's right. What sort of food do you like best?'

Kelly's eyes widened. 'Chips or Wet Nelly or a crust with Conny Onny on it,' she said thoughtfully. Then she added with a sigh, 'Me mam usually gives us bread and dripping or else Scouse.'

Penny felt at a loss. She wasn't even sure what Wet Nelly was. She thought it was a bread pudding of some kind and decided that Conny Onny must be sweetened condensed milk. She had certainly heard of Scouse and that was a cheap stew consisting mainly of vegetables.

She had no idea what Mrs Davies had prepared for their lunch but it certainly wouldn't be any of those, she thought, with an inward smile. She wondered if Kelly would eat what was offered and felt apprehensive about how her mother would react if she didn't.

She didn't have to wait long to find out. A few minutes later her mother came bustling through to the morning room.

'As it is such a hot day and I had no idea at all where you were or what time you would be coming back I told Mrs Davies that cold ham and salad might be the most suitable for lunch. There's fresh raspberries and cream for pudding. Do you think the child will like that?'

'I'm not sure and by the way her name is Kelly,' Penny reminded her.

'Your father will be home at any moment so I think it would be best if you two have your lunch here in the morning room rather than with us in the dining room,' her mother responded. 'It will give the child time to get used to being here and perhaps then she will answer when she is spoken to.'

'Yes, very well, if that is what you wish us to do,' Penny said stiffly.

'I suggest that before either of you have anything to eat you clean her up. After you've had lunch then perhaps you should go into Liscard Village and buy her a decent dress before your father sees her; the one she is wearing is practically in rags. I imagine that everything else she has brought with her will be in much the same state.'

'The only clothes she has are the ones she's wearing,' Penny said quietly.

'In that case you'll definitely have to go out this afternoon and buy her some. For heaven's sake make sure you don't take her into any of the shops where we are known, Penny, or people will start gossiping. They probably will do so anyway if they see you wheeling that horrible contraption she's in.'

'They will probably think that it is something to do with one of the many charities you support and that I'm helping out,' Penny muttered.

From the annoyed look on her mother's face Penny knew she had heard what she'd said but preferred to ignore her sarcastic remark.

Penny felt both angry and dismayed that her mother's reaction to Kelly was so negative. She hadn't dared hope that she would welcome Kelly with open arms but as it was she was barely being civil towards her.

She would have been more welcoming if I'd brought a puppy home, Penny thought resentfully. As soon as they'd had something to eat she would certainly take Kelly out and buy her some new clothes. Perhaps if she was wearing a pretty dress and her hair was washed and trimmed a little shorter she wouldn't look so untidy and bedraggled and her father wouldn't be quite so critical as her mother when he met Kelly for the first time.

Kelly was starving. She tucked into the crusty roll even before Penny had time to put any butter on it or cut the ham on her plate into small manageable pieces. Then, ignoring the knife and fork, she used her fingers to eat everything on her plate.

She looked doubtful and shook her head when Penny asked her if she would like some raspberries and cream. When Penny offered her a taste from her own dish, however, she seemed to like it so much that Penny gave her a very small portion in a dish of her own. Kelly ate it with relish and then held out the dish for some more.

Penny waited until she knew her father had left the house before taking Kelly upstairs to give her a good wash and to try and do something to tidy her hair before taking her out.

Kelly looked round in awe when she carried her into the gleaming white bathroom.

'I only have a bath once a week at home and that's in a tin bath on a Friday night,' she confided in a small voice. 'The rest of the time the bath is on a nail outside the back door. Do you get in that great big white one, miss?'

'Yes, every morning before I have my breakfast,' Penny told her gravely.

'Why? You never get grubby do you?' Kelly said in a puzzled voice.

'You also need to have your hair washed,' Penny told Kelly while ignoring her question.

'I don't like having that done because me mam always gets soap in me eyes and it stings so bad it makes me cry,' Kelly scowled.

'Well it won't today, not the way I'll do it,' Penny promised. 'I'll let you sit in a chair with your head back over the wash basin and I'll use a lovely shampoo and make sure it doesn't get in your eyes.'

Kelly looked puzzled but agreed to do as Penny asked. It was a messy procedure and by the time she'd finished washing and rinsing Kelly's hair Penny felt exhausted. Kelly, on the other hand was exuberant because no soap had gone in her eyes.

'I'd like to fill up the bath and let you soak in the warm water but I can't do that because of your leg, Penny told her. 'Instead I am going to wash you all over and then I'm going to take you shopping and buy you a new dress.'

Kelly shuddered but made no protest as Penny stripped off her clothes and lathered the flannel with soap and began washing her from head to toe.

Penny couldn't believe how thin and frail Kelly was. Her ribs and shoulder blades protruded and her legs and arms were spindly. There seemed to be nothing of her she thought uneasily as she wrapped Kelly up in a big fluffy pink towel and began to dry her.

She felt a sense of revulsion as she re-dressed Kelly in her shabby clothes and wished that there was something else she could wear.

The shopping trip went extremely well. It was rather difficult for Kelly to try things on because she couldn't stand up very well. In both the shops they visited, however, the assistants were very helpful.

Kelly loved the two pretty cotton dresses with matching cotton knickers that Penny chose for her and looked astonished when new white socks and a pair of brown sandals were added to the pile.

'Now all we need are either some pyjamas or a couple of nightdresses. I suppose it will have to be nightdresses because of your leg,' Penny mused.

By the time they reached home again Kelly looked exhausted. She didn't even brighten up when Penny told her that she could put on one of her new dresses and that she could choose which one.

Kelly shook her head, yawned deeply and rubbed her eyes. 'I'm tired, I want to go to bed,' she said.

'You haven't had anything to eat since lunchtime. You are probably hungry,' Penny told her. 'Let's get you all dressed up and then we'll go downstairs for dinner. I'm sure you'll feel much better after that.'

'No!' Stubbornly Kelly shook her head. 'I want to go to bed,' she repeated in a whining voice.

'Oh very well, if that's what you really want to do,' Penny exclaimed in exasperation. 'I'll help you to get ready for bed and then I'll see what I can find for you to eat and bring it up here for you.'

Kelly brightened up, the tears and snivelling stopped. 'Can I have a jam butty?'

'You need to have something more substantial than that. Isn't there anything else you'd like?'

'A chip butty then, and could I have a sausage as well?' she asked hopefully.

'I'll see what I can find,' Penny promised. 'Let's get you into bed first,' she added as she half carried Kelly towards the small truckle bed that had been set up on the far side of the bedroom for her.

'I'll see what I can find is what me mam always says when we say that we are hungry and all she can find for us is bread and scrape.'

'I think I can do better than that,' Penny promised as she helped Kelly to undress and put on one of the pretty cotton nightdresses that they had bought that afternoon, before helping her into bed.

'Now you lie quiet for a few minutes and I'll be back with a glass of milk and something for you to eat.'

'Water'll do if you can't afford milk,' Kelly assured her cheerfully. 'Unless there is some of that lovely lemonade left; you know what you gave me to drink when we first got here this morning.'

Ten minutes later, when she came back upstairs with a plate of tiny sandwiches and both a glass of lemonade and one of milk Penny found that Kelly was fast asleep.

She put the tray down on a stool within reach of the bed so that Kelly would find it if she woke up. Then she straightened the bedclothes and made sure Kelly was comfortable. She looked so innocent and fragile, her dark hair, now clean and shining, fanned out against the white pillowcase, that it brought a lump to Penny's throat.

Captain and Mrs Forshaw were already in the dining room enjoying a glass of sherry when Penny went downstairs.

'On your own, Penny? What have you done with the child?' her mother asked, raising her shapely eyebrows enquiringly. 'Have you taken her back to her own home?'

'Child, what child are you talking about?' Captain Forshaw asked tetchily looking from his wife to Penny and then back again. 'Penny, you haven't gone against my express wishes again have you?' he asked angrily.

'She most certainly has done so!' Leonora Forshaw stated forcibly.

'You mean she's brought that little Liverpool street urchin back here to our home!'

'Yes, Father, I have brought Kelly back,' Penny said defensively.

He stared at her in disbelief. 'After all the warnings I gave you, Penny? I stressed that it was inadvisable to have anything at all to do with the Murphy family. Even Arnold warned you against the idea.'

'I've brought Kelly back because I intend to look after her

until she is better. As I explained to you all, I am doing it so that I am not taken to court over the accident.'

'How long will it take for her to be fit again? Have you any proof that the parents won't take any action? What will happen if they do?' Her father scowled.

'You can't trust that sort of rabble,' he went on giving her no chance to reply.

'She was filthy dirty and absolutely in rags when she arrived here,' Leonora stated with an exaggerated shiver. 'I had to send Penny out to buy some decent clothes for her.'

Penny shook her head. 'She isn't looking like that any longer, Mother. Wait until you see her tomorrow and then you'll realize what a lovely little girl she really is.'

'Where is she now?' Captain Forshaw demanded looking at Penny.

'At the moment she is upstairs in my bedroom. She is sound asleep because she is utterly exhausted by all that has gone on today.'

'She won't remain that way for long,' her father warned. 'You'll need to watch her; she'll be into everything, nothing will be safe. She's probably been brought up to thieve for everything she wants.'

'Father, Kelly is six years old; she has a broken leg and is unable to walk without help.'

'At the moment! Another couple of weeks and she'll expect to have the run of the place. And what about her family? Are we going to have them calling every few days to see how she is?'

'It's not very likely. There are three children younger than Kelly and a boy who is older. I can hardly see Mrs Murphy bringing all of them over here to visit Kelly, can you?'

'Who knows? You can't be sure. If they think they might benefit from handouts of some kind then those sort of people will go anywhere,' he muttered gloomily. 'What has Arnold got to say about it all? Or doesn't he know that you've brought this child here?'

'Not yet because I haven't seen him since I brought Kelly home.'

'I don't think he is going to like it one little bit,' Leonora sighed. 'He was very much against you even going to see this family,' she reminded Penny.

'I know that, Mother. I have to do what I think is right though, don't I.'

'You should have taken my advice,' her father said bluntly. 'If you'd listened to me I would have handed the matter over to Sidney Porter and let him deal with it. Solicitors are used to handling such cases and know how to treat those sort of people. It's still not too late.'

Penny shook her head, her eyes bright with tears. 'No, I can't do that,' she insisted. 'I made a promise to look after Kelly and I intend to keep it.

Six

Penny slept very fitfully because she felt so anxious about Kelly. She wasn't too sure that she'd done the right thing by separating the little girl from her family and familiar surroundings and bringing her over to Wallasey.

Kelly, however, was so worn out with all that had happened to her the previous day that she remained sound asleep until well after daybreak.

When Penny woke up she found that Kelly was propped up in the little truckle bed eating the dried up sandwiches she had left there the night before and drinking the lemonade.

'That milk tasted a bit funny, I think it must have gone sour,' she commented when Penny sat up and greeted her and asked her if she had slept all right. 'The rest of my breakfast is lovely,' she added quickly.

'That was supposed to be for your supper last night, not your breakfast, but you were sound asleep when I came back upstairs with it,' Penny told her with a smile.

'The butties were the nicest I've ever had,' Kelly told her with a deep sigh. 'I wish I could eat them all over again.'

'Well you can have your breakfast as soon as we are both washed and dressed. Which of your new dresses do you want to wear?'

Kelly's eyes lit up. 'You mean I can choose which one,' she said excitedly. Then her face clouded. 'I don't have to get washed all over again like I did yesterday do I?'

'No, you need only wash your hands and face this morning. Why don't you lie there and decide which dress you want to wear while I go and have my bath,' Penny suggested as she slid out of bed and slipped on a blue floral cotton dressing gown.

Kelly regarded her wide-eyed. Is that what you are going to wear today, miss. It's ever so pretty, you look really lovely in it.'

'It's my dressing gown and I'm only wearing it to go to the bathroom.' Penny smiled. 'After I've had my bath I will be putting on a pretty dress the same as you are going to do,' she added as she went over to the chest of drawers. She picked out some clean underwear to take through to the bathroom and then selected a sleeveless cotton frock from her wardrobe.

When she returned dressed ready for the day Kelly regarded her critically. 'I think your dressing gown much prettier than your frock, miss,' she remarked.

Penny smiled. 'Listen, Kelly since you are going to be living here for quite a long time I think you should call me Penny, instead of saying miss, don't you.'

'Penny, Penny,' Kelly repeated the word several times then frowned.

'Shouldn't it be Auntie Penny? You are a grown-up and me mam says I always have to say mister, missus or miss when people speak to me. That's unless they are friends of my mam's and then I calls them Auntie or Uncle. Well, all except policemen and we calls them rozzers or scuffers. The man who calls each week for money is the tallyman. Do you have one of them coming to the door, miss . . . I mean Penny.'

Penny shook her head. 'No we don't, Kelly. Now look, it's time for you to come along to the bathroom. After you're washed I'll help you to get dressed and then we'll go downstairs and have some breakfast. Have you decided which dress you are going to wear today?'

Kelly screwed up her eyes in concentration. 'The pink one,' she said.

Twenty minutes later in her new pink cotton dress and with her clean dark hair tied back with a piece of pink ribbon Penny had managed to find she looked quite different from the scruffy little girl she had been the previous day.

Penny wished Kelly had looked like this when her mother had seen her for the first time. If she had then perhaps her mother would have been far more welcoming.

Her parents were already seated at the breakfast table when Penny carried Kelly into the morning room.

'So this is the child you are proposing to look after is it,' Captain Forshaw said gruffly looking over the top of his newspaper as she helped Kelly on to a chair and pushed it in under the table. 'Well I must say she certainly seems to be far more presentable than I

expected her to be from your mother's lurid description,' he added
dryly.

'Yes, well, you didn't see her yesterday when she first arrived
here from Liverpool,' his wife retorted sharply.

'Say "Good morning Captain Forshaw",' Penny prompted Kelly
in a whisper.

Kelly looked up at her with a puzzled expression on her face.
'Is he your dad?'

'Yes, that's right,' Penny said with a smile.

'Does he live here with you all the time?'

'Yes, of course he does.'

'I never see my dad much,' Kelly sighed and tears came to her
eyes. 'He's a sailor and goes away on a boat. I think it must be
much bigger than the one we were on yesterday because me mam
says he goes all over the world in it.'

'That's very interesting,' Captain Forshaw boomed. He turned
to his wife. 'Isn't breakfast ready yet?'

'Mrs Davies has put the eggs on and Mary will bring them in
any minute now as soon as they are ready.'

'Are we having boiled eggs in their shells for breakfast? Does that
mean that it's someone's birthday today?' Kelly piped up excitedly.

'You'd like a boiled egg would you,' Penny said smiling at
Kelly's enthusiasm.

'Ooh yes! We only have them when it's someone's birthday.
Oh, and at Easter. Sometimes my dad has one when he comes
home from the sea and when he does he gives me the top of it,'
she added dreamily.

'Well you'll be getting a whole one all to yourself,' Penny told her
as Mary came into the room carrying a bowl of freshly cooked eggs.

She handed the bowl first to Mrs Forshaw so that she could
take one and then to Captain Forshaw who selected two. Then
she placed the bowl containing the remaining two eggs in front
of Penny. Penny put one of the eggs into the eggcup on Kelly's
plate and removed the top and then spread butter on a piece of
toast and cut it into strips.

As she ate her own breakfast Penny was conscious of the mess
Kelly was making as she dipped the strips of toast into her egg
before she ate them. She was obviously enjoying them very much
so Penny said nothing, and hoped that her parents didn't notice

that as well as getting it all over her face Kelly was dripping egg on to the blue and white check tablecloth.

Mrs Forshaw was not nearly so reticent and kept on tutting reprovingly, especially when Kelly put her eggy spoon down on the cloth instead of on to her own plate.

Worse was to follow. Kelly reached out for her glass of milk and in an attempt not to spill any of it on her new dress accidentally upset it on the tablecloth. At the same time she placed her elbow in the middle of her plate sending a cascade of crumbs on to the floor.

Penny quickly mopped up the milk with her serviette but not before her father had seen what had happened and frowned in annoyance.

When Mary came into the room to clear away after they'd finished Captain Forshaw instructed her to stay and keep an eye on Kelly because he wished to speak to Penny and his wife before he left for the office.

'Give the child a biscuit or more milk or something if she is tiresome,' he told Mary curtly as he ushered Penny and his wife from the room.

'The child is called Kelly so why don't you use her name when you are talking about her?' Penny said crossly once they were outside the morning room.

Captain Forshaw ignored her comment. In silence he ushered them into the drawing room and closed the door.

'Penny, after this morning's display I hope you realize that the child you are proposing to look after hasn't been trained to sit at table and eat in a civilized manner. From now on I must ask you to feed her in the kitchen or if Martha Davies says that isn't convenient then you must use the morning room after we have finished our breakfast. You will also serve her other meals in there and not with us. Is that understood?'

'I think it is a very appropriate decision,' Leonora Forshaw agreed quickly with a smug little smile of approval.

'That is so unfair,' Penny exclaimed. 'I agree she made one or two mistakes this morning but she is very unsure of herself. All this is new to her. You are treating her as if she was a pet animal. How do you think she is going to feel if she is isolated from us all at mealtimes?'

'Well, I suppose you could ask Mrs Davies to let her eat with them in the kitchen,' Captain Forshaw murmured.

'I'm not sure if that is fair on them,' Leonora stated very forcibly.

'The only other alternative if you don't want her to eat on her own is that you have your meals with her in the morning room,' Captain Forshaw stated, not giving Penny a chance to pursue the argument.

'Yes, that might be a much better idea,' his wife agreed. 'We certainly don't want to upset or inconvenience Mrs Davies because she is such a treasure.'

'If you decide to use the morning room Penny, then in the evenings you had better make sure that the child is fed and in bed by seven o'clock. If you do that then you can sit down and have dinner with us in a civilized manner,' Captain Forshaw added pompously.

'I think you are both being highly unreasonable,' Penny told them heatedly. 'I'm quite sure that seven o'clock is far too early for Kelly to be put to bed. How do you think she is going to feel about that?'

'You should have thought of all these many different aspects before volunteering to look after the child,' her father said dismissively.

'In fact, you should have done what Arnold suggested and put the child in a convalescent home of some kind for a few weeks until she could walk again,' her mother reminded her. 'If you'd done that then we wouldn't have had to have any dealings with her whatsoever.'

Penny took a deep breath then simply shrugged her shoulders in acceptance. She knew it was pointless arguing with them and she felt so angry that she was afraid she might say something she would later regret.

'I'll go and take Kelly out into the garden, she's probably wondering what is happening,' she said resignedly. 'She shouldn't be in anybody's way out there and she can't do much harm to the grass,' she added sarcastically.

'Well clean her up first; she has egg around her mouth and probably sticky hands. And do make sure she doesn't pull the heads off any of the flowers or the gardener will be cross,' her mother warned.

'Shall I carry her through to the garden for you, Miss Penny,'

Mary asked eagerly when Penny said she was going to take Kelly out there.

'Thank you, Mary, but I will be putting her into the pushchair. I need to take her upstairs first so that I can wash her face and hands and to find hats for both of us because the sun is already very hot out there.'

'I'll help her wash her hands down here if you like,' Mary offered.

By the time Penny came back downstairs with two straw sunhats Mary had already settled Kelly into the pushchair and offered to wheel her out into the garden.

'I wish I could stay out here and play with her but Mrs Davies will scold me if I don't get back to the sink and deal with all the dirty breakfast dishes,' Mary said wistfully when Penny thanked her for her help.

'Is Mary your sister?' Kelly asked in a puzzled voice as Penny bent down and fitted the smaller of the two straw hats on Kelly's head.

Penny found it difficult to explain. 'No, Mary's not my sister but she lives here with us and helps Mrs Davies in the kitchen and with the housework.'

'Why do you have someone to do the work? Can't your mam do it? My mam does all ours. And the washing and shopping and there's a lot more of us than there is living here,' Kelly went on.

'Yes, but this is a very big house to keep clean,' Penny explained.

'Why do you need so many rooms? We only have two proper rooms; the bedroom and the living room,' Kelly commented. 'We have a bit of the scullery as well but we have to share that with the people upstairs.'

Penny felt at a loss. 'Let's go and see what there is to look at in the garden shall we,' she said brightly in an effort to change the subject.

'Is all this your garden?' Kelly asked in a bewildered voice as Penny pushed her up the path leading from the patio to the flower garden and then to the kitchen garden where there was a large vegetable patch, fruit bushes, a plum tree and two apple trees that were loaded with ripening fruit.

As they walked back to the patio Kelly insisted on knowing the names of all the bushes and flowers and Penny did her best to name them.

'It's like being in a park, miss,' Kelly said in awe, her eyes shining.

'I thought we agreed that you were going to call me Penny.'

'Sorry, miss. I forgot. I wish I could play ball on the grass,' she said longingly.

'Perhaps you will be able to do so soon. Once your broken leg begins to mend and it is strong enough for you to stand on it then you will be able to use your crutches to walk about,' Penny said encouragingly.

'Penny, do you think my leg will be better again in time for me to go to school after the summer holidays are over?' Kelly asked pensively.

'Oh, I'm sure it will be,' Penny assured her. 'Which school do you go to?'

'I haven't started going to school yet,' Kelly sighed.

'Really? I thought you were already six?' Penny exclaimed in surprise.

'I am,' said Kelly with a giggle.

'In that case you should have been at school for at least a year,' Penny told her.

'Me mam says that once I start going then if I stays away the school board man will come to get me. I don't think she wants me to go at all really because she likes me being at home to help look after Brian and Lily.'

'Do you have to look after them very often?' Penny frowned thinking what a tremendous responsibility it must be for a six-year-old.

Kelly nodded. 'Most of the time me mam only takes the baby with her when she goes out to the shops or to the market,' Kelly told her with a big sigh. 'She says the other two play her up so she can't manage them as well as the baby.'

'Why ever not?'

Kelly spread her arms in exasperation. 'They don't like walking and me mam hasn't got a pram. She can't carry them as well as the baby and all the shopping now can she.'

'So is that why you don't go to school?'

'I suppose. I have to help me mam keep the place tidy, and I used to have to feed little Lily but she can feed herself now.'

Seven

When they went back indoors for their lunch Kelly didn't appear to notice that Mrs Forshaw didn't join them.

After lunch, although it was a very hot day, Penny put Kelly into the pushchair and walked to Vale Park.

'It's nice but not as pretty as your garden,' Kelly told her after she'd been pushed right round it.

'I'll bring you back here on Sunday and then you will be able to listen to the band,' Penny told her. 'This is where they play,' she added as they paused by the bandstand.

She wondered if she would be able to persuade Arnold to accompany them. It would be a wonderful opportunity for him to get to know Kelly right away from the pressure of her mother or father's presence.

Later in the afternoon when Penny arrived back home she found that Mary had already set the table in the morning room for Kelly's supper. There was a plate of egg and cress sandwiches and a piece of chocolate cake.

'Do you want a glass of milk to drink with that?' Penny asked.

Kelly shrugged her thin shoulders. 'Not really, I'd sooner have some lemonade,' she said hopefully.

After she had finished her meal Penny took her upstairs and washed her hands and face.

'I've never gone to bed this early before,' she protested as Penny helped her to undress and put on her nightdress.

'You don't have to go to sleep right away,' Penny told her. 'I'll see if I can find you some picture books to look at.'

'You didn't have your tea with me so are you going downstairs now to have some grub with your mam and dad?' Kelly asked when Penny came back with a pile of magazines.

Penny felt her cheeks redden. 'Yes, that's right,' she said almost apologetically.

'They don't want me down there with them because they don't like me, do they?' Kelly muttered defiantly.

'Of course they like you,' Penny protested. 'It's just that they aren't used to having young children around the place . . . not since I grew up,' she added lamely.

She bent over the bed and kissed Kelly on the brow. 'Would you like me to sit down and read you a story?'

'Do you mean from a comic?' Kelly's blue eyes widened excitedly. 'Sometimes my mam brings one of them home for me when she goes cleaning offices and she finds one thrown out in the rubbish bin.'

'Your mother goes out cleaning?'

'Of course she does; she has to earn money for grub and her booze. She only goes out cleaning at nights though and usually Lily and Brian are asleep by then. She leaves a bottle all ready for me to give the baby when it starts grizzling.'

'Does this happen every night?' Penny quizzed her.

'Nearly every night in the week except on Saturdays; that's when me mam goes to the pub for a bevvy with some of her friends.' Her brow creased into a frown making her look old beyond her years. 'I don't know how she'll manage without me there to look after the little 'uns when she wants to go out. Perhaps she'll make Paddy do it.'

'Paddy? I haven't met him. Is he your older brother?'

'That's right. He always skedaddles off somewhere with his mates when they come out of school and we don't see him until bedtime. If he does that then me mam will have to take the baby with her.'

'You mean she'll leave Brian and little Lily on their own?' Penny asked aghast.

'Yeah and they get scared on their own so they'll probably both be screaming their heads off by the time she gets back home.'

Before Penny could think what to say in response, Mary knocked on the bedroom door. 'Sorry to disturb you Miss Penny but Mr Arnold has arrived and he's asking for you.'

Arnold Watson, smartly dressed in white flannels and a dark green and white striped blazer, was waiting in the hall. He was twirling his panama boater hat with an air of impatience.

Penny paused as she descended the stairs and felt a surge of emotion. He looked so handsome that it made her heart beat faster and a smile played on her lips as she greeted him.

'Why aren't you ready?' he asked looking at her critically as he gave her a quick peck on the cheek. 'We're going to be late at the club,' he added tersely.

'Late for what?' Penny asked a puzzled look on her face.

'You surely haven't forgotten that we have a court booked for this evening for a doubles match with Isabel and Tony,' he said tetchily as he checked his watch.

'Oh!' Penny clapped a hand to her mouth. 'I'm so sorry, Arnold, I forgot all about it. Give me a moment and I'll change into my tennis skirt and collect my things. First though I'd better ask mother if she will keep an eye on Kelly while I'm out.'

'Kelly? You surely don't mean you have that slum child here, in your home!'

'You don't have to sound so surprised. You know that I was planning to bring her here so that I could look after her until her leg was better.'

'Yes, and I suggested putting her in a convalescent home of some kind and your father agreed with me. In fact, if I recall correctly, he even offered to foot the bill.'

'Well, I didn't agree with that and she's here,' Penny retorted with a tight smile.

'Not a good idea, surely,' Arnold frowned. 'Anyway,' he shrugged dismissively, 'we're late so we haven't time to discuss it now; we can talk about it later.'

'Did I hear Arnold's voice? Why have you left him in the hall?' her mother asked when Penny burst into the dining room to explain what was happening.

'He's called to take me to the tennis club and we are running late. I'm afraid I will have to miss dinner,' she told her mother apologetically.

'Oh dear, that's a shame because we are having one of your favourite dishes; are you sure you haven't time? There's plenty so Arnold is very welcome to eat with us.'

'Sorry, Mother but we have a court booked. All I wanted to do was ask if you would listen out for Kelly and check on her sometime during the evening to make sure she is all right.'

'You are asking me to look after that dreadful child,' Mrs Forshaw exclaimed in an exasperated voice, 'No, Penelope, that is quite out of the question.'

'Kelly's already in bed and she'll be asleep in a few minutes. All you need do is look in on her and see that she is all right,' Penny repeated.

'No, Penny. She's your responsibility; we made that quite clear when you defied your father's wishes to put her into some sort of home.'

'Very well, I'll asked Mary or Mrs Davies if they will do it.'

'Oh no, that is also out of the question,' her mother retorted her lips tightening into a disapproving line.

'There is really nothing to do,' Penny persisted. 'She's already had her supper, I've given her a wash and changed her into her nightdress. She'll probably be asleep within half an hour. It's simply a case of looking in on her later to check that she is all right,' Penny repeated.

'And that is your responsibility,' her mother affirmed.

'Does that mean I am going to have to stay in every evening all through the summer even though there are other people in the house?'

'Yes, unless you take the child along with you whenever you go out.'

'Mother, don't be difficult. How on earth do I explain that to Arnold whenever he wants to take me out?' Penny questioned in dismay.

'That's something you should have thought about and sorted out with him before you committed yourself to such an undertaking,' her mother retorted.

'Obviously,' Penny sighed. 'Look, do you think you could do it just for this once? Or can I ask Mary to help out, so that I don't have to upset all Arnold's arrangements for this evening.'

'The answer remains the same, Penny. The child is your responsibility. If you go out with Arnold this evening then you must be prepared either to take the child with you or else leave her to her own devices. Perhaps you had better lock her in your bedroom because I certainly don't want her wandering through the rest of the house.'

Arnold's face darkened with anger when Penny apologetically started to explain why she wouldn't be able to go to the tennis club with him that evening.'

'Yes, Penny, I heard every word your mother said and I simply can't believe that you are putting this little guttersnipe before me!' he exclaimed angrily.

'I'm not; it's not like that Arnold. I can hardly leave her on her own though, can I.'

'She's probably well used to being on her own,' he pointed out. 'Her mother is probably off down to the pub or standing out in the street gossiping to her neighbours every evening.'

'No, as a matter of fact her mother goes out cleaning in the evenings.'

'Well there you are then, exactly what I have just said. She can take care of herself because she is used to being on her own in the evening.'

'No –' Penny shook her head – 'it's not like that. She has to look after her siblings and one of them is only a baby, so she is far from being alone.'

'Perhaps you should have brought them here as well and then she'd have had plenty of company when you wanted to come out with me,' he said spitefully.

They stood for a moment glaring angrily at each other. He's behaving like a spoilt brat, simply because he can't have his own way she thought as she saw his mouth tighten and his jaw jut aggressively.

She had never seen him in such a petulant mood but then until now she had never attempted to defy him. She had always fallen in with his plans even when it meant cancelling arrangements she had already made.

'I don't know what do,' she murmured. 'I really don't think I can leave her on her own when she's only been here a couple of days.' She put her hand on his arm pleadingly. 'Everything in this house is so strange and so different for her.'

'Then take her back to the hovel she came from and let her own mother take care of her. She's not your responsibility; she caused the accident by running out into the road in front of your car,' he told her callously.

'I know that but I have promised to take care of her to try and stop her mother suing for damages and to make sure that our name and yours are kept out of the newspaper,' she reminded him.

'She'll probably sue you anyway no matter what she says to

the contrary. You can never trust those sort of people, that's what they are like,' he told her in a contemptuous voice.

'Look, I am very sorry about letting you down this evening, Arnold. I promise that I'll try and make better arrangements in the future,' Penny told him contritely.

'Don't bother. I can easily find myself another partner at the tennis club and not just for tonight's match,' he said dismissively, as he rammed his straw boater on to his head and, turning on his heel, moved towards the front door.

As the door slammed behind him Penny heard her mother call out to her from the dining room. She was so close to tears, though, that she simply couldn't face another interrogation at that moment, so she fled upstairs to her room.

She stood by the window staring out unseeingly, tears streaming down her cheeks. She felt utterly devastated by Arnold's reaction. He hadn't even kissed her apart from a brief peck on the cheek when he'd arrived.

She thought back over the good times they'd had when they'd first started going out together and wondered if they would ever return to those carefree days. She knew her friends envied her. Arnold was not only from a wealthy family but extremely handsome and very much in demand.

She knew he liked to have his own way and usually she went along with whatever he suggested. Most of their friends did the same. She'd always attributed it to his popularity but now she wondered if perhaps they too had discovered that he didn't like to be thwarted in any way.

She twisted the solitaire diamond ring on her left hand, the ring Arnold had placed there less than a year ago as a pledge of their love for each other.

Their engagement party had been such a memorable occasion. They'd had a party at the Adelphi in Liverpool. As well as their own friends there had been shipping magnates, importers and exporters, business connections of her family and Arnold's. It had been like a pre-announcement of the merger that there would one day be between their two companies.

This was the man she was planning to marry she reminded herself. In a few months' time they would be man and wife and then she would certainly be expected to do whatever he dictated.

What sort of life was she letting herself in for when it was impossible to reason with him and he wasn't prepared to compromise even for one evening? Furthermore, he had let her down at the very moment when she most needed his love and support.

Arnold had made it quite clear that, like her parents, he didn't approve of what she was doing and wanted nothing at all to do with Kelly.

Eight

The argument marked the start of an entirely different regime for Penny. She was kept busy during the day with looking after Kelly and keeping her entertained. Most days she took her out to one of the parks or for a walk along the promenade or kept her amused in the garden.

Whenever her mother invited any of her own friends around for afternoon tea she always insisted that Penny must take Kelly out somewhere. She also stipulated what time she should return home again so that she could make sure that none of her friends ever encountered Kelly.

The evenings were quite another matter. Apart from taking dinner with her parents Penny found herself in complete isolation once Kelly was in bed and asleep. Even though she knew that Mary would have been quite willing to listen out for Kelly in the evenings she had been forbidden by her mother to ask her to do so.

Arnold was conspicuous by his absence and both her parents repeatedly commented on this. Penny did her best to avoid the subject knowing that he was fulfilling arrangements they'd made at the tennis club and that she should have been there with him.

Deep down she was bitterly saddened by his attitude. She had thought that given time he would understand and support what she was doing. She had even envisaged the two of them taking walks in the evening and at the weekends with Kelly in her pushchair. Not only had Arnold made it quite clear the first time she had suggested it that he had no intention of ever being seen with Kelly but he had even stopped coming to the house.

As the days passed Kelly made excellent progress. She filled out from eating good regular meals and having plenty of sleep. Slowly but confidently she was walking short distances using her crutches and she loved nothing better than when Penny took her on the bus to New Brighton.

Once there she was equally happy to sit in the window of

one of the many cafés drinking a glass of lemonade or eating an ice cream and watching all the people passing by, or for them to take a short walk along the promenade or even down on the shore.

'Is that really Liverpool over there?' she would ask in disbelief as she looked across the Mersey and saw the outlines of the Liver Building against the skyline.

Penny wondered if she was homesick but whenever she asked her if she was missing her mother and her brothers and sisters Kelly would give her a big beaming smile and say, 'Not really because it is so much nicer living over here with you.'

'Well, it can't last much longer,' Penny warned her as August drew to a close. 'I will have to return to work soon and that means you will have to go back home to your mother.'

'I don't want to,' Kelly sighed. 'I want to stay here with you for ever and ever.'

'I'm afraid that's not possible,' Penny told her, giving her a hug and a kiss.

'I wonder if I will be able to go to school when I get home even though I still can't walk properly?' Kelly asked.

'Oh, I'm sure you will,' Penny told her brightly.

'What about when we go out to play? If the other kids are rough then I might get pushed over.'

'I am sure that won't happen because you really are getting stronger every day,' Penny told her encouragingly, 'You will have to go and see the doctor at the hospital before then and he will decide if you are fit enough to go to school or whether you need to stay home for a bit longer.'

Kelly's face brightened. 'If he says that I can't go to school then can I go on living here with you, Penny?' she begged in a wheedling tone of voice.

'No, Kelly, as I've already told you I'm afraid that won't be possible because I will be going back to work and that will mean you will have to go home to your mother.'

When she took Kelly to the hospital for a check-up at the end of August they were told by the doctor that it would be best if she delayed going to school for at least another month.

Penny was very taken aback. She wondered if perhaps she should have taken her father's advice and let Kelly go into a convalescent home after all. They would probably have been able to do much more for Kelly than she had done to get her fully mobile again.

Perhaps it still wasn't too late. Then the thought of having to admit to her parents and Arnold how wrong she'd been made her decide that it wasn't the answer. No, she resolved, there was nothing else for it she must take Kelly back to her own home in Liverpool.

Penny thought that Cannon Court looked even more drab and dirty than it had done the first time she'd visited it. She felt a shudder of distaste go through her as she knocked on the basement door of number five.

When Ellen Murphy finally answered the door she looked as grubby and bedraggled as she had done the first time Penny had seen her. The two smaller children, Brian and Lily, were clutching at her skirt.

Ellen didn't look at all pleased to see them. 'You'd better come in,' she said a little grudgingly and giving Penny a rather hostile look.

As they went into the living room Penny found the putrid smell that assailed them was almost overpowering. Although there were damp clothes hanging everywhere, the window was tightly shut and the air was fetid.

Brian and Lily stood staring up at her saucer-eyed but refused to speak or even smile at her or Kelly. The baby was lying half naked on a grubby sheet in the old wicker basket, clutching an empty feeding bottle to its mouth and sucking loudly on it.

With Kelly clinging on to her arm like a limpet, Penny explained to Ellen Murphy that Kelly would have to return home almost at once because as a teacher she herself would be starting back at school in less than a week's time.

Ellen Murphy looked stunned.

'You gave me your word that you would look after my kid until she was proper better,' she stated angrily. 'Now all of a sudden you've decided to go back on your promise.'

'Not at all. I have looked after Kelly for almost a month and in another couple of weeks she will be perfectly fit and ready to go to school.'

'And what am I supposed to do with her until then? Wait

on her hand and foot and help her to get around? I can't have her leaning on me arm while I carry the baby and manage the other two little ones all at the same bloody time.'

'There's no need for Kelly to lean on your arm, she's able to get about quite well on her own using her crutches.'

'She can't help me or carry the baby or the shopping, though, when she's on those things now can she?' Ellen Murphy pointed out.

'True, but since she doesn't need the pushchair any more you can use that for the baby. In fact, Kelly might even be able to walk without her crutches if you let her be the one to push the baby because the pushchair will give her all the support she needs.'

'No, it's no good.' Ellen Murphy remained adamant. 'I've enough to do as it is and it would be more trouble to me than she's worth if Kelly came home now.'

'I'm afraid she will have to do so, Mrs Murphy,' Penny insisted. 'As I keep telling you I have to go back to work.'

'You said you'd look after her until she was better. If you don't then I'm off to see the scuffers. I'll tell 'em all about how you knocked our Kelly down with your motor car and the way you have been trying to avoid going to prison by promising to look after her until she is better.'

'Kelly ran out into the road in front of my car,' Penny said quietly.

'Even so you knocked her down and then went on your way without bothering about her and that's a crime,' Ellen Murphy insisted doggedly.

'You know quite well that what you are saying isn't true,' Penny defended firmly. 'I stayed with her until the ambulance came and then after I had talked to the police I came over here to find out how she was.'

'That's as maybe but we'll see what the scuffers have to say. They'll have made notes about the accident you can bet your boots on that. If they say it was your fault and that you were driving too fast then it will be their word against yours. And you bloody well know who will be believed when the case comes up in court,' she added triumphantly.

Penny knew it was useless arguing with her. Instead she tried bribery. 'Look, Mrs Murphy, if I give you some money each week until Kelly is completely better so that you don't have to go out charring in the evenings then surely that would help.'

'Who told you I go out charring?' Ellen demanded angrily, her sallow face flushing.

'Kelly said something about having to look after the baby and her little brother and sister when you went out on cleaning jobs in the evening,' Penny murmured.

'So it was you as what told the welfare people about it and had them trying to stop the few measly bob they gives me,' Ellen said furiously.

'Not at all, I haven't spoken to anyone about you. I know nothing at all about your affairs. I only want to help.'

'Then stop going back on your promise. You said you'd look after Kelly until she was proper better. She's no use to me until she can help me around the house.'

'I'm sure she will be able to help you a great deal,' Penny murmured.

'If she can't walk proper then she can't carry the other kids around, so she's no use to me at all and I don't want to be lumbered with her. I have enough to do as it is,' Ellen Murphy added as she picked the baby up in an attempt to stop it crying.

'I've already explained that I have to return to work next week,' Penny reminded her.

'Then take her to work with you the same as I have to take these three along with me when I go out cleaning now.'

'If Kelly was back at home with you then she could look after them again while you did that,' Penny pointed out.

'How? She can hardly walk herself so how is she going to carry them around or lift them back into bed if they falls out?'

'Come, come Mrs Murphy, how often does that happen?'

'They can be right little devils so how is she going to stop them from fighting if she can hardly walk,' Ellen Murphy went on, ignoring Penny's remonstration.

'No, you stick to what you promised, miss. You said you'd look after our Kelly until she was better and that's what you'll have to do. Ain't that right, Kelly?'

For the first time since they'd entered the place she looked directly at her eldest daughter and seemed to notice her clean appearance and the pretty dress she was wearing.

'Just look at her all dressed up in her fancy glad-rags and with a ribbon in her hair. You don't want to come back here anyway do you, Kelly. Not after living in a big posh house and prancing around like a lady, now do you, luv?'

'Not really, Mam,' Kelly answered with a grin. 'This is a dirty old hole and you look grubby and dead scruffy.'

'There, what did I tell you,' Ellen Murphy exclaimed triumphantly.

'I got a bed all to myself at Penny's house and their garden is as big as a park,' Kelly went on smugly.

'There, what did I say! Spoilt her rotten you have. She doesn't even want to come back home to her own mam and her family.'

'I'm sure she does,' Penny said lamely. 'She knows that I have to go back to work quite soon and that it is impossible for her to stay with me any longer.'

'You mean your mother doesn't want her there, more likely,' Ellen Murphy said sourly.

'She don't. Her mam hates me, says I'm a little guttersnipe. Her dad don't like me either and nor does her boyfriend Arnold either,' Kelly confirmed.

'That's nice to know now, isn't it? No matter how much they dolls you up in fine clothes, shiny new shoes and puts a ribbon in your hair they still thinks of you as a kid from the Liverpool slums do they,' Ellen sneered.

'Mrs Murphy, I don't think you should say things like that,' Penny said reprovingly.

'Why not? It's the bloody truth, now, ain't it? Poor little bugger she won't know where she is when she gets back here. All the other kids will tease the living daylights out of her for being so bloody stuck up and having such la-di-dah ways.'

Nine

Leonora Forshaw looked utterly astounded when Penny walked back into the house again and she saw that Kelly was still with her.

'I thought you were taking that child back to her own home,' she said reprovingly. 'I hope you haven't forgotten that you are due back at school in two days' time?'

'I know. We'll talk about it later . . . after Kelly is in bed,' Penny said shortly as she helped Kelly out of the pushchair and parked it in an alcove in the hall.

'No, Penny, we'll talk about it right now; I want to know where things stand,' her mother said firmly. 'Why have you brought that child back here again?'

'Kelly's mother is not able to look after her and I did undertake to do so until she was quite better if you remember,' Penny answered in a low voice. 'I don't want to discuss it in front of her.'

'Really! I hope you know what you are doing and I hope you are going to be the one to explain the situation to your father,' her mother said sharply.

'Of course!'

Leonora Forshaw's mouth tightened into a thin disapproving line but she said no more. Turning on her heel she walked away.

'She don't want me here do she,' Kelly pouted. 'I like you but I don't like her one little bit.'

'Hush, I've told you before that you mustn't say things like that,' Penny admonished quietly. 'What about a glass of lemonade and one of those biscuits you like so much,' she added quickly as she saw the tears filling Kelly's eyes.

'You mean those wafer ones that have the chocolate inside them,' Kelly grinned, her face lighting up as she brushed away her tears with the back of her hand.

'That's right, and since it is such a nice day we'll sit outside in the garden.'

Penny settled Kelly in a canvas chair on the terrace and took her out some lemonade and two wafer biscuits. When she returned to the kitchen to collect her own glass of lemonade she was rather annoyed to find that her mother was waiting there for her.

'Let me make it quite clear from the start, Penny, that I have no intention of looking after that child while you are at school,' she said in a firm uncompromising voice.

'I never for one moment thought that you would,' Penny told her as she took a sip of her lemonade.

'So what do you intend to do with her? I'm not prepared to look after her and I will not permit either Mary or Mrs Davies to do so.'

'Thank you, Mother you have already made that quite clear so the answer is obvious.'

'What do you mean? You can't be thinking of taking her to school with you,' Leonora Forshaw exclaimed her eyes widening in alarm.

'That is precisely what I shall be doing,' Penny said determinedly.

'Now you really are being ridiculous. I'm quite sure Miss Grimshaw won't stand for that,' her mother told her scornfully. 'You have only to look at the child to see that she won't fit in with any of the other children who attend there.'

'Well, I'll soon find out if you are right or not since school starts the day after tomorrow,' Penny stated.

At first Kelly was quite excited when Penny explained to her that as she had to go back to work she would be taking her along to the school with her. Then suddenly she went quiet and there was a look of doubt on her face.

'Have you asked me mam if it's all right for me to go to school. She said that once I started I'd have to go every day otherwise the school board man would be hammering on the door to know where I was and she'd be in trouble.'

'I don't think there is any need for you to worry about that,' Penny assured her. 'This is a private school and no one in Liverpool will know anything about it.'

Although she made sure that Kelly had on a suitable dress and that her hair was well brushed and neatly tied back from her face with a ribbon, Mrs Forshaw's prediction was right. Miss Grimshaw was appalled by the idea of admitting Kelly to the school.

'How do you think you can possibly give your full attention to your class if you have a disabled child to take care of at the same time. What on earth are you thinking of Penelope.'

'I caused her injuries and I have promised her mother I will take care of her until she is better,' Penny explained. 'It will only be for a very short time until she is able to walk. Once she no longer needs crutches for support she will be going back to her own home in Liverpool.'

Miss Grimshaw shook her head. 'I'm sorry, Miss Forshaw,' she said formally, 'I cannot countenance it. It would be against all school protocol.'

'It's only intended to be a temporary arrangement,' Penny insisted.

'No!' Miss Grimshaw's face tightened. 'To start with you said yourself that she had never attended school before so she will have no idea about the rules or how to mix with other children.'

I'll make sure that she doesn't transgress any of the rules,' Penny promised.

'No, most definitely no!' Miss Grimshaw stated firmly. 'I'm afraid you will have to make other arrangements; either that or I shall have no alternative other than to temporarily suspend you from your duties.'

'I rather think my father will have something to say about that,' Penny stated, looking Miss Grimshaw in the eye. 'After all this is a private school and he is one of the governors.'

'He may be but there are six others,' Miss Grimshaw reminded her frostily.

Penny could see that she was losing the argument and that getting all heated up was not improving the situation one iota so she decided to change her tactics.

Taking a deep breath she decided that for Kelly's sake she must put her own pride and feelings to one side and adopt a different approach.

'Surely we can give it a try Miss Grimshaw and see how it works out,' Penny begged in a softer more cajoling voice as she looked hopefully at the stern figure facing her.

In her tailored grey cotton dress with its stiffly starched white collar and cuffs, and her dark hair in a tight bun, Miss Grimshaw looked so determined and uncompromising that Penny suspected that her argument was falling on deaf ears.

'I understand from what I've heard from Captain Forshaw that this child is from the Scotland Road area of Liverpool,' Miss Grimshaw stated in a severe voice. 'Now, how do you think the parents of the other children attending our school are going to feel about that?'

Penny groaned inwardly. Obviously her father had already discussed the matter in great detail with Miss Grimshaw and she wondered if he had warned her against allowing Kelly to attend the school.

'I don't understand what her background has to do with it,' she said boldly. 'Kelly is living in our house at the moment. Surely that must count for something.'

'Yes, so I believe,' Miss Grimshaw commented acidly, 'but I think I am right in saying that it is your idea that she is there and that it is not with your family's approval.

'Apart from that,' she went on quickly before Penny could answer, 'the child is hardly likely to settle in here. Our pupils are all from good homes; they are all expected to wear a school uniform and they have all been properly brought up. They are used to a much higher standard of living than this poor little thing,' she added deprecatingly.

'I am quite prepared to buy Kelly a school uniform if that is all that is worrying you,' Penny assured her. 'As for fitting in, well children are extremely open-minded about most things unless they are taught differently. I'm sure Kelly will make friends here in next to no time.'

'I very much doubt that.'

'Please, Miss Grimshaw, can we at least put it to the test by letting her stay on for the moment? I have left her out in the playground with two of the girls from my class looking after her and I must say that they all seem to be getting along extremely well.'

Miss Grimshaw gave an impatient sigh and shook her head dismissively.

'Please, Miss Grimshaw. If she doesn't fit in with the other children, or there are complaints from any of the parents, then I promise that I will make other arrangements.'

'Penelope, I'm very sorry but the matter is out of my hands. Captain Forshaw has already told me that I am not to admit the child to this school.'

'My father has done what!' Penny's voice rose. She felt an overwhelming surge of anger. How dare he interfere. 'What on earth has my father's opinion on the matter have to do with something like this,' she demanded, two spots of high colour staining her cheeks. 'It has nothing whatsoever to do with him,' she added lamely.

'I'm afraid it has,' Miss Grimshaw stated firmly. 'As you have already reminded me, Captain Forshaw is one of the governors and as they all agree it is imperative that we maintain the high reputation of the school.'

'You mean that having Kelly here will affect your high standards?'

'Parents are paying very substantial fees for their children to attend this school and as I have already said they will not want them associating with a child who comes from the slums of Liverpool.'

Before Penny could reply someone knocked on the door calling out Miss Grimshaw's name. When she told them to enter one of the prefects came into her office.

'Miss Grimshaw, there's been an accident. That new girl has been knocked . . . I mean fallen down in the playground and seems to have hurt her arm.'

Together Penny and Miss Grimshaw rushed out into the playground to find out what had happened. A group of children were already gathered round Kelly who was lying on the ground clutching her arm and sobbing noisily. When one of them tried to help her up she screamed and lashed out wildly with her good arm.

Penny knelt down beside her and spoke to her quietly and gently stroked her hair back from her tear-stained face until she was calmer. Then she gently touched her arm to try and see if it was broken or merely badly bruised. From the angle of her hand it was pretty certain that she had broken either her wrist or one of the bones in her arm.

'You'd better take her along to the hospital and have it checked out,' Miss Grimshaw ordered when Penny looked up and told her this. 'Where is your car parked? Do you need any help to get her into it?'

'I'm afraid I don't have my car, I'm not allowed to drive it since the accident,' Penny said in a tight voice.

'Oh, that is irritating,' Miss Grimshaw frowned. 'I'm not sure the child's injuries justify calling an ambulance. I'll try and see if anyone is prepared to drive you to the hospital.'

'No, please don't do that, I would prefer to call a taxi,' Penny stated firmly.

Kelly was still sobbing noisily as Penny and one of the other teachers helped her to stand up. Because of her injured arm she was unable to use her crutches so between them they carried her into the school building and put her on a chair.

She sat there hunched up and crying, her thin shoulders heaving spasmodically, until the taxi arrived.

While they were waiting Penny tried to comfort the sobbing child. She decided that the most sensible thing to do would be to take her straight to the Liverpool Infirmary rather than the local hospital. She hoped that if they went there they would be able to see the same doctor who had dealt with Kelly's broken leg.

Two hours later it was confirmed that Kelly had broken her arm and that it would have to be in plaster and that in all probability it would take about six weeks before she would be able to use it again.

Penny's spirits sank; with her arm in a plaster cast Kelly would be unable to use her crutches and so once again it would mean taking her everywhere in the pushchair. It also meant there would be an even longer delay before Kelly could return home to her own mother.

Ten

Kelly was very subdued as they travelled back to Wallasey in a taxi. She huddled up as close to Penny as she could, sniffling back her tears but not speaking. She had still not explained exactly what had happened out in the playground or how she had come to fall over.

While she'd been waiting for Kelly's arm to be attended to Penny had wondered if she ought to alert Mrs Murphy about this new accident. In the end she'd decided that it would be futile to do so. Kelly was now even more in need of some loving care and understanding and she was pretty sure she wouldn't get that from her mother.

Miss Grimshaw listened in silence as Penny gave her a detailed report about what had happened at the hospital. She frowned forbiddingly when Penny said it meant that she now had no alternative but to bring Kelly to school with her each day.

'I'm sure it will work out all right,' Penny said confidently. 'I will leave her sitting in her pushchair in a corner of the classroom so she will be no trouble at all,' she added.

'That is completely out of the question. I am very surprised that you have even suggested it. It would be far too disruptive for the rest of the class and, as I have already told you, it would be going against Captain Forshaw's instructions.'

Penny squared her shoulders determinedly. 'I'll talk to my father as soon as I get home; I'm sure he will reconsider his decision when he hears what happened today.'

'I very much doubt it,' Miss Grimshaw said sternly. 'The other governors were in full agreement with him. The only thing I can advise you to do Penelope is to take an extended holiday. I will do my best to reinstate you at a later date after you have returned the child to its mother.'

★   ★   ★

As the taxi approached Penkett Road Penny became apprehensive about how her own family would react when they heard the news about Kelly's latest accident.

She blamed her father; if he hadn't interfered none of this would have happened, she told herself. She knew she daren't say that to his face but she felt very resentful because by discussing Kelly with Miss Grimshaw he had made her life so much more difficult.

Arnold would also be furious when he heard the news, she thought worriedly. He had made it clear from the outset that he wanted nothing to do with Kelly and he'd kept his word. Penny knew he couldn't wait for Kelly to recover and to go home to her own family.

Even so she found it very hurtful that she had barely seen anything of him over the last month. She was aware from the many rumours that her mother heard and seemed to delight in reporting back to her that he had been carrying on almost as if she didn't exist.

According to her mother's reports Arnold spent most of his evenings and also his weekends at the tennis club. Whenever he attended any other social function or dance he escorted one of the girls from the tennis club.

'People are talking and wondering what is going on between the two of you,' her mother repeatedly told her. 'The next thing you know he will be breaking off your engagement and I dread to think how upset your father would be if that happened.'

'There's nothing very much that I can do about it since you won't look after Kelly in the evenings. If you did that then I could go out with him occasionally,' Penny had pointed out rather tersely.

'Your father has strictly forbidden me to do so,' Mrs Forshaw stated primly. 'Not that I want to have anything to do with the child anyway.'

'I know you don't want to help with her but Mary or Mrs Davies would do so if only you would let them,' Penny reminded her.

'That is completely out of the question. Both Mary and Martha Davies are employed to work for us, not spend their time looking after some child from the Liverpool slums.'

* * *

'What on earth has happened now, Leonora Forshaw demanded as Mary ran to tell her that a taxi had pulled up outside the house and Miss Penny was helping Kelly out of it.

'I don't know but the little girl seems to have her arm in a sling,' Mary said breathlessly.

As Penny helped Kelly into the house Mrs Forshaw frowned. 'Another accident?' she asked in an icy accusing tone.

'Yes, Mother. I'm afraid Kelly has had another accident and has broken her arm.'

'How very careless. First it was her leg and now it's her arm. Does she do it on purpose?'

Penny bit her lip to stop herself from answering and entering into an argument with her mother. She knew it would be pointless to do so and only antagonize her mother even more.

It had been a long day for both of them and Penny felt quite relieved when Kelly asked in a tired little voice if she could go to bed and have her supper brought up to her.

'Of course you can if you are sure you want to do that,' Penny agreed.

She had to admit that Kelly did look tired and exhausted. There were traces of tears on her face and whether these were as a result from all she had gone through at the hospital that day or because she was upset because she sensed that she wasn't wanted back at Penkett Road, Penny wasn't sure.

'I want to go straight to bed because I feel so tired and now my arm is hurting as well as my leg,' Kelly said in a piteous little voice.

'Yes, I'm sorry about that,' Penny said gently. 'It was my fault for leaving you out in the playground while I talked to Miss Grimshaw.'

'It wasn't your fault,' Kelly defended. 'It was them two girls that did it.'

'What do you mean?' Penny stared down at Kelly in surprise. 'You still haven't told me exactly what happened, have you?' she added gently.

'They pushed me so hard that I fell over. They said they didn't want any slum kids in their class.'

'They did what!' Penny felt indignant. The two girls she had asked to look after Kelly were the best behaved in her class.

She could only surmise that they had overheard their parents discussing the reason why she was looking after Kelly following her accident.

An hour later when Penny came back down the stairs, after consoling Kelly, taking up her supper tray and then tucking her into bed and making her as comfortable as possible, she could hear Arnold's voice and then her mother's coming from the direction of the sitting room.

They seemed to be deep in conversation about something but they both stopped abruptly the moment Penny entered the room.

Arnold stood up and walked over to greet her and gave her a light peck on the cheek.

'I popped in to tell you some good news and to remind you that there is a meeting of the Drama Society tonight.'

'I'm afraid I won't be able to come,' Penny said apologetically, 'I have to stay with Kelly.'

'I thought that you were taking her back to her own mother in Liverpool once you started back at school,' Arnold responded with a frown.

'Yes, that was the plan but the situation has changed. I took Kelly into school with me today and there was an accident in the playground and she has broken her arm and is now in a worse state than ever.'

Arnold frowned as if he didn't understand what she meant.

'Because of her broken arm Kelly can't use her crutches and she isn't able to walk without them so she will be staying in my care until she is better,' Penny explained.

Arnold's handsome face darkened. 'This really is too bad of you, Penny. I've been without a partner at the tennis club all through the summer season because you didn't bother to come out with me and now you've found another excuse.'

'From what I've heard you've managed to find yourself plenty of partners so I hardly think you have noticed my absence all that much,' Penny retorted spiritedly.

Arnold's scowl deepened. 'It is very important that you attend the Drama Society tonight. We are putting on a Shakespearean comedy and as I was telling your mother I have been given the lead part and of course I insisted that you should star opposite me. The rest of the cast are being selected tonight and we will be starting rehearsals next week as soon as we've had a chance to learn our parts.'

'Oh, Arnold, how wonderful,' Penny exclaimed delightedly, knowing how keen he was on amateur dramatics. Then her face clouded. 'But I'm afraid my accepting a part is out of the question because of Kelly.'

He stared at her in disbelief, his dark eyes narrowing. 'Surely, once you have put her to bed at night that is the end of the matter until next morning. You don't have to be here or stay with her,' he snapped.

'That's not quite right. If Kelly needs anything or has to get out of bed to go to the bathroom then I must be here to help her.'

'Absolute rubbish, Penny! Surely one of your maids can see to her?'

Penny shook her head and looked appealing at her mother. Leonora Forshaw's mouth tightened. 'No, that is not possible, Arnold. I'm afraid Captain Forshaw won't countenance it,' she said primly.

'I'm sure you wouldn't mind keeping an eye on the child during the evenings once she is in bed?' he said in a persuasive tone.

Leonora Forshaw squared her shoulders and shook her head firmly. 'No, Arnold. I have already told you that it is quite out of the question. We made it quite clear when we permitted the child to stay here after the car accident that she was Penelope's responsibility.'

'I know, but do you realize that Penny is my fiancée and that she hasn't been out with me for the whole of August,' Arnold pointed out in an exasperated voice.

'I am well aware of that, Arnold, and it is one of the reasons why I have begged her to take the child back to its mother. In fact, if she had done this when I asked her to do so a couple of days ago then the child would never have fallen over and broken its arm.'

'Mother, her name is Kelly; I do wish you would stop referring to her as "the child". As for taking her back to her home I did try to do that before the new term started as you very well know.'

'In that case why was she still here with you when your new term started?' Arnold asked irritably.

'Her mother said she was unable to cope until Kelly is capable of walking unaided.'

'Absolute rubbish! She would have managed well enough if you'd left the child there,' her mother asserted. 'As it was you brought her back here and took her with you to school even though you were asked not to do so – and look what happened. You've brought all this on yourself, Penelope, because you are so stubborn and won't listen to reason or to what we tell you. I have nothing more to say on the subject,' Mrs Forshaw added in an indignant voice as she swept out of the room.'

'I can't believe that you can be so obstinate, Penny,' Arnold said tetchily the moment they were on their own. 'You've ruined my summer and now it looks as if you are intent on spoiling all my chances with the drama group as well.'

Penny bit her lip. 'As I said before, you managed to find someone to partner you at tennis all through the summer so I'm quite sure you won't have any problems finding someone to take on the leading lady role in the play,' she stated.

'That's true enough,' he agreed. 'Katy Wilson was hoping for the part so I'm sure she will be delighted to step into the breach when she hears that you have let me down.'

Penny felt hot colour staining her cheeks. Katy had been her rival in most things when they were at school and even now whenever they met she always took a special delight in flirting with Arnold. In the past she had always ignored this but now, remembering some of the gossip her mother had said she'd been told by some of her friends, Penny felt a surge of jealousy because she wasn't too sure about Arnold's feelings for Katy.

'I'm sorry, Arnold; I would have loved to have played opposite you but I'm afraid that it is out of the question,' she repeated reluctantly.

She laid a hand on his arm and reached up to kiss his cheek but he shook her hand off irritably and pulled away from her.

'Well, that's it, isn't it? You prefer to put this child before me. Since the situation looks like lasting for some considerable time I can see it is a complete waste of my time trying to make any plans for our future together.'

Penny stared at him in stunned dismay. 'What are you implying, Arnold?'

'I would have thought that I was making myself crystal clear,' he said abruptly. 'Since it appears that you intend to make your own arrangements about this child without any consideration for me—'

'That's not true, Arnold,' Penny interrupted him. 'As soon as Kelly is well enough to go back to her own home then I will be free and ready to fall in with any plans you wish to make, the same as I've always done.'

'Until the next lame dog comes along and demands all your attention!' he sneered.

'Arnold!' Penny's voice caught in a sob but he was unrelenting.

'I've pandered to your whims for long enough,' he went on in a hard voice. 'Our engagement is at an end; it's all over between us, Penny. You can keep the diamond engagement ring I gave you as a memento of how foolishly you've behaved.'

As the front door slammed behind Arnold, Mrs Forshaw came rushing into the room.

'Was that Arnold leaving?' She frowned. 'I invited him to stay to dinner.'

'He's gone, Mother and what is more he won't be coming back.'

'What on earth do you mean, Penny. Have you two had a lover's tiff?'

'Rather more than a tiff, Mother. Arnold has broken off our engagement.' Penny said, clenching her hands into fists at her side to stop herself from crying.

'Don't be so ridiculous! I never heard such nonsense. Why on earth has he done that?' she asked in disbelief.

Penny walked over to the window and stared out unseeingly. She couldn't believe that after all this time Arnold had simply walked out of her life. She wasn't sure what she felt about his rejection; possibly more angry than heartbroken, she mused.

'It's because of that dreadful child, isn't it?' her mother exclaimed in an 'I told you so' voice before Penny had a chance to answer. 'I warned you that this could happen but would you take any notice – of course you wouldn't. No man is going to like being pushed to one side simply because you decide to give all your attention to a slum child.'

Penny put her hands over her ears but it didn't shut out her mother's nagging voice.

'What your father will have to say I dread to think. He and Arnold's father had great plans for your future together. They even talked about merging their two companies when they both retire in a few years' time and putting Arnold in charge as managing director.'

'You talk about us as if we were a couple of puppets and you simply pull the strings and we dance to your tune,' Penny retorted bitterly. 'If you were so keen on me marrying Arnold then why didn't you let Mary look after Kelly some evenings so that I could go out with him?'

'You know the answer to that,' her mother retorted. 'If you had done as Arnold and your father wished and put the child in a nursing home then there would have been no problem. As it is you've made a rod for your own back and now your engagement is broken off as a result. I have no idea what your father will say when he comes home and hears about it. It wouldn't surprise me if he turned you out.'

The colour drained from Penny's face. 'You wouldn't let him do something like that,' she said in a small voice.

Mrs Forshaw gave an imperceptible shrug. 'He's head of the house and I have to go along with what he says, surely you realize that by now.'

Eleven

The atmosphere at the Forshaw's dinner table that evening was very strained.

'I thought you told me that you were inviting Arnold to dine with us tonight,' Captain Forshaw stated when Mary brought in the soup. 'Why aren't we waiting for him?'

'Arnold won't be coming. As a matter of fact it seems that we won't be seeing very much of him in the future,' Leonora Forshaw stated in an ominous tight-lipped voice.

'I'm afraid I don't understand what you mean?' Captain Forshaw shook out his napkin, picked up his spoon and attacked his soup.

'What mother means is that Arnold has broken off our engagement,' Penny said in a low voice.

Captain Forshaw reacted in exactly the way Penny's mother had anticipated. Frowning heavily he stared directly at Penny in disbelief.

'Did you say he's broken off your engagement!' he exclaimed. 'That's quite impossible. What are you talking about?'

'Arnold has broken off our engagement,' Penny repeated in a stony voice.

'Don't be so ridiculous, Penny! What has brought this about? A lover's tiff?'

'No, this is quite definite. There won't be any reconciliation,' Penny said tightly. She felt the tears welling up in her eyes; why was she always the one in the wrong. No one seemed to recognize that she had tried to act responsibly and do her duty in order to minimize the damage her accident might have on the rest of her family.

Her father's angry voice cut across her thoughts. 'Utter nonsense! William Watson and I have a great future planned for the pair of you after you are married.'

'Arnold is very fed up with the way Penny has been treating him for the last month or so and really I can't say that I blame him,' Leonora Forshaw piped up.

Marcus Forshaw looked from his wife to Penny and back again as if waiting for further details.

'He's seen practically nothing at all of her this summer because she has been too busy devoting all her time to this child she's taken under her wing,' Leonora explained in a waspish tone of voice.

'I thought that was all behind us. Surely your new term back at school started today, Penny, and we had agreed that you would take the child back to its mother.'

'Instead of which she took the child along to school with her and there was an accident in the playground. Now the child has a broken arm as well as a broken leg,' Leonora told him before Penny could do so.

Captain Forshaw pushed his soup bowl away and dabbed at his lips with his napkin. 'I cannot believe what I am hearing. How could a daughter of mine be so senseless and inconsiderate as to put a child from the Liverpool slums before her own future prospects,' he exclaimed bitterly, wiping his mouth fastidiously.

There was an ominous silence in the room as Mary came in to take away the soup bowls and to serve the main course.

'You know quite well why I did it, Father,' Penny reminded him in a tearful voice as soon as they were on their own. 'I did it because I felt it was my duty to prevent your name and Arnold's being dragged through the courts because of something I had done.'

'What utter nonsense! The case would never have reached the courts,' her father stated as he attacked the lamb chop that had been placed in front of him.

'Mother was worried in case details of the accident were in the newspapers and about the scandal that would result if my name was mentioned,' Penny persisted.

'Do stop trying to justify your foolish actions. I am bitterly disappointed in your inane behaviour, Penny. You defied me and the results have been disastrous. I want that child out of my house immediately.'

'I've already explained to mother that it is absolutely impossible for Mrs Murphy to look after Kelly because now that she has broken her arm she is unable to use her crutches to get about.'

'I'm not interested in the details. I don't want that child here any longer; do I make myself clear? What you do with her is your affair,' Captain Forshaw stated in a clipped angry voice.

'If you insist that she has to go then I'll go as well,' Penny said defiantly.

'That is entirely up to you but do remember that if you do I may not want you back here ever again,' her father told her harshly.

They continued eating their meal in silence. Penny pushed hers around on her plate, her appetite gone.

As soon as he had eaten his desert Captain Forshaw pushed back his chair and stood up.

'I'll have my coffee served in my study,' he said curtly as he left the room.

'Do you think he really meant what he threatened?' Penny asked worriedly, looking at her mother.

'I'm quite sure that he did,' her mother responded firmly, dabbing her lips with her napkin. 'He is extremely upset that you have gone against his wishes. The best thing you can do is to take the child back to Liverpool right now and hope he says no more about it.'

Kelly was still fast asleep when Penny went upstairs. She stood by the side of the truckle bed looking down at her and wondering what to do for the best.

Kelly still looked so thin and so very vulnerable that she couldn't bring herself to do as her father had instructed and take her back knowing the conditions she would have to endure. It would feel as though she was abandoning Kelly when she most needed her help.

Penny was still pondering the dilemma she was in and wondering if there was anything she could do to put matters right when she went to bed herself.

The future looked bleak. She had lost Arnold, so there was no question of turning to him for help, and her father had been adamant that he wouldn't have Kelly living there any longer. Nor was there any hope of Miss Grimshaw letting her have her job back as long as she was caring for Kelly.

Penny woke to a dull wet morning. The sky was grey and overcast and although it was only the start of September it felt as chilly as November.

She had lain awake for a long time during the night thinking back to her own childhood and the wonderful times she had known as she was growing up.

As an only child it had been a very privileged existence. Her earliest memories were of Nanny Pritchard, a plump, loveable woman who had been her constant companion until she was old enough to go to school.

It had been Nanny who had comforted her when she felt sad and who had dressed her in pretty dresses when there were guests and had taken her down to the drawing room to meet them. Afterwards, when she escorted her back to the nursery she would listen to her childish prattle as she undressed her and put her to bed.

It was Nanny who accompanied her on her first day at the private school her parents had chosen for her. Nanny who had patted her shoulder encouragingly and then struggled to hide her own tears when she had to leave her there.

Nanny had always been at the school gate to meet her at the end of each day. She had listened attentively to her account of all the things that had happened to her at school.

It had been a sad day for both of them when a few weeks after Penny's seventh birthday Mr and Mrs Forshaw decided that she no longer needed a Nanny and Mrs Pritchard was sent on her way.

She always remembered to send me a birthday card and another one at Christmas for the next ten years, Penny thought with a smile.

She recalled how she'd been heartbroken when the cards had stopped coming and her father had told her that it was because Mrs Pritchard had died.

By then she'd been in her teens and so many other things were occupying her time. Not long afterwards she had met Arnold and he had become the centre of her life.

As Kelly woke up, Penny's mind switched to the problems that faced her now. She wondered if she was overreacting and if she should simply carry on as normal and when they were both washed and dressed go down for breakfast as if nothing had happened.

If her father was there would he forget all about what he had threatened the day before or would he still insist that she should take Kelly and get out of his house, she wondered.

There was really only one way to find out, she decided, as she went along to have her bath and then help Kelly to wash and get dressed ready for the day.

The morning room was empty when she and Kelly went in there. 'What would you like to eat this morning?' she asked Kelly as she sat her down at the table. 'Is it to be porridge or shredded wheat or would you sooner have an egg and some toast?'

Before Kelly could make up her mind Mr Forshaw appeared in the doorway and his look was thunderous as his gaze rested on Kelly.

'Have you forgotten every word I said last night?' he asked Penny in an angry voice.

Penny took a deep breath before answering. 'No, Father but I wasn't sure if you really did mean what you said,' she ventured in as steady a voice as she could manage.

'I meant it; every word of it and you have defied me yet again. I want you and this child to leave immediately . . . and this time for good. Is that understood!'

'Very well, we'll go as soon as we've had breakfast,' she said as calmly as she could although inwardly she was shaking. He had never threatened her before and she found it hard to believe that it was happening.

'No, you will go now! You have ten minutes to pack a bag and I don't want to see either of you back here ever again. Do you understand?'

Penny stared at him in disbelief. 'You can't turn me out; this is my home. I have nowhere else to go,' she protested spiritedly. 'Think how upset Mother will be!'

'Your mother is in complete agreement with my decision. She is staying upstairs in her bedroom until she knows you have left the house.'

Penny felt too choked to answer. Her legs felt weak as she lifted Kelly from her chair and carried her in her arms as she went towards the door.

'I'm hungry, I haven't had any breakfast yet,' Kelly wailed petulantly.

'We're both going out to a café for our breakfast,' Penny mumbled, her voice shaky.

'You mean because there's nothing here for us to eat because your ma's run out of food like mine does?' Kelly said resignedly.

Penny nodded but didn't attempt to answer. Upstairs she tried to gather her wits and decide what to do. She had no idea where they could go except to Liverpool and she found it difficult to know what to take with them.

She counted out the money she had in her purse and checked the balance in her bank book; money she had been saving to buy things for her forthcoming wedding. She wouldn't be needing it now, she thought ruefully, then shuddered when she saw how little there was in either of them. There wasn't enough to last them for more than a week, or two at the most, unless she could find some sort of work.

Reaching down a brown leather suitcase from the top of the wardrobe she packed Kelly's few items into it. Then, almost in a panic, she rammed in as many of her own clothes as she possibly could. That done she dressed Kelly in the new warm coat she'd bought for her for the coming winter and then put her mackintosh on over it.

'You wait here a moment while I take these downstairs,' she told Kelly as she picked up the suitcase and one of her own winter coats.

Before she came back upstairs to collect Kelly she phoned for a taxi.

As she put on her own raincoat and hat she took one last look round her bedroom. Tears came into her eyes as she saw all the many books, pictures, family photographs and other precious belongings she was being forced to leave behind. As she moved towards the door she couldn't help wondering if she would ever see any of them again.

Kelly seemed to be aware that something dreadful was happening and her eyes were full of fear. Much as she wanted to explain and comfort her Penny couldn't find the right words to do so.

There was a lump in her throat as she picked Kelly up in her arms and carried her down the stairs and settled her into the pushchair.

Before leaving the house she looked into the dining room and the drawing room in the hope of seeing her mother but both rooms were completely empty.

The entire house seemed to be deserted and she assumed her father was in his study. Mrs Davies and Mary had probably been ordered to stay in the kitchen and her mother must still be upstairs in her bedroom.

'Can you manage to balance this on your lap?' she asked Kelly as she loaded the suitcase on top of her. 'It will only be for a few minutes,' she assured her when Kelly started to grumble about being squashed.

There was no one to say goodbye and wish them well and Penny felt as if her heart was breaking as they made their way out into Penkett Road to wait for the taxi.

Twelve

'Are you quite sure that this is the right address, miss?' the taxi driver asked in a perplexed voice as he unloaded the pushchair and the suitcase on to the rubbish-strewn pavement in Cannon Court.

'Yes, I'm quite sure,' Penny affirmed with a brief smile. She helped Kelly into the pushchair, balanced the case on it as well, and then paid him.

She waited until he had driven off before wedging the pushchair against a wall, picking up the suitcase and telling Kelly she would be back for her in a minute.

She was apprehensive about what sort of reception she would get from Mrs Murphy. Her heart was thudding as she carried the suitcase down the cracked steps to the battered black door in the basement. Then she went back up and helped Kelly down the steps and then returned for the pushchair. After she had settled Kelly back into the pushchair she took a long deep breath before knocking on the door.

Ellen Murphy opened the door with the baby in her arms and Brian and Lily clutching at her skirt. The top buttons of Ellen's grubby blue cotton blouse were undone and the baby was clawing inside it as if it had been interrupted while feeding. Penny wondered if Ellen ever put the baby down or whether she was still clutching it and feeding it when she went to bed at night.

'What do you want this time?' Ellen rasped, pushing the baby's hands away from her chest and struggling to fasten her blouse. 'I thought I made it plain that I didn't want our Kelly back here until she can do things for herself.'

'I know what you said, Mrs Murphy, but the situation has changed,' Penny said wearily. She felt tired and dispirited and the last thing she wanted was an argument.

'Changed? What do you mean by that?' Ellen Murphy asked, glancing at Kelly with a scowl on her face. 'She still ain't able to walk by the look of things and what's wrong with her arm? Why has she got it in a sling?'

'Kelly's had another accident and I'm afraid she has broken her arm. Don't worry, she's making good progress,' Penny added hastily, 'and I'll take care of her until it is better.'

'So what's this change you're on about then?' Ellen Murphy asked suspiciously.

'I've left home and—'

'Left home? You mean your folks have kicked you out more likely,' Ellen sneered. 'So where does that leave my Kelly?'

'I told you I would look after her until she is better and I will keep to my promise,' Penny told her sharply. 'I wondered if she could stay here for a short while and I also wondered if perhaps—'

'You ain't moving in here with us so you can put that idea out of your head right away,' Ellen interrupted.

'I can assure you I have no intention of doing so. What I was hoping was that you might be able to tell me where I could rent a couple of rooms fairly cheaply.'

'Its got to be on the cheap has it,' Ellen said disparagingly.

'Well yes, it will have to be somewhere at a fairly reasonable rent until I can find a job,' Penny explained.

'You mean you've lost your job as well as being kicked out of your home,' Ellen said in a shocked voice.

'Yes, and she's lost her bloke who's called Arnold,' Kelly piped up. 'I'm hungry, Ma, because her dad wouldn't let us have any breakfast so have you got any grub?'

'You mean all this has happened today and your folks have turned you out all because of you looking after my Kelly?' Ellen Murphy exclaimed a look of disbelief on her face.

'I'm afraid so. Now, can you tell me where I might find some accommodation?'

Ellen Murphy humped the baby on to her other arm. 'Not really, not the sort of place where you'd want to live,' she said slowly.

'Surely there must be some place you can recommend, someone you know who has a couple of rooms they would be willing to rent out,' Penny persisted.

Ellen shook her head; then her face brightened. 'Old Ma Reilly might take you in. She's very good-hearted and she's known all of us for years,' she added.

'Give me her address then and I'll go and see her and find out if we can stay there.'

'You can leave Kelly here while you do that just so long as you comes back for her,' Ellen Murphy said grudgingly.

'No, I'll take her with me and my suitcase as well so that this Mrs Reilly knows exactly what to expect.'

'She knows our Kelly and what happened to her so she won't need any explaining to be done. In fact, Ma Reilly knows about most things that go on around here. It's because she'm very well in with Father O'Flynn even though she doesn't go to Mass as often as she should.'

Blenheim Road was only a short distance away but Ma Reilly's terraced house was completely different from the Murphy's in Cannon Court.

The two steps leading up to the front door were scrubbed and whitened, the brass knocker and the letterbox shone like gold and the windowpanes gleamed like crystal. Lace curtains protected the privacy of the occupants from anyone standing at the front door.

Penny parked the pushchair at the bottom of the steps and told Kelly to sit still as she would only be a few minutes. When she knocked on the door she saw the lace curtains twitch slightly so she knew someone was in.

Within seconds the door was opened by a small stout woman with grey hair and a round apple-cheeked face who looked to be somewhere in her sixties. She was wearing a voluminous black skirt and a starched high-necked white cotton blouse fastened with a large cameo brooch.

'Mrs Reilly?'

'Ma Reilly; yes that's me. Was you wanting something?' Her sharp black eyes were questioning as she studied Penny closely.

'I – I'm looking for a room and I was told you might have one to let.'

'Is that so now; and who would be telling you such a thing as that may I ask?'

'Mrs Murphy who lives in Cannon Court told me. I'm looking . . .'

'Aah, sure, I knows you now.' Her face creased into a broad

smile. 'You're the young lady as what knocked over young Kelly Murphy when she was going for a day out at New Brighton and you've been looking after her ever since.'

'That's right. Well, she's had another accident and broken her arm so she is going to need looking after for a while longer, I'm afraid.'

'So why are you wanting to rent a room over here? I was told that you were caring for young Kelly at your own home over in Wallasey.'

'Yes, I have been doing that up until now but it's no longer convenient.'

Ma Reilly regarded her shrewdly.

'So you want a room for yourself and for her until she is fit again, is that it?' she said at last. 'Well, you'd better come inside and let's talk about it over a cuppa, not out here on the doorstep where the whole world can hear our business.'

'Is it all right if I bring Kelly in as well? She's sitting in her pushchair and I'm sure she must be feeling squashed because our suitcase is balanced on top of her.'

'Of course you must bring her in, you can't leave her out in the street like that! Fetch her on in and all your luggage as well. I'll go and put the kettle on. Do you need me to help or can you manage to get that pushchair up the steps?'

'Yes thank you, I can manage,' Penny assured her confidently.

Ma Reilly's kitchen was very bright and welcoming; everywhere was spotless and sparkling. It was obvious she took a pride in making sure that her home was neat and tidy and everything had a place of its own.

'So young Kelly has had another accident has she and her own mam can't be doing with looking after her as well as all the other little ones,' she commented as she moved the suitcase and the pushchair into a corner of the hallway.

'Well I suppose that's understandable but why are you coming over here to look after young Kelly? As I said before I was given to understand that she was staying with you at your big house over in Wallasey.'

'Well, yes, she was . . .' Penny hesitated, biting her lip, uncertain how to go on.

'Your folks have got fed up with having her there, am I right?' Ma Reilly commented, giving Penny a shrewd look.

'Something like that,' Penny mumbled.

'It's because they don't like me,' Kelly chimed in with a grin.

'I thought you were a schoolteacher,' Ma Reilly went on, ignoring Kelly's remark.

'Yes I am . . .'

'They sacked her because she took me to school with her and two of the girls there pushed me over in the playground and broke my arm,' Kelly butted in. 'When her bloke heard about it he dumped her as well because she couldn't go out with him because of looking after me and then her mam and dad got real cross and—'

'Kelly, that's enough. Shush!' Penny exclaimed in embarrassment.

'I reckon she's told me all I need to know,' Ma Reilly said chuckling. 'We'll say no more about it. Now, about that room you want to rent. I do have a room vacant and it's a fairly large one with two single beds in it so there's plenty of room for you both in there.'

'That sounds wonderful,' Penny said, a look of relief on her face.

'Come on then, I'll take you upstairs so that you can see it for yourself before you make up your mind about whether you want to take it or not.'

'I'll leave Kelly sitting down here if you don't mind,' Penny said.

'Yes, it will only take us a minute or two and she's heavy for you to carry around,' Ma Reilly agreed.

'It's in the front of the house and it's got a nice big window and there's always plenty going on out in the street for Kelly to watch,' Ma Reilly commented. 'You can both have your meals down in my kitchen with me,' she added as they made their way upstairs.

'The room was fairly big and spotlessly clean. It had two single beds side by side, a good size dark oak wardrobe and a matching dressing table with a big glass over it. As Mrs Reilly had told her, the window was very large and made the room appear light and airy.

'This will be fine as long as I can afford it,' Penny told her as she looked round. 'At the moment I'm not working,' she explained.

'Oh, I see.' Ma Reilly looked thoughtful. 'I thought you said you were a school teacher, so why not get yourself a teacher's job over here?'

'It's not as easy as that, Mrs Reilly. I was teaching at a private school and because of what happened to Kelly when I took her along with me the headmistress may not even be prepared to give me a reference.'

'Don't you worry your head about that. I'll have a word with Father O'Flynn, sure I will. They're bound to be needing good teachers.'

'That's very kind of you but I'm afraid I'm not a Catholic.'

'Ssh! We'll not talk about such things. If he needs a teacher then he needs a teacher and that's all there is to it. You leave it to me. I'll let you know in a day or two. Now what about that room? Are you going to take it? You can leave paying me until you get some wages,' she offered.

'Oh no, there's no need for you to wait. I can pay you, I do have some money,' Penny assured her. 'Not a great deal, mind,' she added with a wry smile.

They settled the details and Ma Reilly insisted on them having a cuppa to seal the deal.

'I haven't had me breakfast yet, her dad wouldn't let us have any,' Kelly told Ma Reilly when she put the kettle on for their cup of tea.

'Is that so, now. Then I'd better make you a butty to go with your glass of milk,' Ma Reilly told her. 'Which sort do you want a batty butty or a jam butty?'

'Ooh, lovely. I'm starving so can I have one of each?' Kelly asked, her face lighting up.

'Fish paste in one of them and strawberry jam in the other,' Ma Reilly murmured as she reached into the bread bin for the loaf of bread.

They sat for almost half an hour drinking their tea and chatting while Kelly munched her butties. Then Penny carried the suitcase upstairs to their room and unpacked it and put away their clothes while Kelly stayed down in the kitchen with Mrs Reilly.

When she'd finished unpacking Penny looked round with a feeling of satisfaction. She felt relieved that they had a roof over their head and knew she had been very fortunate to have found such good clean accommodation in such an area.

Although it was very different from what she was used to she felt hopeful that things would turn out all right eventually once they had settled in.

Thirteen

Penny soon found that living with Mrs Reilly at Blenheim Road in Liverpool was something of an eye-opener after her own comfortable home in Wallasey.

Although Ma Reilly's house was spotlessly clean there were still a great many differences and most of them were a disadvantage.

There was no bathroom or inside lavatory. This meant that she had to go out into the back yard to use the lavatory that was housed in a small wooden shed. Furthermore, it was shared not only by all the occupants of Ma Reilly's house but by the people who lived next door as well. Even at night she either had to go out there or else use the enamel chamber pot that was secreted underneath her bed.

Personal washing was also difficult. Having a bath was out of the question and Ma Reilly told her that if she really had to have a bath then she would have to go along to the public baths that were in Upper Frederick Street.

Penny discovered that the public baths were reasonably clean but as she looked around at the people waiting their turn to use them she found herself shuddering. It wasn't that they were poorly dressed or spoke in such a thick Scouse accent that she could barely understand what they were saying, it was because they all looked so very dirty.

Penny made one visit and then decided that in future it was better to have a daily strip wash at home, even if it was only from a bowl of tepid water in her bedroom.

It didn't take Penny long to realize that the standard of cleanliness in Ma Reilly's home really was the exception. The lodgers she let out rooms to were also of a different type than the majority of people living locally.

'I don't have any long term lodgers,' Ma Reilly explained to Penny a few days after she arrived. 'Most of my regulars are commercial travellers who are only in Liverpool for a couple of nights at a time on business, and most of them have been coming here to stay for years. The others are people needing a stay over for a night or two because they are catching a boat to Ireland or somewhere abroad. They come from outside Liverpool and are recommended by people who've stayed here before.'

Although Ma Reilly was barely five feet tall, she had a very strong will and personality and seemed to have the ability to get most people to do as she told them.

Father O'Flynn, who was a regular visitor to the house, was tall and thin with a rather morose expression on his lined face. He and Ma Reilly would sit in her kitchen enjoying a glass of good Irish whisky together while they gossiped about what was going on in the world and in particular the latest happenings in the Scotland Road area of Liverpool.

Between them they seemed to know everyone's business and, although they had heated discussions about what the various people should do to improve their lot, there was never any malice in their judgement.

True to her promise Ma Reilly introduced Penny to Father O'Flynn and immediately asked him to find her a teaching post. In the next breath she demanded to know when Penny would be starting.

'My prayers have been answered,' Father O'Flynn exclaimed clasping both Penny's hands between his own thin ones. 'She can start right away. It's not permanent, of course, merely filling in for a teacher who is off sick,' he explained when he saw the look of surprise on Penny's face.

When Penny thanked him but said that it was impossible for her to start work immediately because much as she needed to earn a living there was no way she could leave Kelly on her own.

Ma Reilly shook her head and tutted Penny to silence.

'You don't have any problem about that,' Ma Reilly told her firmly. 'I'm always here so I can be looking after young Kelly while you are out at work; that is until she is well enough to go to school. It will only be for a few more weeks, to be sure. Once her little arm is strong enough to take her weight she'll be able to use those crutches to get around again. By then her leg will be almost better so it will.'

Kelly seemed to be happy enough with the arrangement,

especially when Ma Reilly promised that she would let her help with the cooking and even show her how to make cakes.

For Penny her new job was very exacting; absolutely everything was done differently from the way she had been used to doing it at the private school in Wallasey.

What Father O'Flynn had failed to tell her was that all the other teachers were nuns and when Penny appeared in a cream blouse and a dark green skirt instead of a long black gown and starched white wimple the children were bemused and not at all sure that she really was a teacher.

Not only were the teaching methods alien to her but religion played such a major part of each school day that she wondered if she was going to be able to cope with it all.

Added to that, the children were themselves very different from those she had been used to teaching. They were mostly ragged and some were downright dirty. On several occasions she had insisted on one or the other of them going to the cloakroom and washing their hands before handling the exercise books.

When it came to lessons, in some ways it seemed the children were extremely backward for their age and she often felt exasperated when they were unable to read fluently or carry out simple mathematical calculations.

On the other hand both the boys and the girls in her class seemed to be extremely wily and were quick to catch on to any loophole that provided an excuse for their behaviour. Sometimes it was for their bad work, or for not doing the homework that had been set for them to do; at other times it was for missing school altogether.

The sisters seemed to take all this behaviour in a bland almost dismissive manner and to Penny's mind never seemed to administer adequate punishment. They never ordered any of the children to stay in after school and do the work correctly but merely told them to go away and remember to say 'three Hail Marys' or read a passage from their catechism before they went to bed.

Penny was sure that behind the nuns' backs the children laughed about their punishment and that very few of them did as they'd been told.

The sisters were also equally dismissive of any new ideas Penny put forward to try and make lessons more interesting for the pupils.

'None of them really want to learn,' Sister Ambrose sighed. 'They know they have to come to school because otherwise they will be in trouble with the authorities but many of the ones who play truant are aided and abetted by their parents.'

'Whatever do you mean; why would they do that?' Penny questioned.

'Well, the children are more use at home. They can be set to work running messages or looking after their little brothers and sisters while their mother goes out charring.'

Remembering how much Ellen Murphy counted on Kelly looking after the younger children Penny said no more. She also recalled that Kelly had not even started school yet although she had turned six. Father O'Flynn must be well aware of this fact, she thought, and yet he had not reported it or, as far as she knew, even said anything to Ellen Murphy about it.

Penny had only been teaching for a couple of weeks when she arrived back at Blenheim Road to be greeted at the front door by Ma Reilly announcing, 'There's a visitor to see you so I've put him in the parlour.'

Puzzled, she followed Ma Reilly through to the best room. It was in the front of the house and only used on very special occasions. Every piece of furniture in it was highly polished yet even so it smelled musty. She was very taken aback to find that Dr Bryn Cash from the hospital was in there talking to Kelly.

He stood up immediately, but his dark eyes were hard and his greeting was extremely cool and straight to the point of his visit. 'Kelly should have attended my clinic at the hospital over a week ago, Miss Forshaw, in order for me to check the progress she is making so why didn't you bring her?' he demanded.

'Do you mean for her arm or her leg?' Penny asked, feeling flustered. 'I'm so sorry, Dr Cash, I completely forgot about it. There's been so much else happening,' she added in an apologetic voice.

'So I understand from what Kelly has been telling me. However, it is still no excuse for neglecting to bring her to my clinic,' he told her curtly. 'Furthermore, you didn't even inform me or let the hospital authorities know that you'd changed your address.'

'That has only just happened and it was also unforeseen,' she explained with an apologetic smile. 'I really am sorry, Dr Cash.

As you can see, Kelly is progressing extremely well so I don't think there is any cause for concern.'

'Not on your part perhaps, Miss Forshaw, but in order for my clinical records to be accurate and up to date it is imperative that Kelly is kept under observation until she is completely better. Then, and only then, will I discharge her from my clinic at the hospital.'

He seemed to be so angry that Penny felt at a loss for words. She was relieved when Ma Reilly appeared in the doorway to ask, 'Would you be taking a cup of tea with us doctor?'

Bryn Cash frowned and took out his pocket watch and studied it for a moment. 'Thank you but I'm extremely pressed for time.'

'Then it's a good job I've gone ahead and brewed it. Come on through to the kitchen. I've already poured you out a cup and you can drink it while you're talking; you too Penny, I've poured one out for you as well. Young Kelly will be needing a biscuit and a glass of milk after all this palaver so come on through to my kitchen the lot of you.'

A quarter of an hour later they were still in Ma Reilly's kitchen talking and drinking tea. Bryn Cash no longer seemed to be an ogre but a very charming young man.

Penny was surprised to hear that he lived in Liverpool not all that far from Blenheim Road. She also discovered that he belonged to a tennis club and felt rather pleased when he invited her along as his guest even though she knew it would be impossible for her to go.

'Right, I must be off. I'll pick you up on Saturday afternoon at about two o'clock,' he told Penny as he picked up his trilby and doctor's bag and prepared to leave.

'I'd love to accept but I'm afraid it's impossible,' Penny told him with regret. 'I have Kelly to consider and I really can't leave her on her own.'

'Don't worry about that; you won't mind keeping an eye on Kelly for the afternoon will you, Mrs Reilly?' Bryn Cash said, smiling at her confidently. Before either of them could say any more he was gone.

'That young man is not only rather handsome but he has a very forceful way with him,' Ma Reilly said with a smile. 'Still, it will do you good to mix with some of your own sort even if it is only for a couple of hours. After all,' she added with a chuckle when she saw that Penny was about to speak, 'you will have to go because it's "doctor's orders".'

Their outing was a great success and the first of many. When the tennis season ended in late September he invited her to all sorts of other events. Gradually it became an accepted arrangement that Bryn Cash would be calling to take Penny out somewhere most Saturdays and that Ma Reilly would keep an eye on Kelly.

The more Penny saw of Bryn the more she grew to like him and enjoy his company. He seemed to have a dual personality; a somewhat curt manner as a doctor and a warm benign manner when he was off duty. They shared the same interests and sense of humour and Penny particularly enjoyed their visits to the theatre or to the Philharmonic Hall to listen to a concert.

By the end of October Kelly was fully recovered. The plaster cast had been taken off her arm and with gentle exercise she quickly regained full use of it. She no longer needed her crutches and could walk and even run. She had also been discharged from the hospital clinic.

Penny knew that Kelly was fit enough to go home to her own mother but she delayed saying anything or taking any action about it because she realized how much she was going to miss her. It also meant that she would have to take a decision about her own future.

Once she was no longer responsible for Kelly there was nothing to keep her at Blenheim Road. Also, the teacher she had been filling in for was due to return to school after Christmas so she would no longer have a job there.

After thinking about it for several days she broached the subject of Kelly starting school. Ma Reilly thought it would be a very good idea but she wasn't at all sure that Kelly's mother would be in agreement.

'Ellen Murphy counts on young Kelly being at home to look after the other nippers so that she can go out to work,' she pointed out.

'Yes, I know that but that's only in the evenings when she goes charring, isn't it? Kelly will be at home then so it shouldn't make any difference.'

'Well, there's Kelly herself to be considered,' Ma Reilly went on. 'Never had a lesson in her life, so how do you think she is going to feel about it?'

'Perhaps if we stayed on here with you for a little while longer then Kelly could start school while I am still there and that would give her more confidence,' Penny suggested. 'She's very bright, you know, and I could help her to catch up with the lessons.'

'Well, I suppose that could work,' Ma Reilly conceded. 'It might be best if you had a word with Father O'Flynn and see what he has to say on the matter.'

Father O'Flynn was in full agreement with the idea and Kelly was quite excited when she heard the news that she would be starting school. She was equally delighted when she discovered it meant that she wouldn't be going back to her own home for a while longer.

'I will only be staying on at the school for a month or so, Kelly, so it is up to you to learn all you can in that time,' Penny warned her.

Kelly assured her that she would try to do so and she was as good as her word. She worked extremely hard and by mid-December was reading quite well. She was also able to spell more than one hundred words and write her own name although her handwriting was atrocious.

Penny knew that the time had come for Kelly to be reunited with her own family; even so she hesitated when Ma Reilly brought the matter up and said she thought Kelly ought to return to her own home for Christmas.

'I suppose you are right,' Penny agreed. 'I was hoping that we could make this a very special Christmas for Kelly by spending it here with you,' she confided to Ma Reilly.

'Sure now and I'd like nothing better, Penny, but the poor child ought to be with her own family,' Ma Reilly said with a deep sigh.

They argued about it in a friendly way for several days and finally decided to ask both Father O'Flynn and Dr Cash for their opinion. Penny couldn't help feeling slightly ruffled when both of them agreed with what Ma Reilly had already said; namely, that by rights Kelly should celebrate Christmas at her own home with her family.

As a form of compromise Penny agreed that Kelly could go

back to her own home before Christmas but promised that she would go on living at Blenheim Road at least until the New Year in case things didn't work out for Kelly.

Penny and Ma Reilly also made plans to have a party for Kelly the week before Christmas and asked her whom she wanted to invite. To their surprise, it wasn't any of the little girls in her class at school but Dr Bryn Cash and Father O'Flynn.

Fourteen

Two days before the little party that Penny and Ma Reilly had planned to hold for Kelly they received an unexpected visit from Dr Cash.

He came straight to the point. 'Penny, I'm afraid I have some bad news. Your mother has had a heart attack and is seriously ill and you need to go to her right away.'

'My mother? What are you talking about? How do you know that?'

'I received the news from Dr Ian McAllister, your mother's doctor. He was trying to get in touch with you on behalf of your father. He thought that as I lived and worked in the Scotland Road area I might know the whereabouts of the Murphys and through them I might be able to find out where you were living.'

'Are you sure about this?' Penny stared at him in astonishment remembering all that had happened between her and her parents only a few months earlier and her father's anger on the day he'd turned her out.

'Your mother is asking for you and your father is desperate for you to return home,' Bryn Cash confirmed.

'On my own?'

Bryn frowned. 'He didn't say anything about that but Kelly is fully recovered from all her injuries now so there is no reason why you should feel you need to take her with you.'

'Hold on a minute both of you,' Ma Reilly interrupted. 'I'm listening to what you're saying but there's no way that I am prepared to have young Kelly staying with me on her own, indeed I'm not. I don't mind keeping an eye on her for an hour or so when the two of you want to go out but I'm far too old to be taking sole charge of her. Now that she's off them crutches there's no knowing what she'll be up to or where she'll be going off to on her own. No, I'm not having that.'

'There's no need for Kelly to stay here any longer if you don't want her to do so,' Bryn Cash assured her. 'She's perfectly fit now so she can go back home to her family whenever you wish. You were thinking of sending her home for Christmas anyway weren't you?'

'Yes, that's quite true,' Penny admitted reluctantly. 'As yet though we haven't mentioned the matter to her,' she added, a trifle worriedly.

'Kelly is perfectly able to cope on her own so I really think you should be considering your own family's needs, Penny, and putting them first,' Bryn Cash insisted firmly, locking his eyes with hers.

As she met his steady dark gaze Penny felt some of the tension ease and although she felt too choked to speak she nodded in agreement.

'I'll take Kelly back to her mother and explain the situation so that she understands what is happening,' he assured her with an understanding smile. 'From the way Dr McAllister spoke, your mother really is desperately ill and I don't think we should waste any time.'

She thought how different he was from Arnold. Arnold would merely have shrugged and said it was up to her what she did; Bryn was helping her to reach a decision in a thoughtful constructive way.

'I think I ought to be the one to tell Kelly about why she is being taken back to her family,' Penny prevaricated. 'I don't want her to feel I am simply walking away from her.'

'Very well, but we'll do it together. I don't want her cajoling you into changing your mind.'

'Well now, there's glad I am that that's all settled,' Ma Reilly said with a sigh of relief. 'I'll go and make a pot of tea and find some biscuits for Kelly. She'll take it better if we can sit down comfortably and explain the situation to her in a friendly manner,' she added firmly.

Kelly was in tears when they called her into the kitchen and told her the news.

'You're like all the others – you're fed up with me,' Kelly sniffled when Penny put her arms around her and hugged her, trying to console her. 'I don't care though,' she gulped, pushing Penny away. 'I hate you, I hate all of you and I hate having to live here with you,' she stormed, looking round the warm comfortable kitchen.

'You don't mean what you're saying Kelly and it is not Penny's fault,' Bryn Cash told her quietly. 'Penny's mother is very ill and so she has to go home and look after her.'

'Her ma wouldn't even say goodbye to her when we left their house and her dad told her never to darken his door again,' Kelly reminded them stubbornly.

'Grown-ups often say things they don't really mean, especially when they are very upset,' Bryn explained.

'Yeh, like she did after she knocked me down with her motor car. She said she was going to look after me until I was better,' Kelly responded glaring at Penny.

'Now then young lady, that's not a fair thing to say,' Ma Reilly interrupted. 'Penny has been like a fairy godmother to you and don't you ever forget it. She's cared for you for months and months, spent her own money looking after you and buying you new clothes. She's given you a far better time than you would have had at home. Don't let me ever hear you say bad things like that about her ever again. Understand?'

'She made promises and you made promises and now neither of you want me,' Kelly gulped with tears running down her cheeks.

'Of course they care about you,' Bryn Cash told her firmly. 'It's just that other things have happened that have changed the situation.'

'You're all grown-ups so you can do whatever you like,' Kelly snuffled, wiping away her tears with the back of her hand and glaring round at them.

'If it was your mother that was ill and asking for you then you'd want to go and see her now wouldn't you,' Penny said gently, pulling the child into her arms again.

Kelly wriggled uncomfortably and shrugged her thin shoulders. 'P'rhaps,' she muttered giving a loud sobbing sniff.

'Well, it's what I want to do,' Penny said gravely. 'I'll come back to see you again as soon as my mother is well enough for me to leave her and I'm sure you will be seeing Mrs Reilly from time to time.'

'I want to see you again and I want to know now when that will be.'

'I can't tell you that until after I have seen my mother and found out how ill she is. I tell you what I'll do, I'll write and let

Mrs Reilly know how my mother is getting on and when I will be able to come back to see you,' Penny promised. 'She will tell you what is in the letter when you pop round to see her. She might even let you help her to make some of those special fairy cakes for our tea when I tell her I am coming to visit you.'

'Penny, we really should be on our way,' Bryn said worriedly. 'I'll take Kelly and her belongings round to Cannon Court while you pack your suitcase. I should only be about ten minutes so be ready to leave when I get back.'

Throughout the journey over to Wallasey Penny felt very apprehensive about what sort of reception she would receive from her parents. Her mother might want to see her, especially if she was ill, but she was not at all sure that her father would make her welcome. When he had turned her out he had been so emphatic that he didn't want to see her ever again and he wasn't the sort of man who changed his mind.

When she confided as much to Bryn he reassured her that Dr McAllister had been extremely relieved at tracking her down. He'd also mentioned that her father had stressed how important it was that she should return home as soon as possible.

'Yes, he might have said that because my mother was asking for me . . .'

'Look, why don't you stop worrying about it and wait and see what happens when we arrive,' Bryn advised as they reached Penkett Road and walked down the drive of the house she indicated. 'I'll stay until we are sure that you are welcome,' he added reassuringly.

Mary let out a tiny scream when she opened the door to them. 'There's glad I am to see you, Miss Penny. Mistress has been asking over and over again for you.'

Hearing the commotion, Captain Forshaw came out of his study to see what was happening. There was one brief moment while father and daughter stood looking at each other in uneasy silence. Then suddenly they were in each other's arms and he was hugging her close and thanking her for coming back home.

She introduced him to Bryn Cash and as the two men shook hands Bryn explained that he had to get back to Liverpool immediately as he had a clinic to attend at the hospital. 'I'll call again in a day or so to make sure that Penny is settled in,' he said as he prepared to leave.

'There is no need to waste your time doing that,' Captain Forshaw assured him forcibly. 'This is her home remember; she'll settle in all right, it's where she belongs. Thank you for bringing her home.'

Bryn nodded but there was a twinkle in his eye as he said goodbye to Penny and gave her hand an extra squeeze as he saw the apologetic look on her face.

The minute the door closed behind him, Penny headed for the stairs anxious to go up and see her mother but her father laid a restraining hand on her arm.

'Take it slowly,' he cautioned. 'Your mother has been gravely ill, Penny, and she is still extremely frail. Too much excitement would not be good for her.'

When she went into the bedroom Penny was shocked by her mother's emaciated appearance. She appeared to be sleeping and Penny's breath caught in her throat and tears filled her eyes as she stood by the bedside staring down at the thin white face that looked almost like a mask.

Her mother's hands were lying on top of the bedspread and, as she gently picked one of them up and held it between her own, she noted how the blue veins stood out emphasizing her mother's frail condition.

'Penny . . . Penny . . . where are you?'

The words were spoken so softly that for a moment Penny wondered if she was imagining her mother had said them because she still appeared to be sleeping. Then the sad little plea came again, almost as if the words came out automatically from between her lips as she breathed.

'I'm here, Mother,' Penny murmured, gently squeezing the hand she was holding. 'I've come home.'

Her mother's eyelids fluttered and with a tremendous effort she managed to open them and focus her gaze on Penny. She stared in a disbelieving way, uttering a little sigh of pleasure and then with a great effort she reached up to stroke her daughter's face.

Over the next few days Penny spent every moment she possibly could with her mother. When she was awake Penny helped to feed her or sat by her bedside, holding her hand and talking to her.

A nurse came in regularly to attend to Mrs Forshaw's personal needs. While her mother was being bathed and dressed in clean clothes ready for the day, Penny usually sought out her father's company or went down to the kitchen to chat to Mrs Davies and Mary.

They didn't attempt to celebrate Christmas. They did eat the turkey, which had already been ordered, and as Mrs Davies pointed out there was no point in wasting it since they had to eat something.

Penny found it strange to be back in her own home and her very own bedroom with all her favourite things around her. She was more than ever conscious of how cramped her living conditions had been during the past months while she had been living at Blenheim Road and sharing a room with Kelly. One of the things she had missed most of all was being able to take a bath and now she was able to do so whenever she felt like it.

Bryn came to visit her occasionally despite her father's comment that there was no need for him to do so. He never stayed very long but he brought her news from Ma Reilly.

Whenever she asked after Kelly he told her not to worry. 'Kelly is doing fine; she's young and adaptable so she'll settle back in with her family in next to no time,' he assured her.

His answer failed to set her mind at rest. She promised herself that as soon as her mother was stronger and she felt she could leave her for a few hours then she would go across to Liverpool. She wanted to see for herself whether or not Kelly really had settled back at her home in Cannon Court and was happy there.

Her waking hours, however, were so taken up looking after her mother that Penny found she had no time for her own life.

Mary and Mrs Davies were very supportive but they had their own work to do in running the house and preparing meals. It was left to Penny to fetch and carry for Mrs Forshaw who was becoming more and more demanding as her strength returned.

The days became weeks and Penny was well aware that she had still done nothing about her proposed visit to Liverpool. When she mentioned her intention to her father he frowned and told her not to be too hasty.

'You're place is here; your mother still needs you,' he pointed out. 'It's done her so much good having you here looking after her, so it's your duty to put her first, Penny.'

Fifteen

It was almost mid-February before Leonora Forshaw was able to get dressed and come downstairs for a little while each day. She looked very pale and fragile and was still quite weak and rather unsteady on her feet.

She still made constant demands on Penny and expected her to be on hand to fetch and carry for her. She also insisted that Penny must always be at her side when she walked so that she could lean on her arm for support.

Gradually, however, her strength returned and by the beginning of March she was managing not only to stay up all day but to have dinner with her husband and Penny before retiring for the night.

Captain Forshaw was relieved by his wife's progress. Not only was his home life gradually returning to normal but he knew that as Penny was there to look after her he was able to go to work with a clear conscience concerning his wife's welfare in his absence.

A few days before Easter, without a word to either his wife or Penny, he invited Arnold Watson to dinner.

Leonora was delighted when Arnold arrived. He looked immaculate in a dark grey well-tailored suit, crisp white shirt and a discreetly patterned blue tie. He greeted her with a large bouquet of exotic flowers.

He also conveyed a message from his own parents to say how relieved they were that she was now almost fully restored to health. They hoped that she would be well enough to visit them very soon.

Arnold also brought a bottle of a special brandy liqueur for Penny's father, which pleased Captain Forshaw immensely.

Penny was taken aback to see him and immediately wondered if his visit had been engineered by her father in the hope of bringing about some sort of reconciliation between herself and Arnold.

If that was so then it had been a mistake, she thought. She

recalled only too well the way Arnold had treated her throughout the previous summer and the abrupt way in which he had ended their engagement. She also remembered his total rejection of Kelly. Not only that but they had been apart now for so long that she was a different person and no longer had any feelings whatsoever for him.

She received him coolly and was aware that for a brief moment, when he handed her a box of expensive chocolates, Arnold seemed slightly embarrassed by their encounter.

As they gathered in the drawing room to have a glass of sherry before dinner was served she noticed that he avoided speaking directly to her whenever possible.

As they were about to move into the dining room they heard the doorbell ring. A few minutes later Mary came into the drawing room to say that there was a gentleman at the door asking for Miss Penny.

Much to Penny's astonishment she found that it was Bryn Cash.

'We haven't spoken for such a long time that I thought I owed you a visit,' he greeted her. 'I was hoping that I could take you out for a meal somewhere and we could catch up with all our news,' he added.

'Oh dear, I'm afraid that's not going to be possible. We were about to start dinner and we have a guest.'

'Oh, I am sorry. I should have telephoned to let you know I was coming,' Bryn admitted with a rueful smile. 'So when will you be free?'

Before Penny could answer her father came out into the hall to find out why she was detained. He frowned heavily when he saw who their unexpected visitor was.

'Bryn came to take me out,' Penny explained. 'I was about to suggest that he should join us for dinner.'

There was a moment's hesitation before Captain Forshaw agreed. It was done in such a very grudging manner that Bryn quickly refused and said that he would contact Penny the following day.

'If you've come all this way then of course you must stay and have dinner with us,' Penny insisted. Linking her arm through his she propelled him towards the dining room.

As she introduced Arnold and Bryn to each other Penny saw a look of irritation on Arnold's face. Remembering her father's reluctance to ask Bryn to stay to dinner, she was even more convinced that her father had inveigled Arnold's visit to try and get them back together again.

Arnold regaled them over dinner with details of the play staged by the Amateur Dramatic Society in which he had performed the lead role and how brilliant the girl who had played opposite him had been. He then went on to tell them about the many other social activities that he had indulged in since he had last seen them.

Penny was well aware that he was doing this on purpose to make her realize how much she had missed out on over the past few months.

Throughout the meal she found herself comparing Arnold with Bryn Cash. They were about the same age and both men were tall and good-looking but in many different ways.

Arnold had a long face with chiselled lips beneath his trim moustache. He had an elegant appearance and a somewhat supercilious manner that could be irritating.

Bryn was more sturdily built with wide shoulders, square features and a firm jaw and he was far more reserved and pragmatic.

Their backgrounds were equally different, she reflected. Arnold's father was a prosperous shipping magnate and Arnold had enjoyed a very privileged and cosseted background. He'd been sent to private schools from a very young age and always made aware that he was a very special person. As an only child his mother had doted on him and he'd been thoroughly spoilt. From his very earliest days he'd been given everything he asked for and indulged in every way.

The moment Arnold left the expensive private college he'd been sent to he was appointed to a position in his father's company; one that gave him both power and authority. He was also given a company car and a generous business allowance as well as his salary.

Bryn came from a farming family in North Wales and had known a hard realistic childhood. They had lived in a stone farmhouse south of Beddgelert at the foot of the majestic Snowdon mountain range. His father had bred sheep which had roamed the nearby mountainside.

Bryn had three brothers. They were all older than him and from the time he was eight years old he had been expected to do his share of chores on the farm. This had included tending the sheep and helping to herd them down from the mountainside every year at the start of winter.

Bryn had grown up self-resilient and sturdy. He was not afraid of hard work but unlike his brothers he wanted something more from life than merely being a sheep farmer. When he was given the opportunity of going to university and then later on of studying to be a doctor he had accepted the challenge with alacrity.

Nevertheless he was extremely proud of his Welsh background and he was steeped in local folklore about Mount Snowdon and the numerous legends of King Arthur and Merlin that were associated with the area.

He had related many of these legends to Kelly and her favourite had been how the village he came from had earned its name. She never seemed to tire of hearing him tell it to her time and time again.

According to legend Prince Llewelyn ap Iorwerth decided to go on a hunting trip and left his infant son in the charge of his faithful dog Gelert. When the Prince was greeted by Gelert on his return, he noticed that the dog's muzzle was soaked in blood, and his son was nowhere to be seen.

Outraged that the dog he had loved and trusted had betrayed him Llewelyn attacked the dog, and it fell to the ground gravely injured. However, within minutes the prince heard a cry and stumbled through nearby bushes to find his son, safe in his cradle. Beside the cradle lay the body of a giant wolf covered with wounds, the result of a fight to the death it had fought with the hound Gelert.

'So why did they call the village Beddgelert and not just Gelert?' Kelly asked each time he told her the story.

'The word "bedd" means grave and it is where the dog's body was buried,' Bryn would remind her patiently.

Patience was one of his strengths, Penny reflected. She had witnessed it not only with the way he treated Kelly but also with the way he spoke to patients whenever she had attended his clinic at the hospital.

He had told her that one day he hoped he would be able to afford to buy into a family practice or even have a practice of his own. Until then he was quite prepared to work in a hospital.

He'd aimed for one in a large working-class area because he felt that afforded him a greater degree of experience than a smaller hospital would have done. He also felt that living as well as working in the same area gave him a deeper insight into understanding the specialized needs of local people.

Arnold on the other hand, was so self-opinionated that he never considered other people's viewpoint to be of any value. Whenever someone tried to tell him anything he would listen impatiently and then dismiss what they said as being of no interest.

She wondered what Arnold was like at work and whether his colleagues found him overbearing. Since he was the boss's son they probably kept their opinions to themselves. Most of them would fall in with his wishes and try to please him no matter what he asked them to do.

Remembering his comment about thinking of it as delegating responsibility when she had jokingly complained that her mother seemed to be intent on making all their wedding arrangements she suspected that delegating was what he did most of the time.

He was far too impatient to deal with trivial matters so he probably left all those to his secretary who, or so he said, was extremely efficient and couldn't do enough for him.

During dinner as she compared Arnold's inconsequential chatter about his own personal activities to Bryn's calm, direct, straightforward answers when he was asked a question, she realized how shallow Arnold was.

The thought of being married to him was now quite repugnant and far from feeling hurt or sad because he had broken off their engagement she was aware of an overwhelming sense of relief.

It was almost as if she was now freed from an invisible yet overpowering threat that had hung over her like a grey cloud. Now she was completely free and could do whatever she wanted to do. Once again she was heart-whole and had the opportunity to make a new life for herself.

This time, she promised herself, she would make quite sure

that she made the right choice and not let herself be talked into any arrangement that didn't suit her.

As she looked up and saw Bryn looking at her across the dining table she felt the colour staining her cheeks. She wondered if he had sensed what she'd been thinking.

Once again she found herself comparing him with Arnold. He was so much more concerned with other people and their problems than he was with himself. His work was far from easy yet she had never heard him grumble or ever heard him say that he had delegated responsibility.

She looked round the table and saw how they were all listening to Arnold who was glowing with pleasure that he was so popular. Even her own parents seemed to be under his spell and were avidly interested in what he was telling them.

Or were they? Or were they merely being polite, she wondered.

Remembering what her mother had said about her father and William Watson amalgamating their companies when they both retired, she suspected that her father was most definitely counting on a reconciliation between her and Arnold.

She knew he dreamed of the day when this would be possible and he could retire. Had it not been for the motoring accident and her involvement with Kelly she knew she would have accepted his plans; what was more, she would have felt that it was her duty to do so.

Now she felt a shudder go through her as she realized what the outcome would have been. Arnold would not only have had supreme power and control over both companies but over her as well.

Sixteen

Penny chose a Saturday for her visit to Liverpool. It was the one day of the week when she knew she could rely on her father being at home to keep her mother company.

She bought the biggest chocolate Easter egg she could find to take as a present for Kelly. It was wrapped in brightly coloured shiny foil and she could imagine how Kelly's eyes would light up when she saw it.

In the spring sunshine Cannon Court looked even more grimy and dismal than she remembered it. Mrs Murphy was wearing a stained dark red dress and her hair was straggling around her face when she answered the door after Penny had knocked several times. As usual she was clutching the baby in her arms, and the other two were hanging on to her skirt. She frowned darkly when she saw who her visitor was.

'Young Kelly ain't here, she's out somewhere with her brother Paddy,' she stated before Penny could even greet her.

'I see. Do you have any idea where they may have gone?'

'No, as I just said, they're out somewhere,' Mrs Murphy repeated. 'That something for her?' she asked staring at the large brown paper bag Penny was carrying.

'Yes, it's an Easter egg but I was hoping to give it to her myself,' Penny said, as rather reluctantly she handed the bag over to Mrs Murphy.

Penny watched helplessly as Brian grabbed at it and snatched it from his mother's hand. Lily joined in and the egg tipped out on to the floor. They both scrabbled for it, pushing and giggling. As they started to tear at the bright shiny foil Ellen Murphy cuffed them both over the ears and retrieved the egg and put it back in the paper bag.

'You will tell Kelly that I will be calling back later because I very much want to see her and to find out if she has settled back in.'

'She's had to hasn't she,' Mrs Murphy said tartly. 'Took her a bit to drop all her airs and graces, though. You spoilt her something rotten while she was living with you at your place, didn't you?'

Penny didn't answer. There seemed to be no point in entering into an argument with Mrs Murphy. With a tight smile she said goodbye.

As she was walking away Mrs Murphy called after her, 'If you're lucky you might find them somewhere in town. I think that's where Paddy said they were going.'

Penny was on the point of asking why they would go there but decided it was probably a waste of time to do so.

As she made her way back into Scotland Road, picking her path through the litter that seemed to be strewn everywhere, she wondered if it was Mrs Murphy's way of getting rid of her. It was obvious that she didn't want to invite her in and have her hanging around on the off-chance that Kelly would soon be home and she wondered if it was because she didn't want her to meet up with Kelly for some reason.

It made her all the more resolute to do so. It was such a lovely spring morning that she decided that a walk into Liverpool city centre would be no great hardship. If, as Ellen Murphy had said, that was where Kelly and her brother had gone then she might meet them on their way back.

Lord Street was busy with shoppers and as Penny approached the Kardomah Café in Church Street she stopped in surprise when she spotted Kelly standing outside the doorway singing. A gangly looking lad that she assumed must be Paddy was with her and he was passing his cap around and taking a collection of coins from the small crowd of bystanders that had gathered to listen to Kelly.

To her dismay Penny saw two policemen approaching and she dreaded what might happen next.

Kelly and her brother had also spotted them. As the two children tried to make their escape a man in the crowd stopped them. He grabbed Kelly by the arm but her brother managed to avoid his grasp and within seconds was lost in the maze of nearby streets.

Penny stepped forward and touched the policeman's arm as he was about to march Kelly away. 'Don't worry, officer, I know who she is and I'll take her home. I'm sure it was simply a childish prank. I'll make sure she doesn't do it again.'

The policeman stared from Kelly in her torn dress and grubby bare feet to Penny in her neat dark green suit and crisp white blouse. He frowned as though trying to establish a connection between the scruffy little street urchin and the smartly dressed well-spoken young lady.

'Come along, Kelly, it's time for us to go home,' Penny said with a forced smile. She reached out and took hold of Kelly's hand to lead her away but the policeman's hand tightened on Kelly's shoulder.

Recognizing her, Kelly grinned broadly as she twisted away from the policeman's grasp and then grabbed tight to Penny's hand.

The policeman looked slightly bewildered then raising his eyebrows commented sternly, 'Very well, miss, I'll overlook it on this occasion but make sure you don't let her do this sort of thing again.'

Once they were clear of the crowd that had lingered to see what was going on Kelly squeezed Penny's hand. 'Have you come back for good because your ma is better?' she asked hopefully her small face wreathed in smiles.

'No, I came over to visit you because I wanted to make sure that you had settled in with your family and that you were well and happy.'

Kelly's face clouded. 'I hoped you were back for good and I could live with you at Ma Reilly's house again,' she said in a sulky voice.

'I've brought you a present, an Easter egg, a really big one,' Penny told her. 'I've left it with your mother.'

When Kelly didn't answer Penny said brightly. 'Shall we go and see Mrs Reilly before I take you back to Cannon Court?'

Kelly stubbed her toe against a lamppost angrily. 'No,' she shouted, 'If you are not coming back for good and you aren't going to let me live with you then I never want to see Ma Reilly or you ever again.'

Before Penny could stop her Kelly had scampered off down the road dodging among the crowds and in seconds she was lost to view.

Penny hesitated wondering if she should try and follow her but realized it would be futile. Kelly probably knew all the back-streets to get home and would reach Cannon Court well ahead of her.

Feeling defeated Penny made her way to Blenheim Road to see Ma Reilly. As they enjoyed a cup of tea in Ma Reilly's warm cosy kitchen Penny related what had happened.

'Perhaps you should forget all about her,' Ma Reilly advised. 'You did your bit looking after her all those months after the accident. It was a sight more than most folks would have done.'

Over the next few weeks Penny tried to put Kelly out of her mind but it was not very easy. Her mother was making such good progress that she required less and less attention. She had reached the stage where she wanted to do things for herself and it meant that Penny was beginning to find time hanging heavily on her hands.

Several times she thought of asking her father if he would have a word with Miss Grimshaw about her returning to her teaching post but her courage failed her. At the moment things were going so well between herself and her parents that she didn't want to stir up the past.

The highlight of her week was when she went out with Bryn Cash. Usually she met him in Liverpool and once the tennis season restarted they played tennis at his club. If it was raining they went for a meal or to the pictures instead.

When he came over to see her they either went for a walk along the promenade at New Brighton or out to a restaurant for a meal.

She toyed with the idea of taking him to the tennis club she belonged to in Wallasey but there was always the chance that they might bump into Arnold. She hadn't seen or heard from him since the evening he had come to dinner and he and Bryn had met. Although she no longer had any feelings for Arnold she thought it might be embarrassing for all of them if the two men met again.

Each time she and Bryn met she asked after Kelly. He always said that as far as he knew she was all right and not to worry about her. Now that Kelly no longer had to attend his clinic at the hospital the only time he saw her was when he caught sight of her out in the street.

'Stop being so concerned about her,' he chided, a frown on his rugged face. 'You can't go on worrying about Kelly forever, you know. You did everything you possibly could when she needed care and looking after and you most certainly got her back on her feet again.'

'Yes, I know but I feel responsible for her. I have only been to see her once since I went home to look after my mother. My visit was such a complete fiasco that I feel guilty about it,' Penny confided.

'I remember and that's why I think it might be best for you not to visit the Murphys again. Leave things as they are,' he advised.

'I know, but in some ways I still feel accountable for Kelly. I often wonder if I've unsettled her and made her discontented by showing her a different way of life,' Penny persisted.

'What utter nonsense! If you go somewhere for a holiday it doesn't make you discontented for ever afterwards now does it. You simply enjoy the experience at the time and retain a happy memory of it.'

'Yes, you are probably right,' Penny agreed. Her face brightened. 'Actually, that's given me an idea. Perhaps I could take Kelly away somewhere for a week during her school holidays in August.'

Bryn shook his head. 'Think about it very carefully before you make a decision,' he advised. 'You don't want to do anything you might regret later on.'

Before she could make up her mind, Bryn brought her some very worrying news about Kelly. She and her older brother had been apprehended by the police for stealing from a shop in the city centre and had to appear at the magistrates' court.

'Oh my goodness,' Penny gasped. 'Whatever will happen to her now? Do you think it would help if I went along and offered to take her back to live with me?'

'Are you sure that your parents would agree to you doing that?' he asked cautiously.

'I didn't mean that I would take her home! I'm sure that wouldn't be possible. No, I would have to move back to Mrs Reilly's place in Blenheim Road and look after her there.'

Bryn frowned. 'Do you want to do that and to have to live in such cramped conditions again, Penny?'

They discussed it at great length but in the end Penny felt she had no choice. When Kelly and her brother Paddy eventually appeared in court they were both found guilty. In the brother's case it was not his first offence and so they were both sent to remand homes.

Penny felt quite devastated; she even went as far as discussing the matter with her father. After carefully explaining all that had happened she plucked up the courage to ask him if he could intervene in some way.

'Really, Penny! I'm surprised you have even dared to ask me to do such a thing. You know perfectly well what I think about your behaviour when the child was knocked down,' he said dismissively.

'Surely that's all in the past,' Penny sighed. 'This is a completely new development and I really feel I ought to do something to help her.'

'If you have some foolhardy idea of volunteering to look after that child again then you can forget about it,' he said abruptly, his face becoming florid with anger. 'In fact I forbid it. I don't want you living back in the Scotland Road area ever again. Furthermore, I most certainly have no intention whatsoever of harbouring that slum child here in this house,' he added angrily.

'I feel it is my duty to do something,' Penny said stubbornly. 'I feel I am responsible to some extent for what has happened because I showed her a better way of life.'

'Yes, you should feel guilty about that,' he agreed forcibly, 'Your action has caused damage enough so don't make things any worse.'

'I want to help her; I want to put things right,' she said quietly.

'Penny, apart from probably disrupting that child's life you also caused havoc in your own family. Arnold has broken off your engagement so you have sacrificed the opportunity of a good marriage. Furthermore, the distress that you caused worried your mother so much that she had a heart attack.'

'I know all that and I do feel terrible about it,' Penny said apologetically.

'Your duty is to think of your mother instead of trying to change things in other families. Furthermore, if you insist on supporting

this child I can well see that you will lose your new friend,
Dr Cash.'

Penny bit her lip. Remembering Bryn's caution she knew there
was a grain of truth in what her father was saying but she refused
to let it pass unchallenged.

'I don't think for one minute that Bryn would react as Arnold
did. They are completely different in the way they look at life.
Bryn practises in that area of Liverpool and he understands the
plight of the people living there.'

'He works there as a professional man but it doesn't mean he
has to be a friend of all the people he meets there or assume
responsibility for them when they digress.'

'Well—'

'Cut along, Penny. This conversation is over,' Captain Forshaw
said impatiently. 'Go and read to your mother and forget all about
this wretched child.'

Seventeen

Kelly Murphy felt miserable and disorientated. She was so unhappy that she vowed to herself that she would escape from St Saviour's Home for Wayward Girls as soon as she could find a way of doing so.

She still had nightmares about her day in court and hearing the terrible words that she was to be put into the care of St Saviour's.

Her brother Paddy had fared even worse than her; he had been sent to a remand home somewhere outside Liverpool. She couldn't remember how long he was going to have to stay there any more than she knew precisely how long her own sentence was to be.

She hated everything about St Saviour's. The three-storey dark grey building was so forbidding that it had sent shudders through her as she was brought there straight from the magistrates' court.

She'd thought that the towering spire of St Saviour's church that loomed over it was like a warning finger threatening what might happen once the huge wooden doors clanged shut behind you.

The nuns in their dark grey garb and their solemn faces that were almost obscured by starched white wimples were equally frightening. Sister Sampson not only looked forbidding but was extremely rough.

On Kelly's arrival at the home it had been Sister Sampson who had frogmarched her straight to the washroom. There she'd made Kelly strip off all her clothes and sit on a hard wooden stool. Another nun had cut her long dark hair so short that it barely covered her head.

Despite her protests she'd then been made to get into a bath – of almost cold water where Sister Sampson proceeded to scrub her all over with carbolic soap. She'd gone from the top of her head right down to her toes until Kelly felt raw and sore.

Sister Sampson had then handed her a coarse grey towel and

told her to dry herself. She'd given her a cotton vest and knickers and a drab blue dress to put on. After that she'd taken her along to the main hall where Sister Thomas told her to sit with the other girls already there.

Kelly had never felt so frightened in her whole life and longed to be back home. She was used to taunts from gangs of older kids in the streets around Cannon Court. She knew how to stand her ground and answer them back. They never tried to bully her because they knew that her brother Paddy was always somewhere around to come to her aid.

This was very different. Talking was not permitted. When she whispered to one of the other girls they remained silent and looked cowed. Within minutes she learned that the nuns each carried a thin cane and that they would use them given the slightest opportunity. Kelly found that they had a sting sharper than any wasp.

Kelly discovered the daily routine was strictly regimented and constraining. Their time was planned for every minute of every day. They had no freedom whatsoever. Because she was used to going her own way and doing things in her own time Kelly resented this aspect of her new life more than anything else.

The day started at six each morning when Sister Margaret flung open the dormitory door and rang a handbell loud enough to waken the dead. Along with the fifteen other girls in the dormitory Kelly learned that she had to be up and dressed with her hands and face washed, her hair combed and her bed made and to be down in the main assembly hall twenty minutes later in time for prayers.

She was warned on her first morning that if she was late for prayers it meant she would not have any breakfast. Even though breakfast was only a bowl of stodgy porridge and a mug of weak tea she always felt so hungry that to miss it was unthinkable.

The day's work started at seven thirty sharp. More prayers, then the tasks for the day were read out and everyone had to be at their designated cleaning job by eight o'clock.

Scrubbing or sweeping the floors, shaking the mats, cleaning the windows, clearing out the ashes from the grates, bringing in the wood and coal, laying the fires, cleaning down the stairs, dusting and polishing; the tasks were endless.

All their work had to be done in silence and completed by midday when they assembled again for prayers. Those who had failed to do their allotted task to the high standard demanded by Sister Thomas were punished.

Kelly frequently found that she was singled out for a beating either with the long thin cane that Sister Thomas favoured or the leather belt that Sister Sampson used. She refused to cry out, even when tears of pain streamed down her face and angry red wheals appeared on her skin. This seemed to make the nun administering the beating hit her even harder to make sure she was fully aware that she had transgressed.

The midday meal consisted of a bowl of grey looking soup or stew with stodgy chunks of vegetables in it and a slice of stale bread. Pudding was either lumpy rice or tapioca.

At the end of their meal they had to take their dirty plates and rinse them clean in the large bowl of tepid water that stood on a stool at the end of each table and then leave them in a wooden rack to dry.

In the afternoon they attended lessons. Kelly greatly enjoyed reading and writing but found that no matter how hard she tried she seemed to lack understanding when it came to doing arithmetic, so most of her lessons ended in a beating.

Classes ended at four o'clock and then there was an hour of recreation. If the weather was good they were sometimes allowed out into the yard otherwise they sat and chattered to each other indoors. This was one of the times Kelly hated. It was when some of the older girls picked on her. They taunted and teased her or else pulled her hair, pinched and even punched her.

When, in tears, she threatened to report them, they jeered at her and threatened what they would do to her if she dared to say anything to any of the sisters.

After evening prayers they had the last meal of the day, usually bread and jam. Then it was back up to the dormitory that she shared with the other girls. Lying in the small narrow iron bed she thought about the life she had known with Penny and about her brothers and sisters and wept into the thin hard pillow.

The routine was always the same, day in day out, except on Sundays. Then, as soon as breakfast was over, they were all assembled and marched in a long line into St Saviour's Church for Mass.

Their meals on Sunday were also special. At midday it was usually some kind of roast with potatoes and cabbage and this was followed by suet pudding. At teatime as well as a slice of bread and jam there were stale cakes that had been donated by the local baker or a piece of overripe fruit from the greengrocer.

Kelly missed the freedom of roaming the streets, eating whenever she felt hungry and going to bed when she was tired which could be almost any time. She even missed having to look after her little brother and sister and the baby.

Above all she hankered after the time she had spent with Penny after her accident. First it had been at her posh home in Wallasey and then at Ma Reilly's. She'd been forced into a routine at both of them but it hadn't been anywhere near as irksome as life was in St Saviour's and she'd never been punished in any way at all.

In fact, she reflected, she had been the centre of attention most of the time and she had grown quite fond of Penny. It was only now that she realized what a terrific sacrifice Penny had made in giving up her own comfortable home in Wallasey in order to come over to Liverpool to look after her.

Most nights before she fell asleep she thought that if only Penny's mother hadn't been taken ill they would probably have still been together at Ma Reilly's. That had been the reason she'd had to go back to her own home at Cannon Court. If that hadn't happened then she wouldn't have got into such a scrape because her brother had made her go stealing and she wouldn't have been arrested and ended up where she was.

She comforted herself with the thought that once Penny heard about what had happened she'd come and get her out. The problem was how she could let Penny know where she was.

Penny couldn't put Kelly out of her mind. Even though both of her parents had forbidden her to make any further contact with Kelly she constantly thought of doing so.

When she mentioned visiting St Saviour's to Bryn he did his utmost to dissuade her saying that it was best to leave things alone. He promised to let her know as soon as he heard that Kelly had been released and was back at her own home.

For Penny it was not enough and finally one afternoon without a word to her family or Bryn she decided to go and visit Kelly. She couldn't rest until she made sure that Kelly was being well cared for and above all that she was reasonably happy.

As she travelled on the ferry boat from Seacombe to Liverpool she felt guilty about going against her family's wishes. But her feeling of responsibility for Kelly's welfare and her sense of where her duty lay were so strong that she managed to persuade herself that she was doing the right thing.

The grey granite exterior as she reached St Saviour's Remand Home for Wayward Girls sent a shudder through her. It was so depressing that as she rang the bell she had an ominous feeling of dread. It increased when the door was opened and she found herself face to face with a nun in dark grey garb and a stiff white wimple who regarded her impassively.

'Good afternoon, I'm Penny Forshaw and I was wondering if I could see Kelly Murphy,' Penny stated nervously.

'Have you made an appointment with Mother Superior to do so?'

'No, I'm afraid not,' Penny said with an apologetic smile. 'I suppose I should have telephoned first. The trouble was I wasn't too sure when I would be able to come.'

'You'd better come inside and I will enquire whether you will be allowed to speak to her.' Reluctantly the nun opened the door a little wider to permit Penny to enter.

The polished wooden floor and dark red walls of the reception hall were quite bare apart from a large framed picture of the crucifixion that hung on one wall. The nun indicated the solitary straight-backed wooden chair and motioned to Penny to sit down. 'Will you wait here, please,' she murmured before she disappeared.

She was left waiting for such a long time that Penny wondered if the nun had forgotten about her. Then as silently as a ghost she reappeared and asked Penny to follow her.

They walked in silence along stone corridors to another waiting room where she was told to, 'Please wait, Mother Superior says you may speak to Kelly Murphy for five minutes.'

This room was equally bare and cold. The window looked out on to a tarmac yard and a few girls were out there walking around aimlessly. They were all dressed alike in drab blue dresses and several of them were hugging their bodies with their arms as if they were cold.

When the door opened again Penny looked up expectantly then gave a gasp as she recognized the thin little figure in the uniform drab blue dress who had come into the room.

'Kelly.' Impulsively she held her arms wide and without a moment's hesitation Kelly ran towards her choking back a sob as she found herself encompassed in Penny's embrace.

'Have you come to take me home, Penny?' she gulped, the tears streaming down her peaky little face.

'No, I'm afraid I can't do that . . . not at this moment.'

'You will come back for me, though; I hate it here with all the rules and the praying. The nuns are always punishing me and the big girls tease me and pinch me and pull my hair and . . .' the rest of her words were muffled as she clung on to Penny sobbing almost hysterically.

'Shush! Calm down, Kelly, or they won't let me stay and talk to you,' Penny admonished.

'You will come back again and next time take me home with you,' Kelly pleaded as she snuffled back her tears. 'Don't make me stay here, Penny. I hate it and I'm so afraid.'

Before Penny could answer the nun appeared. 'Come along, Kelly, back to the classroom.'

'Can't we have a few more minutes together?' Penny asked.

'No. Unless she joins the others now she will be late for prayers and if she misses prayers then she will not be able to have any supper,' the sister told them.

'I don't care about missing supper, Penny, as long as I can stay here with you a bit longer,' Kelly insisted.

Penny saw the nun's mouth tighten and remembering what Kelly had said about discipline she knew it was in Kelly's interest to do as they'd been asked.

'You'd better go now, Kelly,' she said in a low voice. Reluctantly she hugged and kissed the little girl goodbye and promised to come and see her again quite soon.

As the nun shepherded Kelly from the room and sent her on her way, Penny said, 'I would like to have a word with Mother Superior.'

'That won't be possible. Mother Superior is already at her evening devotions,' the nun told her dismissively.

'I'm not in a hurry; I can wait until she has finished.'

The nun shook her head. 'I'm afraid it is far too late in the day for her to receive you. You will have to make an appointment and come back some other time.'

Penny bit down on her lower lip, unsure of what to say or do. She wanted to act immediately because she was sure there would be considerable delay before she was allowed to remove Kelly from their care. She knew that Kelly was desperately unhappy which was why she wanted to put the wheels in motion right away.

'If you will follow me then I will show you out,' the nun stated in stiff unrelenting tones that brooked no argument.

Realizing that it was useless to plead, Penny followed the nun back down the forbidding corridor to the front door. As she heard it clang shut behind her she was more than ever determined to get Kelly out of there.

Eighteen

Penny was aware of the tense atmosphere when she returned home and they assembled in the dining room for their evening meal. She assumed it was because she had been absent from home all afternoon without mentioning to her mother that she would be out.

Since she had been looking after her mother she had always told her if she was going out and roughly how long she would be gone. Now that her mother was so much better she really didn't feel that it was necessary to do so.

In addition she had considered that it was wiser to say nothing about visiting Kelly because she was quite sure that her mother would have done all in her power to prevent her from going.

Memories of Kelly's tear-streaked little face and her impassioned plea to get her out of the cold stark convent school filled Penny's mind as she took her place at the table. She couldn't bear the thought of what the little girl must be suffering. Even her impoverished home in Cannon Court must seem better to Kelly than where she was, Penny thought sadly.

As Mary brought in a mouth-watering steak and kidney pie together with two tureens, one of potatoes and the other of assorted vegetables and placed them in the centre of the table it made her even more aware of Kelly's predicament.

It wasn't until they had all been served and Mary had finally left the room that her father dropped his bombshell by asking her why she had been visiting St Saviour's Remand Home earlier in the day.

'Don't say you weren't there because Arnold was driving past and saw you knocking on the door,' he told her curtly when she searched for an answer.

'I went over there to visit Kelly,' Penny confessed, the colour rushing to her cheeks.'

'After we had both forbidden you to do so,' her mother said in a hurt voice.

'Mother, I'm an adult, you can't dictate what I do. You can't run my life for me.'

'You are certainly not acting in a grown-up way,' her father stated angrily. 'You had a chance to forget all about that child and her family, put it all behind you, and what do you do? You go and visit her. What on earth for? She's being taken care of by people who know how to handle that sort of child, so why can't you leave well alone?'

Penny laid down her knife and fork ready to launch into details of what Kelly had to endure at St Saviour's, then thought better of it. Her parents wouldn't believe her even if she told them. They would probably say that the strict routine was good for Kelly. They didn't seem to think that she had the same sort of feelings as they did.

The problem about Kelly remained uppermost in her mind and she remained silent for the rest of dinner. Her only hope now, she reasoned, was to persuade Bryn Cash to help her. As a doctor, surely he would understand the effect being in a place like that would have on Kelly.

'There's no point in sitting there sulking simply because you can't have your own way,' her father told her as they finished their meal and he stood up to leave the dining room. 'You are not to bring that child back into this house ever again. Is that understood?'

Penny remained silent biting down on her lower lip to keep her anger under control.

'Your father means it, Penny, and I am in full agreement with his decision,' Mrs Forshaw stated the moment the door closed behind her husband. 'You should never have got involved in the first place; it has upset us all, especially dear Arnold. Your father will never forgive you for breaking off your engagement and ruining all the wonderful plans he had for your future together,' she added with a deep sigh.

Penny's thoughts were in turmoil as she went up to her bedroom. She knew she was disappointing her family by not marrying Arnold but since he had agreed with them and not with her when it came to caring for Kelly after the accident she felt no remorse.

It had opened her eyes to the type of man Arnold was. She

was positive that he had only wanted to marry her because it would prove financially beneficial to him in the future. She felt that he was far more in love with himself and his career prospects than he was with her and as far as she was concerned he had proved to be selfish and mercenary. In some ways it was a relief to have found this out and to realize that she didn't love him before they were irrevocably bound together in marriage.

Unfortunately it left only one person she could now turn to and that was Bryn Cash. They had become firm friends and she trusted him and his judgement.

Her feelings for Bryn, she reflected, were not simply admiration and gratitude for his support but something much deeper and more meaningful. She sometimes wondered if perhaps she was falling in love with him and hoped that one day he would reciprocate her deeper feelings. As yet, however, although he was now taking her out on a regular basis, she was sure he only thought of her as a good friend.

Once again, she decided, she was going to have to appeal to him to help her to do something about Kelly's future. She wasn't at all sure what that was to be. The only solution she could reach was that since her parents would not entertain the idea of having Kelly living there then she must do the same as she had done before. She would have to find a teaching job and somewhere to live so that she could make a home for Kelly. Since she wanted to be able to keep in touch with Bryn then it would have to be in Liverpool.

Now that she had been living back at home for so long the thought of giving up the comfort and luxury that surrounded her and going back to Ma Reilly's seemed grim. Even so, she resolved, if that was what it took then that was what she would do.

Her mother would be distraught when she said she was leaving home again but she had no one to blame except herself. If Mother had sided with her and told Father that she didn't mind Kelly living here with them then Penny was quite sure it would have been possible to persuade him to reconsider his harsh decision.

Now, everything rested on what Bryn thought of her idea and how much support he would be prepared to give her.

★   ★   ★

Bryn listened attentively, his square, good-looking face inscrutable, as Penny outlined her idea of moving back to live at Ma Reilly's in Liverpool so that she could look after Kelly.

'It won't be easy, you know,' he warned. 'Apart from all the home comforts you will be giving up you will have to find a job so that you can support yourself and Kelly.'

'I know, that's why I thought that the first step was to talk it through with you. If you think it is a feasible idea then I'll see if Father O'Flynn can arrange for me to go back to teaching at his school and then I will go and see Ma Reilly to find out if she has a room that I can rent.'

'That's the easy part. What is a much greater milestone is persuading the authorities to release Kelly from St Saviour's.'

'Surely if I offer to be responsible for her and I am earning my own living and can provide somewhere for her to live there will be no problem,' Penny countered with a frown.

'The case will probably have to go before a magistrate before a decision can be made,' Bryn explained.

'Really!' Penny's blue eyes opened wide in surprise. 'Even if I am offering to be responsible for her and prove that I can give her a secure home environment?'

'Oh yes. What's more, you will not only have to have the court's permission but in all probability Mrs Murphy will have to agree to the arrangement as well.'

'I'm sure she won't object,' Penny said dryly. 'In fact she will probably be relieved that she doesn't have to worry about Kelly any more.'

'Don't be too sure. Kelly is coming up to an age where she can be a great help around the home and in next to no time she will be old enough to go out and earn some money.'

'Or beg for it, or steal it,' Penny said bitterly. 'I want to show her a very different way of life than that. I can take her right away from Liverpool if you think that might be a better idea.'

'I'm not sure she would settle or be happy if you did that,' Bryn mused.

'So I have to make sure that Father O'Flynn says I can have my teaching job back, and that Ma Reilly lets me have my room back and also agrees to keep an eye on Kelly if she comes home from school before me. If I do all that then do you think the court will agree to releasing her?' Penny repeated, listing them off on her fingers.

'It might be worth a try.'

'You'll speak up for me in court and say that I am a suitable person to be responsible for taking care of Kelly?'

He gave her a warm smile. 'Yes, of course! You know I will do that.'

'What if they won't believe you?' she asked, doubt creeping into her voice.

'I'm sure they will but if they don't then we'll worry about that when the time comes,' Bryn told her.

'In that case then let's get things moving,' Penny urged him. 'I know that Kelly is extremely unhappy and the sooner I can get her out of St Saviour's the better.'

It was almost six weeks before everything was in place. Father O'Flynn had promised her a teaching post at the start of the new term in September and after a great deal of persuasion Mrs Murphy had eventually agreed that she was willing for Kelly to live with Penny and that she would stand up in court and say so if she was asked to do so.

Mrs Murphy had been the most difficult and it had taken quite a lot of persuasion. As Bryn had foreseen, she kept reminding them that Kelly was now old enough to be of considerable help to her and that by rights she should be back home where she belonged.

'You know they will never allow Kelly to come back here to live after what happened,' Penny reminded her, 'and she is extremely unhappy in St Saviour's.'

'Well, so she might be, but she can't get into any mischief while she's in there. If she's living with you then there's no knowing what she might get up to.'

'Kelly didn't get into any trouble when I was looking after her before,' Penny pointed out, 'so why on earth should she do so now?'

'No, but she was in a pushchair then for most of the time,' Ellen Murphy retorted as she shifted the baby from one arm to the other.

Eventually, with Bryn's intervention, Ellen Murphy reluctantly agreed that Kelly could live with Penny provided she was allowed to come home and look after her younger brother and sisters from time to time if ever she needed her to do so.

Penny shivered as she went into the courtroom. She found the formal atmosphere and the high-backed polished wooden seating rather overwhelming. She thought how frightening it would have been for Kelly and she felt relieved that she had not been expected to attend today.

When her name was called, Penny managed to make her statement about why she thought it would be beneficial for Kelly to be in her care rather than in St Saviour's Home in a clear firm voice. She also dealt with the many questions that were fired at her as to where she would be living and how she would support herself and Kelly, in a confident manner.

She was trembling when she finished speaking and was relieved to be able to sit down again on the hard bench seat because her knees felt so weak.

It was then Bryn Cash's turn and although he gave Penny a glowing character reference the magistrate still seemed to be unconvinced.

'I feel it will be very difficult for a single woman to support herself and a child. In addition there is Kelly's reputation to be taken into account. It would seem that this particular child must have far stricter supervision than an ordinary child would need.'

As Bryn sat down there was a long silence in the courtroom as the magistrate consulted the papers in front of him and then conferred with a colleague.

Sensing that he was on the verge of refusing to release Kelly from St Saviour's Bryn Cash rose to his feet again. 'I would like to offer a further extenuating reason before you make your final decision.'

There was a silence as if the magistrate wasn't sure whether to allow this or not. Eventually he said very firmly, 'No, Dr Cash, I doubt whether anything further you might wish to say will make any difference. I have decided to adjourn this case for further consideration.'

Outside the courtroom Bryn and Penny looked at each other in dismay.

'How long will that take?' Penny asked. 'It's July now. The

new school term starts in September. If I'm not going to be able to look after Kelly then there is no point in my coming over here to live.'

'Yes, I suppose that's true,' Bryn agreed. 'I was looking forward to you moving to Liverpool, though,' he added with a wry smile.

'If I decide I'm not coming then I will have to let Father O'Flynn know so that he can find someone else for the teaching post he has offered me.'

'Don't be too hasty,' Bryn warned. 'It's not all over yet, they haven't settled anything. They are still considering the situation, remember.'

Penny shook her head, 'I know that but I don't feel too optimistic about what the outcome will be.'

'Look –' Bryn took her hand – 'I've taken the rest of the day off so why don't we go and have a meal. It will give us the chance to talk things over and see if we can think of anything else we can do. There must be some way we can persuade them to let you take care of Kelly.'

Nineteen

Penny and Bryn sat in the restaurant until it was on the point of closing. They talked over the predicament they found themselves in over Kelly's future and tried to find a solution.

She thought how different he was from Arnold. Arnold would merely have shrugged dismissively and said it was up to her what she did or else to forget all about it.

'Perhaps my father was right and I should never have interfered in the first place,' Penny sighed as they made ready to leave the restaurant. She stood up and slipped her arms into the light linen jacket that Bryn was holding for her, and then picked up her handbag from the table.

'Now I will probably be in trouble again for staying out so late,' she sighed as they went out into the street.

'Then why not stay at my place. I have a spare bedroom and you can telephone home to let your family know that you won't be back there until morning.'

Penny hesitated for a brief moment then shook her head. 'I think that might make matters worse, especially if they ever found out where I stayed. No, I'll go home and face the music.'

'Then in that case I will take you there,' Bryn told her.

It was almost midnight when they reached Penny's home in Penkett Road.

'Don't worry, I'll make enquiries to see if there is any other way of getting Kelly released from St Saviour's,' Bryn promised as he put an arm around her shoulders and gave her a reassuring hug.

She opened the front door as quietly as she possibly could and crept inside. Her heart beat faster as she saw that a glimmer of light showed from the drawing room. Removing her shoes she padded in her stockinged feet towards the stairs but her arrival had already been heard and before she could reach them her father was in the hallway.

'Where the devil do you think you have been until this time

of night?' he demanded. 'Don't bother lying because I can guess; you've been with that doctor fellow. I suppose you were too ashamed to come home after what you did today.'

Penny looked at him in bewilderment. 'What I did today?' she asked in a puzzled voice.

'I don't suppose you thought I would find out. You seem to forget that as a magistrate my name and address are well known in legal circles and when you appeared as a witness in a case that was being heard the clerk took the trouble to inform me of the fact,' he told her pompously.

The colour drained from Penny's face and there was a hard knot of anger in her throat. 'So that was why the case was adjourned,' she said bitterly. 'You had him pass on a message to the presiding magistrate.'

Captain Forshaw didn't answer.

'That was an evil thing to do,' Penny told him in a strident voice.

Her father held open the drawing room door. 'You'd better come in here if you are going to yell at me like a fishwife; I don't want your mother disturbed. She is dreadfully upset that all this worry concerning this wretched child has come up again. We thought it had all been taken care of when she was put into a remand home.'

'I'll go up and talk to Mother,' Penny said, moving towards the door.

'No, stay here and leave well alone,' Captain Forshaw said curtly. 'I said I would wait up until you came home. I persuaded her to take some sleeping tablets and go on up to bed and I trust she is now sound asleep and settled for the night.'

'So now I suppose you are going to lecture me about Kelly,' Penny said wearily.

'I most certainly am,' Captain Forshaw scowled, his face growing florid. 'Why are you ruining your own prospects in this way, Penny? I am in the process of persuading Miss Grimshaw to give you back your job in September . . .'

'That wasn't necessary,' Penny interrupted. 'I already have a job to go to in September.'

'Where?' her father demanded. 'You're not thinking of going back to that Catholic school in the Liverpool slums, I hope.'

'Yes, I am.' Penny squared her shoulders. 'Father O'Flynn has offered me a teaching post starting in September.'

'Then you can ring him up in the morning and tell him you won't be accepting it. You will be going back to Miss Grimshaw's school.'

Penny squared her shoulders defiantly, her blue eyes flashing. 'That very much depends on whether you and Mother will be prepared to have Kelly living here with us and also arrange for her to attend Miss Grimshaw's school,' she told him.

'Don't talk nonsense! I have said we are not prepared to have anything further to do with that child and I mean it. Anyway, there is no question at all of her being released from St Saviour's Remand Home.'

'She would have been released into my care today if you hadn't interfered,' Penny said bitterly.

'Stop being so insolent and talking such nonsense, Penny,' Captain Forshaw said angrily, his florid face becoming even redder. 'You don't expect me to stand by and do nothing while you continue to ruin your future just because you have some stupid idea about saving this child.'

'I am not trying to save her; I merely want to try to give her a better chance in life.'

'She's the produce of the slum that she's been born into and that has been proved. The moment she was out of your influence she was in trouble with the police.'

'Maybe, but it was not of her own volition. It was her older brother's influence over her that caused the trouble,' Penny defended.

'Leave her where she is. The nuns may manage to straighten her out in the remand home; something you will never be able to do.'

As Penny was about to reply he held up his hand to silence her. 'No more; this discussion is at an end. Go to bed, Penny, and resolve to make a new start tomorrow and let all of us put this sordid matter behind us.

Penny couldn't sleep. She tossed and turned going over and over in her mind all that had taken place in the courtroom and since. She kept thinking of how dreadfully disappointed Kelly would be when she was told that her hopes and dreams had been shattered and that she was not going to be released from St Saviour's.

She knew that the nuns would offer no words of comfort to Kelly when they told her of the court's decision and her heart ached for Kelly knowing how let down she would feel.

When Penny finally fell asleep it was almost dawn and she found herself embroiled in a terrifying nightmare involving an argument between her father and Kelly.

The quarrel between them didn't make any sense to her and yet she felt herself becoming involved deeper and deeper in their conflict. Try as she might she couldn't calm either of them because they ignored everything she said. It was almost as if they were in another dimension and although she could see and hear everything that was going on between them they couldn't hear her voice. She kept wishing Bryn was there to help her deal with them but although she called out his name time and time again he never appeared.

When she finally woke up in panic the sun was streaming in her window and as her senses levelled out she felt a sense of relief that it had all been a dream.

Her parents were both in the breakfast room when she went downstairs. Although they were cordial in their greeting there was a tense atmosphere between the three of them.

Penny had barely started her breakfast when Mary came into the room to say that she was needed on the telephone.

'Do you know who it is, Mary?' Captain Forshaw frowned.

'Dr Cash, sir.'

'Then tell him Miss Penny will call him back after she has finished her breakfast.'

'He said it was important,' Mary said looking questioningly at Penny.

'It's all right, Mary, I'll deal with it now,' Penny said quickly, wiping her lips with her napkin and standing up.

Before her father could stop her she hurried from the room and into the hall.

'Hello Bryn, is something wrong?' she asked, as she picked up the phone.'

'Yes, I'm afraid there is. I've just had a visit from Father O'Flynn. It seems Kelly has run away from St Saviour's.'

'When did this happen?'

'They're not sure. She was there last night when one of the nuns told her about the court's decision to adjourn a decision. It seems that Kelly took it rather badly. She was in tears and saying over and over again that it meant she'd never be able to come and live with you.'

'Oh dear!'

'This morning, when they took the roll call before early morning prayers she wasn't there. At first they thought she was sulking and deliberately being late. Then when they checked the dormitory and the classrooms they couldn't find her. It seems they've looked everywhere for her and she is definitely not in the building.'

'Has she taken refuge with Mrs Reilly, do you think?'

'No, the police have already paid her a visit and she hasn't seen anything of Kelly.'

'Then perhaps she has gone to her own home in Cannon Court.'

'No, she's not there. Her mother hasn't seen her since she was sent to St Saviour's. They were going to contact the police in Wallasey to call at your house but I asked them to let me telephone you first because I didn't think you would want your father to be involved.'

'Thank you for that although of course he will be informed. I found out last night that it was because of his intervention that the magistrate adjourned his decision.'

'Are you sure about that?' Bryn sounded taken aback.

'Quite sure. He told me so last night as soon as I got home. Someone at the court recognized my name and the address I had given and telephoned him. Well, you can guess the rest.'

Bryn was silent for such a long time that Penny asked, 'Are you still there, Bryn?'

'Yes, I was trying to work out what to do next. We must be careful not to make things even worse for Kelly.'

'Where do you think she might be? If she hasn't come to you for help and she hasn't gone back to her own home or to Mrs Reilly then she must be wandering around Liverpool. Do you want me to come over and help look for her?'

'No; I think it might be best if you stay where you are

because she might be trying to make her way to you,' Bryn said thoughtfully.

'It would be difficult for her to do that because she won't have any money,' Penny pointed out. 'She would need some in order to buy a ticket to come over on the boat,' she added.

'True, but knowing Kelly she will find a way to mingle with the crowd and somehow manage to slip on board unnoticed.'

'And then she would have to walk all the way here, to Penkett Road, from Seacombe Ferry.' Penny added in a dubious voice.

'If she is determined to find you she will and I am pretty certain that is what she has in mind,' Bryn insisted.

'So what do we do now?'

'Well, as I said, I think you should stay where you are because I am sure that she will turn up there eventually. Mind you, I don't think she will walk straight up to the front door so keep an eye open for her.'

'In the meantime you'll keep looking for her over in Liverpool?'

'Yes, but I have a clinic this morning at the hospital and another this afternoon so I won't be free to do very much until this evening.'

'You will phone me if you have any news?' Penny said anxiously.

'Of course I will and make sure you phone and let me know if she turns up. You can always leave a message for me if the receptionist is unable to put you through.'

The rest of the day seemed endless to Penny. She couldn't concentrate on anything but found herself startled by every sudden noise. She kept popping out into the driveway to peer this way and that up and down Penkett Road to make sure that Kelly wasn't there. She was afraid she might be hanging around and hiding behind one of the trees until she felt it was safe to come to the house.

Bryn phoned twice but he had no fresh news to tell her about Kelly. He'd asked several of his patients if they had seen her but no one had. He'd even found time to pay a visit to Ma Reilly's and also to go to the Murphy's house in Cannon Court in case she had gone there after the police had called but neither Ellen Murphy nor Mrs Reilly had seen or heard from her.

'They must both be very concerned about what has happened

to her and where she is, especially Mrs Reilly,' Penny said, her voice conveying how very worried she was herself.

Towards teatime the sky became overcast and it began to rain. At first it was merely a heavy drizzle, then the clouds became heavier and the rain lashed down. Within a few minutes it was accompanied by deep rumbles of thunder followed by brilliant flashes of lightning.

Penny remembered how frightened Kelly had always been whenever there was a thunderstorm and hoped that she was able to take cover somewhere safe.

As Penny went round the house closing all the windows she peered out in case Kelly had crept into the garden and was sheltering under one of the shrubs.

It was almost seven o'clock and the storm was starting to abate when there was a knock on the door.

'I'll get it,' Penny called out as she rushed to open it, pushing Mary to one side as the girl came out of the kitchen and into the hallway.

Her heart was thudding, hoping that it was Kelly, but to her surprise it was Bryn standing on the doorstep and he was soaked from head to foot.

For a moment they stared at each other in silence before she invited him inside.

'I came over on the ferry and then walked here from Seacombe. I was trying to trace Kelly's footsteps in case she had come over to see you and was sheltering somewhere from the storm,' he explained as he stood in the hallway, water dripping from him on to the floor. 'I was hoping I might find someone who had seen her.'

'Talk about looking for a needle in a haystack,' Penny said with a smile. 'How could you possibly expect anyone to remember one small girl among the many hundreds of people who make the crossing every day.'

'She will still be wearing that drab blue dress and most people in the Liverpool area know that it's the uniform they wear at St Saviour's Remand Home,' he reminded Penny. 'Furthermore her picture is featured on all the newsstand placards as well as the front page of the *Liverpool Evening Echo* stating that she has run away from the home.'

Penny clamped her hand over her mouth in dismay. 'Oh Bryn, how awful! I didn't know that; it makes her sound like a criminal.'

'I know; that's why it is so important that we find her. Not only the police but the general public will be keeping an eye out for her now and if any of them find her first it will be straight back to St Saviour's for her.'

'Come in, take off your wet coat and while we talk about it I'll get Mary to make some hot coffee to warm you up.'

'Perhaps Dr Cash would like to stay and have dinner. That would give all of us the opportunity to have a serious chat.'

Penny looked round, startled, as her father suddenly appeared in the hallway.

'Good evening, Captain Forshaw. That's very kind of you but I am afraid I can't accept because I have far too many other commitments,' Bryn said firmly.

'Then you and I had better have a little talk on our own,' Marcus Forshaw insisted. 'Do take off your wet coat and then come into my study.'

Bryn looked at his watch and then shook his head. 'I'm extremely sorry but I don't have the time to stay any longer. Perhaps some other time.'

Before anyone could speak Bryn had turned, opened the front door and was gone.

Twenty

Penny and her parents had only just sat down to dinner when there was an urgent knocking on the front door. They heard Mary scurrying along the hallway to answer it followed by a babble of voices.

'That's Kelly's voice,' Penny exclaimed, relief and excitement mingling in her voice. She pushed back her chair and hurried out into the hall.

Penny drew in her breath sharply as she saw Bryn and Kelly standing there; for a moment she wondered if she was imagining it. The next minute Kelly was in her arms, sobbing and clinging to her desperately.

'What the devil's going on now?' Captain Forshaw demanded angrily as he followed Penny out into the hallway.

'You're back again!' He stared aggressively at Bryn. 'And you've brought that damned child with you.'

'Kelly was on her way here and I met her out in Penkett Road,' Bryn explained, looking at Penny as he spoke.

'This is wonderful, I am so glad you found her,' Penny breathed as she smoothed the soaking wet strands of dark hair back from Kelly's eyes and planted a kiss on her brow.

'She's not staying here,' Captain Forshaw interrupted. 'You found her Dr Cash so you can take her back to Liverpool with you and return her to St Saviour's Remand Home, which is where she belongs,' he said, addressing Bryn forcibly.

'No, no! I don't want to go back there I want to stay with Penny,' Kelly screamed in a terrified voice and threw her arms around Penny. She began to sob noisily. 'Don't make me go back there. I want to be with you, Penny,' she pleaded looking up into Penny's face.

Penny looked helplessly from her father to Bryn and back again.

'Surely Kelly can stay here until the morning so that she can have a good night's sleep and then we can all talk things over tomorrow and decide what to do for the best,' Bryn suggested.

'I've already decided what is best,' Marcus Forshaw stated abruptly, 'and that's to get that damned child out of here right away.'

'If you turn her out then I shall go with her,' Penny told him defiantly.

'Are we going through all that nonsense again? Think of your mother and how it will affect her. It's your duty to stay here and care for her; she needs you.'

'Mother is quite fit again and she doesn't need me to be here, so I'm leaving unless you are prepared to allow Kelly to stay here with me,' Penny said quietly.

'Very well,' she added when her father remained silent. 'I'll go and tell Mother what is happening and collect my things. Kelly you wait with Dr Cash, I will only be a few minutes.'

Upstairs Penny reached down a suitcase and tried to think what she needed to take with her. Her mind was in turmoil as she packed things into it haphazardly including a bundle of Kelly's clothes that she had bought for her earlier in the summer and still had. It was almost like a rerun of all that had happened before and she hoped that her leaving wouldn't have an adverse effect on her mother.

Kelly had fallen into an exhausted sleep by the time they reached Liverpool. Bryn carried her from the boat up the floating roadway and along to the taxi rank at the Pier Head.

'Blenheim Road,' he told the driver as they settled into the cab.

Ma Reilly looked taken aback when ten minutes later they knocked on her door.

'I'm so relieved that you've found her,' she commented, her wrinkled face softening into a smile as she looked down at the sleeping child in Bryn's arms. 'She looks absolutely exhausted. Had she got very far?'

'She'd made her way to Wallasey to try and find Penny,' Bryn Cash explained.

Ma Reilly suddenly seemed to notice the suitcase that Penny was carrying and a look of consternation registered on her face.

'Oh gracious me, you're wanting to stay here with me again are you! I wasn't expecting you . . . leastways not until September,' she said looking directly at Penny. 'I haven't an empty room until then.'

'Oh heavens!' Penny looked from Ma Reilly to Bryn in dismay. 'What ever are we going to do until then?'

'I'm sorry, luv. There's nothing I can do, I'm all booked up until September,' Ma Reilly repeated worriedly.

'Don't worry, Mrs Reilly. It's no problem,' Bryn said quickly. 'We only called to let you know that we had found Kelly and that she was safe and sound. Come on, Penny, we must get this little sleeping beauty tucked up in bed.'

'What on earth am I going to do now, Penny asked worriedly as they walked away. 'Do you know of a cheap hotel?'

'What's wrong with my spare bedroom,' Bryn asked. 'You are more than welcome to stay there,' he reminded her.

'I don't know,' Penny said hesitantly. Then she looked at Kelly's tear-stained face and made her decision. 'Very well, as long as you are quite sure you don't mind us doing that.'

'I don't mind at all. There's only one bed in there so Kelly will have to sleep with you tonight. Tomorrow we can buy a bed for her.'

Bryn's living accommodation was a large flat above a newsagent's in Scotland Road. It was spotlessly clean but rather sparsely furnished. In the spare bedroom that he was offering them Penny found there was a four-foot bed, a chest of drawers and a wardrobe that was built into the alcove on one side of the small iron grate.

'I think it might be best if Kelly went straight to bed,' Bryn said as he carried the sleeping child straight through to this room and put her down on the bed.

'I wonder when she last had something to eat or drink?' Penny mused as she put her suitcase down and slipped off her coat.

'She can have something to eat if she wakes up later on. For the moment though, I think she is so exhausted that we should let her go on sleeping,' Bryn insisted.

'We'd better try and remove her wet dress; it's bound to be damp and we don't want her catching a chill.'

As they started to undress her and remove the drab blue uniform dress, that was now torn and grubby, Kelly stirred and stared up at them in a bewildered daze.

'We're only taking your dress off because it's rather wet,' Penny explained.

Kelly immediately held up her arms so that Penny could slip it off.

'I'm cold,' she snuffled, shivering and wrapping her arms around her thin little body.

'One more minute and then you'll be snug and warm,' Bryn promised.

He fetched a small light blanket and wrapped Kelly in it before taking her through to his living room and settling her down in an armchair

Kelly looked round frowning at the unfamiliar surroundings. 'Where are we?' she asked in a puzzled voice. Then, before either of them could answer she asked, 'Can I have a drink of water?'

'Of course you can,' Bryn told her. 'Or, better still, how about a mug of hot cocoa and a buttered crust to eat with it?'

Half an hour later Kelly had stopped shivering and was yawning and rubbing her eyes in an effort to stay awake.

'Ready for bed?' Bryn asked as he picked her up in his arms and carried her through to the bed in the spare room.

Penny followed and helped to tuck her in. For a moment they stood there looking down at her, each immersed in their own thoughts. Then Bryn touched Penny on the shoulder and together they left the room, quietly closing the door behind them.

'I bet you're ready for something to eat and drink yourself?' he murmured as they went along the passageway into his small galley kitchen.

'I think I ought to pop round to Cannon Court first and let Ellen Murphy know that Kelly is safe and sound. While I'm there I can collect some clean clothes for Kelly. I'll put this horrid blue dress into the bin. I'm quite sure she will never want to wear it ever again,' she chuckled.

'Hold on, she may have to do so,' Bryn frowned. 'We have to let the police know that we've found Kelly and they will probably insist that she goes back into care.'

Penny looked shocked. 'You mean she will have to return to St Saviour's Remand Home?'

Bryn nodded, his face grim.

'We certainly can't let that happen,' Penny protested.

'I don't see how we can prevent it,' he told her quietly.

'Well, for a start, we don't tell the police that we have found her or that she is here.'

'We can't do that, Penny. At this very moment there are probably dozens of them scouring Liverpool looking for her.'

'Let's think about it,' Penny pleaded. 'Let's talk it over while we are eating.'

'Very well,' Bryn sighed. 'Do you want to cook or shall I get something ready?'

'I'll leave it to you to prepare the meal while I nip round to Cannon Court.'

Kelly was awake when Penny returned; awake and crying.

'Whatever is the matter,' Penny asked sitting down on the side of the bed and putting her arms around the little girl's shaking shoulders.

'I woke up and you weren't here and I thought you'd gone away again,' Kelly snuffled.

'Of course I haven't,' Penny assured her, holding Kelly's trembling body closer. 'I went round to your home to let your mother know that we had found you and that you were safe.'

'What did me mam say? Did she want me back there with her?' Kelly asked wiping the tears from her cheeks with the back of her hand.

'We'll talk about all that tomorrow,' Penny prevaricated.

'You ain't going to send me back to St Saviour's are you?' Kelly asked suspiciously.

'Come on, let's go and eat; it smells good doesn't it,' Penny exclaimed as the savoury smell of bacon and cheese wafted into the bedroom.

'You'd better put on one of the cotton dresses I bought you because you can't sit at the table wrapped up in a blanket,' Penny went on as she opened the suitcase and brought one out.

Bryn had prepared a dish of macaroni cheese and topped it with rashers of crisply grilled bacon. He had uncorked a bottle of wine for himself and Penny, and for Kelly there was some lemonade.

All three of them ate hungrily and mostly in silence. When they did talk, Penny and Bryn avoided mentioning anything about what was to happen to Kelly.

While Bryn cleared away after their meal, Penny persuaded Kelly to go back to bed. As she tucked her in and kissed her goodnight Penny was more determined than ever that she would do everything in her power to stop Kelly being taken back to St Saviour's.

She stayed in the bedroom for several minutes smoothing the creases out of the clothes as she unpacked them from her case and laying them out ready for next morning.

Bryn was still in the kitchen. He had prepared a tray with a jug of coffee, cups, sugar, milk and biscuits.

'We need to talk. Come and make yourself comfortable in the sitting room and I will bring this in,' he told her as he rolled down his shirtsleeves and picked up the tray.

Penny chose the red armchair near the fireplace and after carefully placing the tray down on a low table Bryn settled himself on the settee. Leaning forward he poured out the coffee, added milk to both cups and placed one within reach of Penny. Then he held out the sugar bowl so that she could help herself.

Penny sipped her coffee and looked at Bryn speculatively. She admired his innate honesty and down-to-earth manner so much but this was one occasion when she felt it would be easier if he was not so conscientious. She knew he was right and that it was their duty to let the authorities know that they had found Kelly and, in due course, they would return her to St Saviour's if ordered to do so.

The thought of how unhappy Kelly had been there and her fear of the nuns and dread of going back again made Penny anxious to find some way to contravene that course of action.

Perhaps if she and Kelly moved away to some other part of the country, or even over to Ireland, she could avoid the arm of the law.

She needed money to do that, of course, and she had only a few pounds. Would Bryn lend her the money to carry out her plan, she wondered?

Putting down her coffee cup she cleared her throat and put the proposition to him.

Bryn stared at her in silence, his dark eyes unfathomable. He drained his coffee and put his cup back on the tray.

'It would only be a loan. I would pay you back as soon as I was able to find work and was on my feet again,' Penny promised.

'How would that be possible when you would have the police

of both countries hot on your heels? It would not only be Kelly they were looking for but you as well. You would probably be accused of kidnapping or abducting her, and also find yourself on the wrong side of the law.'

'Then I'll take her to France or Spain or even to America. I don't mind where it is as long as Kelly doesn't have to go back to that awful place. I went there to see her and it was so grim that I haven't been able to put it out of my mind. The older girls bullied her and those nuns, in their sombre garb and their faces framed by stiff white wimples, were so cold and unsmiling that they even frightened me.'

Bryn ran his hands through his thick dark hair. 'No, Penny, I can't go along with your idea because it's far too risky.'

'I'd pay you back, I promise,' Penny insisted.

'It's not the money! I don't give a damn about that. If I thought your plan would work I'd let you have every penny I could raise.'

'Then trust me. We must do something and I am sure it is the only way we can ensure that Kelly is safe.'

'It's you and your future I'm concerned about; you mean far too much to me, Penny, for me to let you do this and put yourself on the wrong side of the law.'

Penny stared at him in disbelief, wondering if she had heard aright.

He stood up and crossed to the armchair and looked down at her. Then pulling her to her feet he held her so close that she could feel the heat of his body through her own clothes.

'You must know how I feel about you,' he said softly. Placing a hand underneath her chin he tilted her head back so that he could look into her eyes. 'I live in hope that someday you will feel the same way about me,' he whispered softly.

For a long moment they gazed at each other and then, as he read the answer he wanted, Bryn bent his head and kissed her firmly on the mouth.

Twenty-One

Penny woke to find Bryn placing a cup of tea down on the small table by her bedside.

'I thought I'd better warn you that I have a clinic at the hospital this morning so I will be leaving very shortly,' he told her.

Penny rubbed sleepily at her eyes and smothered a yawn. 'What time is it?'

'Half past eight. There's no need to hurry,' he murmured. 'Have another sleep if you feel you need it, I merely thought I should let you know what was happening just in case you had forgotten where you were and were startled by all the noise from the newsagent's shop downstairs.'

Penny pulled herself up into a sitting position and looked bewildered for a moment. She ran a hand through her tousled hair, pushing it back from her face.

'Where's Kelly?' Bryn asked

Penny had slept deeply but now as the events of the night before came rushing back and as she became aware of the empty space in the bed beside her she felt a frisson of alarm.

'I don't know.'

'How strange; I haven't seen anything of her.' He frowned.

'She's probably in the bathroom.'

As she spoke Penny threw back the bedclothes, intending to go and look, then conscious that she was only wearing her brief slip she pulled them back over her again. 'Bryn would you go and see if she is in there, please?' she asked.

'Of course, but I'm pretty certain she isn't,' Bryn stated.

As soon as Bryn left the room Penny pulled the coverlet off the bed and wrapped it round her before going out on to the landing.

'Have you found her?'

'No!' Bryn looked perplexed. 'She's not in the bathroom and I'm sure she's not in the living room but I'll check to make sure.'

Penny went back into her bedroom and hurriedly pulled on

the clothes she'd been wearing the night before. She felt a sense of dread as she heard Bryn coming back.

'She's not there,' he said, shaking his head in bewilderment.

'You're sure you've looked everywhere?'

'Yes, I've looked in every room in the flat, even the airing cupboard; everywhere except in my bedroom.'

Penny followed him to the door of his room. Like all the other rooms in the flat it was sparsely furnished and contained only a single bed, a washstand, a bedside table and a fitted wardrobe. There was absolutely nowhere for Kelly to hide.

As he was about to come out of the room Bryn stopped by the bedside table.

'What is it?'

'I left some money there last night; it was about three pounds in small change.'

They looked at each other their eyes full of unasked questions knowing that there was only one person who could have taken it.

'Wait a minute.' Penny went back into her own bedroom and then came out again almost immediately.

'Her clean clothes are gone. I think she's run away again,' she said uneasily.

'It certainly looks like it. Why? Why on earth would she want to run away when she has found you?'

'Maybe she overheard us talking about her last night and you saying that we must inform the police and that she would be taken back to St Saviour's Remand Home again.'

'You could be right,' Bryn agreed. 'I wonder where she's gone this time?'

'I have no idea at all. It means we'll have to start looking for her all over again.'

'I can't do anything this morning because I have patients waiting to see me,' Bryn reminded her. 'All I can do is telephone the police and let them know what has happened.'

'Don't do that, not yet. Give me a chance to look for her,' Penny begged. 'I'll go round to the Murphys and see if they can help. Even if Ellen doesn't know, young Paddy may have some idea where she might be.

*   *   *

It was almost mid-morning before Penny went to see Ellen Murphy. First of all she called round to see Ma Reilly and question her about where Kelly might be hiding out.

'Well she's not here,' Ma Reilly assured her. She frowned in concentration. 'I can't think where on earth the little varmint would be. Have you asked her mother?'

'No, I'm on my way there now but I wanted to speak to you first and see if you had any ideas,' Penny explained.

'Well, you'd better come on in and have a cuppa while we talk about it. I might be able to think of somewhere.'

Seated in Ma Reilly's clean and comfortable kitchen drinking a cup of tea, Penny felt some of her tension ease.

'Now, why would young Kelly scarper again,' Ma Reilly ruminated as she stirred some sugar into her tea and looked questioningly at Penny.

'I have no idea why she's gone or where she is,' Penny stated.

'I wonder if she's gone over to Wallasey, back to your place?' Ma Reilly asked.

'She certainly wouldn't do that,' Penny said quickly. 'She didn't settle there,' she added by way of explanation.

'No, so I gathered,' Ma Reilly said with a grim smile. 'From what she told me your folks thought she was a little guttersnipe.'

She took a mouthful of tea then placed her cup back in its saucer. 'Have you told the police about what's been happening?'

'No!' Penny shook her head vehemently. 'Not yet we haven't.'

'You intend to do so though?' The old woman's sharp eyes demanded the truth.

'We were talking about it last night but I persuaded Bryn to put off doing it until today. Then this happened,' Penny admitted, her voice trailing off uncertainly.

'Do you think that Kelly might have heard what the two of you were saying?'

'I don't think she did. She was tucked up in bed and we had gone into the sitting room. As far as I know she was asleep.'

'As far as you know!' Ma Reilly smoothed down her skirt. 'She's a crafty little thing. I'd bet my last tanner she was listening and heard every word you said.'

Penny frowned. 'And you believe that is why she has run away?'

Ellen Murphy was no help at all. She came to the basement door with the baby clutched in her arms and peered through her curtain of bedraggled hair at Penny in a suspicious manner.

'Well, what is it you want this time,' she asked ungraciously, making no attempt to ask Penny to step inside.

'Has Kelly been here or do you have any idea where she might be?' Penny asked bluntly.

'I haven't seen sight nor sound of her. You called last night to say you'd found her,' Ellen said irritably. 'What with you and the rozzers banging on the door asking me questions about her I don't get a minute's peace.'

'Have the police been here today?' Penny asked ignoring Ellen's sullen manner.

'Course they have; they're still looking for her aren't they or so they says.'

'You didn't tell them that she was staying at Dr Cash's place with me did you?' Penny asked in alarm.

'What sort of nark do you take me for?' Ellen asked huffily. 'I've spent too many years protecting my lot from the rozzers to do a daft thing like that. Anyway, why've you come here asking me where she is; she's with you isn't she?'

'Kelly's run away again.'

'When she do that?' Ellen scowled, humping the baby on to her shoulder and patting its back.

'We're not sure. She was sharing a bed with me but when I woke up this morning she'd already gone. She's also taken some money belonging to Dr Cash.'

'Bigger fool him to leave it lying around when he knew he'd got a little tea leaf in the place,' Ellen Murphy chortled.

'I've been round to Mrs Reilly's but Kelly's not been there; she's not seen her.'

'So? What do you want me to do about it?' Ellen Murphy asked belligerently. 'You said you'd look after her the same as you did last time and look what's happened again.'

'Have you any idea where she might have gone?' Penny persisted, ignoring the taunt.

'I've already told you that I haven't seen her and don't know where she is. Now go away and leave me in peace.'

'What about Paddy, would he know where Kelly might be?' Penny asked as Ellen Murphy made to shut the door.

'How the hell can he know anything about where she is when he's locked up in a remand home?' Ellen countered.

'Sorry that's true. What about his friends, would Kelly have gone to one of them to help her?'

'He ain't got any friends. Now bugger off and leave me and mine alone. There's trouble of one kind or another every time you comes here.'

Resignedly, Penny climbed the basement steps back into Cannon Court. As she walked away and turned into the main road someone touched her on the arm.

'I know where Kelly Murphy is,' a voice muttered softly.

'You do?' Penny stopped abruptly and looked searchingly at the scruffy youth who had approached her. He was down at heel and wearing a ragged striped shirt and dirty grey flannels. His face was pockmarked from acne and she noticed that one of his front teeth was broken.

'Tell me then, where is she?'

'What's in it for me?' he asked eyeing her up and down in a calculating way.

'I don't understand what you mean?' Penny asked hesitantly.

'Make it worth my while and then I'll tell you.' He grinned, moving so close to her that she felt intimidated.

'You mean you want me to pay you for the information?' she asked as she drew back to get away from the smell of his foul breath.

He nodded and held out a grubby hand.

Penny opened her handbag and took out her purse. She looked at him questioningly; she had no idea how much she ought to offer him.

'Give us a tenner,' he demanded.

'Ten pounds!'

'Go on, you can afford it,' he leered.

Penny hesitated. She wasn't sure about handing that much money over to him without some proof that he really did know where Kelly was. She had a feeling that once he had the money in his hands then he would probably make off and she'd never see him again.

'Ten pounds,' she repeated slowly. 'I tell you what: I'll give you half now and the other half when you take me to Kelly,' she offered taking a white five-pound note from her purse.

'No, I want it all now, up front,' he said in a surly voice. 'I ain't going to be seen going over to New Brighton with the likes of you.'

'Why ever not?'

'Rozzers would think I was going to nick something off you and would pick me up before we even got as far as the Pier Head.'

Penny looked thoughtful. She knew there was a grain of truth in what he said but she still wasn't sure if he really knew where Kelly was. If he did, then could she trust him to tell her the truth, she wondered.

She looked down at the money she was still holding in her hand. He had made no attempt to snatch it from her, she reasoned, so perhaps she was judging him too harshly simply because of his appearance.

'Very well,' she agreed. 'If you tell me exactly where Kelly has gone, and how you know, then you can have all the money, the whole ten pounds you've asked for.'

He grinned widely, showing so many brown broken teeth that it sent a shudder through her.

'Kelly Murphy's gone across to New Brighton,' he told her. 'She's joining up with Bilkie's Circus over there.'

'How on earth do you know that?' Penny gasped sceptically.

'Spoke to her earlier on this morning. I was down by the docks and I saw her. She was wandering around like a stray cat.'

'You saw her go on to one of the ferry boats?'

'Better than that, I took her over there. We went on the *Royal Daffodil*. She said that the police were looking for her and she was running away because if they found her then they'd send her back to St Saviour's Remand Home again. I felt sorry for her so I told her the best thing she could do was to join the circus.'

'And she believed you?' Penny asked incredulously.

'She's gone ain't she and you and that doctor fellow don't know where she is.'

'Why would she want to join the circus?' Penny mused.

'To get right away from Liverpool and St Saviour's and so as the rozzers can't find her.'

'If she's only in New Brighton it will be easy enough for them to find her,' Penny pointed out.

'The circus is in New Brighton now but they'll be packing up any day and moving back to Spain because that's what they always do when the season is over.'

'You say they are called Bilkie's?'

'That's right. Everyone knows them. They're a star attraction and they're in the grounds of the Tower Ballroom. They've got a circus of wild animals as well as roundabouts, swing boats, coconut shies, boxing booths and all sorts of other sideshows. Ask for Ferdy Bilkie; he's the big boss man and he'll know where she is.'

'How do you know all this?' Penny repeated dubiously.

'Everybody as what goes to New Brighton knows them,' he said scornfully.

'You seem to know a lot about them, though,' Penny persisted. 'Why did you tell Kelly to go there and how do you know the name of the man who runs it?'

'I used to work for them; taking tickets on the carousel.'

'Really!' Penny looked at him in surprise. He was so scruffy that she couldn't imagine anyone employing him. 'What happened? Why don't you work for them now?'

The boy looked uncomfortable, then he grinned. 'Ferdy caught me nicking some of the takings so he booted me out,' he explained with an air of bravado.

Penny bit down on her bottom lip wondering how much of this scruffy boy's story she could believe. Somehow, even to her critical ears there was a ring of truth in it.

'What makes you think that this Ferdy would let Kelly join his circus?' she queried.

'He's always on the lookout for midgets and the like. She's small enough for what he wants. He dresses 'em up as fairies and then trains them to dance or perform some acrobatics on the back of the elephant or on one of the horses.'

'If you really are telling me the truth and Kelly has gone to join his circus then where would she live?'

'In one of the caravans his lot have, along with all the other kids and dwarves. You satisfied now?' he asked impatiently stretching out a grubby hand to take the money from her.

'I want to know your name,' she said, pulling back as his foul breath hit her in the face making her cough.

'Not bleeding likely. You'll tell it to the rozzers and I'd find myself locked up in a remand home the same as Paddy Murphy is.'

Twenty-Two

'I'm afraid he still isn't free. There are still four patients waiting in Dr Cash's clinic to see him,' the receptionist told Penny when she went along to the hospital and asked if she could speak to him.

Frustrated, Penny didn't know what to do for the best. She wondered whether to wait until Bryn was available or if she should set off on her own to New Brighton.

She didn't altogether trust the boy who had told her where Kelly was and his story about taking her over there himself. He'd looked so dirty and his manner had been so shifty, yet it was the only lead she had as to Kelly's whereabouts.

If what he'd told her was true then she was certainly worried about what might happen to Kelly. She had never visited Bilkie's Circus although she knew where it was sited. She didn't like the sound of Ferdy Bilkie and she felt unsure about what his real intentions were for Kelly.

Perhaps, she resolved, it would be better to talk it over with Bryn and see what he thought about it all before doing anything.

She went back to Bryn's flat in Scotland Road and prepared a simple meal and then made a jug of coffee. She had just put everything out on the table when he came up the stairs.

As they ate their lunch Penny told him that she had again gone to see Ma Reilly and Ellen Murphy and that neither of them had seen Kelly or been able to help in any way.

'So we've nothing at all to go on,' he said morosely.

'Well,' she said hesitantly. 'I do have some news. A young lad stopped me as I was leaving Cannon Court and told me that he knew where Kelly was. He said she had gone over to New Brighton to join the circus.'

Bryn looked startled. 'Good heavens! How on earth did he know that? Or know who you were for that matter?'

'I'm not sure how he knew me,' Penny said lamely, 'except that he had probably seen me coming away from the Murphys' place.'

'You say this lad stopped you in the street and told you that he knew Kelly had gone over to New Brighton to join the circus,' Bryn mused thoughtfully.

'That's right. In fact he said he had taken her over there,' Penny asserted.

'He'd taken her there,' Bryn repeated. 'That sounds like a very strange thing for him to do.'

'He obviously knows her and her family and he seemed to know all about Kelly and her brother Paddy being sent to remand homes. He probably knew she had run away from St Saviour's and he was probably trying to help her.'

'You've no idea of his name?'

'No.' Penny shook her head. 'He wouldn't tell me what it was.'

Bryn pursed his lips. 'I don't trust his motives. Did he ask you for any money?'

'Oh yes! He wanted money before he would tell me where Kelly was.'

Bryn frowned. 'I hope you didn't give him any?'

'Yes, I did. I gave him ten pounds,' Penny admitted.

Bryn's eyebrows shot up. 'His information didn't come cheap!'

'No, but at least we know where Kelly is,' Penny defended.

'True! So what do you propose we do about it? I suppose we ought to tell the police and let them deal with the situation.'

'No, we can't do that,' Penny protested. 'If we tell the police then it means they will go over there and pick her up and take her straight back to St Saviour's.'

'That's going to happen anyway sooner or later,' Bryn pointed out as he helped himself to a second cup of coffee.

'I know, but perhaps it would soften the blow a little if we found her first and explained things to her. She might take it more calmly if we told her that although she has to go back there for the moment we will be doing everything in our power to get her released.'

'Or we could leave her where she is and let the circus people take her with them when they go back to Spain,' Bryn mused.

'We can't do that, Bryn! We don't know what would happen to her; we don't know anything about this Ferdy Bilkie,' Penny exclaimed her voice full of concern.

'No, but it's certainly the easiest solution!' Bryn countered. 'We can't simply walk up to him and ask for her back. This young scallywag who approached you this morning has probably made him pay out good money for her.'

'Are you suggesting that this boy I spoke to has sold Kelly to the circus people!' Penny exclaimed in a shocked voice.

'If he asked you for money before he would tell you Kelly's whereabouts then you can bet your boots he asked this Bilkie fellow for money before he handed her over.'

Penny shook her head. 'He wouldn't do that, surely.'

'If he went to the trouble of taking her over to New Brighton himself I'm pretty confident that he's traded her,' Bryn assured her. 'Otherwise why bother to go all the way over there with her? He could have told Kelly where to go and who to ask for and left it to her to make her own way.'

'So what do you think we should do now?' she questioned. 'Perhaps we ought to go over to New Brighton right away and see if we can persuade this Ferdy Bilkie to let us have her back,' she added quickly before Bryn was able to reply.

Bryn shook his head. 'That would probably be a complete waste of time,' he warned. 'The minute you mention Kelly's name this Bilkie fellow will deny all knowledge of ever having seen her.'

Penny chewed on her lower lip in dismay. 'There must be something we can do,' she protested heatedly.

'Yes, inform the police of her suspected whereabouts and let them handle it,' Bryn responded gloomily.

'Or we could go along to one of the circus performances,' Penny suggested. 'If we actually saw that she was there then Bilkie couldn't deny knowledge of her, now could he?'

'I'll think it over.' Bryn pushed back his chair. 'I must go; I have another clinic this afternoon. We'll talk about it again when I get back. I still think the most sensible action, and the right one, is to inform the police.'

As Penny tidied away the remnants of their lunch she felt more and more concerned about Kelly's safety. The boy had hinted that Kelly would be trained to become one of the performers in the circus and she wondered if she could believe this. After all, Kelly was only six years old, so what sort of role could she possibly undertake in the circus? What would they train her to do; become an acrobat or perhaps a dancer? Or would she merely become a skivvy at the beck and call of all and sundry.

She was so young that somebody there would have to look after her so perhaps Bryn was right and letting Kelly go with them to Spain might well be the answer. But what if they were simply kidnapping her?

The thought of what her fate might be if that was the case worried Penny so much that she couldn't rest. Finally she put on her jacket and went out again to see if she could locate the boy she'd spoken to earlier that day.

She walked the full length of Scotland Road, then to Ma Reilly's in Blenheim Road and from there to the Murphys in Cannon Court. She didn't knock on either door knowing that it was pointless to do so but she kept hoping she might see the lad she had spoken to earlier that day.

She even walked round to the church to see if she could find Father O'Flynn and ask his advice but everywhere looked deserted. She was tempted to knock on the vestry door but she was afraid that if someone other than Father O'Flynn answered the door then they would want to know why she wanted to see him.

The fewer people who knew about her concern over Kelly or her suspected whereabouts the better, she reasoned, in case they said anything to the police.

She determined she would persuade Bryn to come with her to New Brighton and face this Ferdy Bilkie and find out the truth. It was the only way they would be able to find any answers to their many questions.

She waited impatiently for Bryn to come home but he was so late that evening that although he finally agreed with her decision their visit had to be postponed.

'We're so short of doctors that I'm having to do double duty,' he explained.

He was kept extremely busy the next day, working right into the evening, making it far too late for them to visit New Brighton when he came home.

'Provided nothing unexpected comes up that demands my attention and keeps me working late then we'll go this evening,' he promised her the following day as he ate a hurried snack at midday before hurrying back to the hospital.

Penny dawdled after Bryn had left. She poured herself another cup of coffee and sat there wondering about Kelly. She was annoyed by the unfortunate delay because she felt that by not taking some positive action sooner she had failed Kelly.

She picked up the *Liverpool Echo* in order to check what time the evening performance started so that she could make sure they arrived there in good time. To her surprise she saw that there would be a matinee that very afternoon.

On impulse she decided to take matters into her own hands. She scribbled a brief note for Bryn so that he would know where she'd gone and in it suggested that he should follow her as soon as he arrived home. She hoped he would understand. Then she piled the dirty dishes up in the sink and snatching up a jacket and her handbag she made a dash for the door.

With any luck if she managed to get a ferry boat direct to New Brighton she would reach the circus before the matinee started, she thought, as she hurried towards Water Street and headed for the Pier Head.

It was late August, a warm, sultry day and time seemed to stand still for Penny as the crowded ferry boat ploughed its way up the Mersey towards New Brighton.

She should have taken action much sooner she reproached herself. It was almost three days since Kelly had disappeared. It was so near the end of the season for the circus people that some of them may have already packed up and gone back to Spain. If so, they might well have already taken Kelly there with them.

She found this thought very disturbing and she realized that it was ridiculous to worry about it when all the time Kelly was probably still in New Brighton, so she turned her mind to more pleasant things.

Bryn declaring his love for her had been something she'd dreamed about for so long that she still found it hard to believe that it had come true and that he really did feel the same way about her as she did about him.

Their concern over Kelly's disappearance had rather over-shadowed them showing their feelings for each other since that night, she thought sadly.

Once they knew that Kelly was safe they'd celebrate in some way, she told herself, and wondered what her parents' reactions would be. She sensed that although they tolerated Bryn they were by no means as enamoured by him as they had been by Arnold.

Arnold had been very much the blue-eyed boy and it seemed could do no wrong in their eyes They seemed to be blind to his faults and to his selfishness like she had once been.

In countless ways, she reflected, he was the exact opposite of Bryn. Arnold only cared about himself and his own prospects. Thank goodness she had discovered his true nature before it was too late.

Twenty-Three

Penny made sure that she was at the very front of the disembarking crowd waiting impatiently for the gangway to be lowered as the *Royal Daffodil* pulled in alongside the landing stage at New Brighton Pier.

In the distance she could see the outline of the circus Big Top and as she hurried off the boat and made her way towards the grounds of the Tower Ballroom she could hear the music coming from the adjacent funfair.

Apprehensively she bought a ticket and made her way into the huge tent. It was packed and the fanfare of trumpets announcing that the start of the show was imminent had already blared out by the time she'd climbed up the narrow wooden steps and found her place on the hard tiered seats that surrounded the ring on all sides.

It was such a sweltering hot day that once inside the tent the smell of human bodies mingled with the stench of animal droppings that pervaded the air was almost overpowering.

As an introduction to the main attractions clowns were performing a variety of tumbling tricks around the arena. They were being loudly clapped and cheered by hordes of children who were making the most of the last few days of their summer holidays.

The first main event brought screams and gasps from the audience. A huge iron cage covered by a green cloth and obviously carrying some great animal inside it was wheeled into the centre of the ring to a fanfare of music. A ringmaster wearing a smart black and gold uniform and a black top-hat that was also trimmed with gold braid whipped away the covers. He then began wielding a very long gold-topped cane to stir the sleepy lion inside the cage and make it get to its feet.

As it stood up it shook its huge mane and then let out a tremendous roar that had the older children clutching at each other and screaming. Many of the younger ones burst into tears or hid their faces in their mother's skirts because they were so frightened.

They all watched with bated breath as the ringmaster took his life in his hands and stepped inside the cage. He then coaxed the lion to climb on to a stool, reach out a paw, take food from his hand and finally to lie down and go to sleep again.

When the lion's cage was wheeled away it was replaced by a huge black bear that sat on a stool and threw things into the air and then caught them again; this was followed by a gaggle of monkeys who had the children in fits of laughter as they performed their naughty antics.

Between each act there were tumblers and acrobats as well as dancers of all shapes, ages and size to keep the vast crowd entertained. Penny avidly watched every movement in and around the arena as they performed hoping she might catch sight of Kelly but to no avail.

She began to wonder if the boy had been lying and he hadn't brought Kelly over there at all. The only thing she could do now, she decided, was to wait until the performance was over and then go to the back of the tent and ask to see Ferdy Bilkie himself and find out what he could tell her.

As there came a lull in the proceedings Penny was about to leave her seat to go and see if she could find Bilkie when the ringmaster stepped into the centre of the arena. There was a hush of anticipation as he took off his top hat, bowed to the audience, and held up a hand for quiet.

'We now come to the star event,' he announced. 'This is something so very special that it will make you gasp in amazement. Today, we have a new artiste who is appearing for the very first time. She is a beautiful angel and she has come down from heaven to entertain you.'

There were cheers, clapping and catcalls from the audience until the ringmaster once again held up his hand for silence.

A huge grey elephant its great head decorated with embroidered trappings and tinkling bells was then led into the circus ring. On its broad back was a decorated raised dais that was draped with gold tassels that bobbed against the elephant's sides as it lumbered into the ring.

Perched high up on this seat and sitting on a purple velvet

cushion was a tiny figure dressed in a skintight pale pink leotard. There were gossamer wings edged with silver fixed to her back and on her head was a glittering silver crown. She was waving a thin, gleaming wand, topped by a large silver star, in time to the music, as the enormous animal moved slowly around the ring.

The crowd sat mesmerized. Penny leaned forward in her seat trying to see more clearly. Instinct told her that this new attraction, this so-called little angel, was none other than Kelly, but even so she wasn't sure.

Then the music stopped and there was a loud fanfare from a bugler. Once again the ringmaster asked for quiet. The crowd held their breath expectantly as a dwarf who was dressed as a clown and wearing a pointed floppy hat with a silver bell on the end that jangled as he moved led a high-stepping jet black horse into the ring.

'On the count of three the clever little angel will fly through the air from the elephant's back and land on the horse,' the ring-master told the audience. 'Are you ready?'

There were shouts of agreement and encouragement. Then in unison the audience began counting aloud, 'One; Two; Three.'

Dexterously the elephant swung his trunk round and picked up the tiny little angel and wafted her through the air and deposited her on to the horse's back. For a moment she wobbled precariously struggling to keep her balance as she tried to stand up. Then as she finally managed to do so the crowd cheered her loudly.

Penny's heart was in her mouth as she watched. The high stepping horse, prancing and dancing, was paraded round the ring with the angel on its back waving her wand in the air.

Despite all the tinsel and glamour Penny was more than ever convinced that the little 'angel' was Kelly.

Suddenly there were screams and shouts; panic broke out among the audience after a press flashbulb exploded, frightening the horse.

In the pandemonium that ensued the horse reared up and broke away from the leading rein and made straight for the exit. The dwarf ran after him trying to grab the leading rein that was now trailing on the ground.

The little angel lost her balance and began screaming

hysterically and grabbing at the horse in an effort to keep on its back. She managed to twine her fingers into its mane but they were not strong enough to hold her weight and she began to slide down the side of the horse.

The ringmaster lunged at the horse and, grabbing hold of the trailing rein, managed to stop the horse as it reached the barricade but not before the little angel, screaming and crying, had been dragged face down through the sawdust all the way across the ring.

Her screams were so familiar that Penny now knew for certain that it was Kelly. Ignoring the protests from people all around her Penny pushed and elbowed her way through the crowd to Kelly's side.

Kneeling down and cradling the little girl in her arms, she tried to calm and console her, anxious to ascertain how badly hurt she really was.

Kelly was sobbing and her thin body was shaking with fright. Gently Penny tried to brush away the sawdust and grime from her little face, talking to her and trying her best to comfort her all the while.

Kelly appeared to be covered by cuts and grazes and many of them were bleeding profusely. They were not only on her face but also on her bare arms and legs.

'Here, use this.'

Without looking round Penny took the large clean white handkerchief that was being pressed into her hand and gently dabbed at the lacerations. As she did so the little girl stared up at her in bewilderment.

'Penny? Is it you? Are you really here?' she snuffled, clinging on to Penny's arm. 'Don't leave me, I'm so scared of that horse, don't let them make me go on its back again,' she pleaded as she shuddered.

'Yes, I'm here, Kelly, so don't worry, I'll stay with you. You've had a nasty fall but we'll soon have you better again,' she promised.

'I hurt my bad leg again when I fell off that horse,' Kelly whimpered.

Very gently Penny ran her hand down Kelly's leg where she said it hurt. The skin was badly grazed but it didn't feel broken.

'I think it is all right,' she consoled her.

'If I've broken my leg again will you look after me like you did before?' Kelly pleaded in a frightened little voice.

'Of course I will, Kelly,' Penny assured her as she started to sob again when a flashlight bulb went off so close to them that it made her flinch.

Penny looked round to thank whoever it was that had so kindly passed her his handkerchief. As she did so she found herself looking up into the powerful features of a man who had deep-set, magnetic black eyes in a swarthy, handsome face.

He was in his mid-forties, wearing a smart dark brown suit and a brown and beige check shirt.

'Kelly seems to know you; she called you by name,' he stated.

For a moment Penny felt a frisson of alarm in case he was a policeman looking for Kelly and wondered if he had been following her hoping she might lead him to her.

'I'm Ferdinand Bilkie, the owner of this circus,' the man informed her. 'And you are Penny . . .?' He paused waiting for her to finish the sentence.

'My name is Penny Forshaw and Kelly is my responsibility,' Penny said stiffly.

'Really?' He looked at her suspiciously. 'You mean you are a relation?'

'Not exactly. She is temporarily in my care,' Penny said awkwardly.

'Really!' There was disbelief in his voice and on his face but Penny was not prepared to go into details.

A fresh burst of sobbing from Kelly brought them both back to the need for action.

'Well, if you will permit me, Miss Forshaw, I will carry Kelly across to my van where someone will attend to her cuts and grazes.'

Penny hesitated, frowning, unsure what to do for the best. She felt reluctant to let him do this and wished Bryn was there to take charge

'It will also mean that she is away from the rabble and all the publicity,' Ferdinand Bilkie added grimly as the crowd pressed closer, eager to see what was happening.

Without waiting for Penny to answer he bent down and lifted Kelly up in his arms. As he did so there was another flash as a press photographer took more shots of the scene.

Without another word Ferdinand Bilkie strode out of the tent with Kelly in his arms.

Penny hurried after him. Now that she had found Kelly she was determined to stay with her at all costs. She had no intention of letting this man whose motives she was unsure about whisk Kelly away out of her sight.

Twenty-Four

Penny felt very uneasy as she followed Ferdinand Bilkie out of the circus tent. As they hurried past the sideshows and various other funfair attractions and across to the far side of the Tower Ballroom grounds she wondered exactly where he was taking Kelly. Then her heart lightened a little as she saw the long row of caravans parked there.

His van stood slightly apart from the others and was by far the largest one there. Inside it was opulent with Axminster carpet on the floor, heavy velvet drapes at the windows and well-polished built-in furniture.

Kelly was still whimpering and complaining that her bad leg was hurting as Ferdinand Bilkie very carefully set her down on a dark green leather couch.

'I think I had better telephone Dr Bryn Cash and ask for his advice; he attended her before when she broke her leg,' Penny said quickly.

'Do you think it might be broken again?' Ferdinand questioned, his deep voice full of concern.

'I hope not. It happened about a year ago and—'

'It broke because you knocked me down with your motor car,' Kelly snuffled loud enough for him to hear.

Ferdinand Bilkie raised his eyebrows questioningly and Penny felt the hot colour rush to her cheeks but she didn't offer any explanation.

'If you direct me to a telephone I will call Dr Cash and ask his advice,' she repeated.

Ferdinand Bilkie shook his head.

'If you suspect her leg is broken let us take her straight to the Liverpool Infirmary. I will drive you there,' Ferdinand Bilkie told her.

'No, that's not necessary; I can manage perfectly if you find me a taxicab.'

'I will take you myself. After all, the accident happened in my circus,' he said sharply.

Penny bit down on her lower lip. She didn't want him accompanying them but she couldn't think of how to refuse. In some ways she supposed he was right in what he was saying and for the moment at any rate Kelly was his responsibility.

Ten minutes later Penny was sitting in the back of Ferdinand Bilkie's huge dark green Citroën motor car. She was cradling Kelly, who was wrapped in a rug, and trying to console her as Ferdinand Bilkie drove as fast as possible.

'Where are you going?' Penny asked anxiously, leaning forward and tapping him on the shoulder as he drove towards Poulton and then over the Penny Bridge in the direction of Birkenhead.

'To get on the ferry, of course. The ones that take cars don't operate from Seacombe. I thought you would know that.'

'Yes, of course,' Penny murmured. She had been so concerned about Kelly that she had forgotten all about this and felt rather foolish because for one moment she'd been quite scared about where he was taking them.

She breathed a sigh of relief when they eventually reached Liverpool, drew up outside the hospital and Ferdinand Bilkie was out of the driving seat and opening the back door of the car. He lifted Kelly out of Penny's arms and strode inside with her.

Penny hurried after him and reported to the admission desk. The receptionist immediately summoned a porter and instructed him to take them straight to Dr Cash.

The porter took them into a small consulting room and indicated to Ferdinand Bilkie to put Kelly down on the examination couch.

'Don't leave me, Penny,' Kelly begged, clutching at Penny's hand. She was still sniffling and crying and complaining that her leg hurt but she calmed down when Bryn Cash entered the room.

Penny saw Bryn's jaw stiffen as she introduced him to Ferdinand Bilkie even though he shook hands with the other man and greeted him cordially.

'So what have you been up to this time, Kelly?' he asked in a cheerful manner as he walked over to the examination couch and bent over her.

As he pulled back the rug he stared in surprise. 'Why are you dressed like this?' he asked when he saw the leotard with the gossamer wings attached that Kelly was still wearing.

'I'm an angel and I have been riding on the back of an elephant in the circus,' she sniffled.

'And you fell off?'

'Not off the elephant! I fell off the horse but it was the horse's fault not mine,' she said defensively. 'He stood up on his hind legs and I lost my balance and couldn't hold on. He dragged me all across the ring and now my broken leg's hurting bad again.'

'Then I'd better have a look at it and see if I can make it better,' Bryn told her.

After he'd examined Kelly he listened intently to Ferdinand Bilkie's detailed account of what had happened at the performance that afternoon and asked one or two relevant questions.

'If you two would like to go to the waiting room,' Bryn said focusing his attention back to Kelly, 'I will arrange for Kelly to be X-rayed to make sure that she hasn't damaged her leg in any way or broken any other bones.'

The waiting time seemed to be interminable and Ferdinand Bilkie paced restlessly up and down the room reminding Penny of one of the caged animals he kept in his circus.

'If you need to get back to New Brighton I can always get a message to you later, Mr Bilkie and let you know how Kelly is,' she told him.

'No. I would prefer to wait and hear what the doctor has to say,' he said firmly.

When Bryn eventually came to the waiting room his manner was curt. 'Kelly hasn't broken any bones but she is very badly bruised.'

Ferdinand Bilkie looked relieved.

'Thank you, Dr Cash. I will take her away and see that she is well looked after,' he assured Bryn. 'One of my staff has nursing experience so she will be in charge of her recovery. We retain a professional nurse; we need one with all the minor tumbles and falls our acrobats get from time to time,' he added with a deprecating laugh.

'Kelly will be staying here in hospital overnight,' Bryn said firmly. 'She is still suffering from shock and it is important that we keep her under observation for at least twenty-four hours.'

Ferdinand Bilkie looked slightly taken aback. 'In that case I will return tomorrow and collect her.'

'It is not quite as simple as that, Mr Bilkie,' Bryn prevaricated. 'Kelly has had an accident and it is one that must be reported to the authorities.'

Bilkie's manner changed abruptly. 'Surely that's not necessary,' he blustered. 'I'll make sure she is looked after and in a couple of days the incident will be forgotten.'

'No, Mr Bilkie, I'm afraid it is the rule that when an accident occurs in a public place it has to be reported. I don't intend to contravene it,' Bryn Cash stated firmly.

As Penny watched the two men standing there like stags at bay arguing about what had to be done, her own thoughts were more concerned by what was best for Kelly.

If the police were informed about the accident Kelly had been involved in there would be an enquiry about how she came to be at the circus in the first place. And then, when they discovered who she was and the rest of the details, she would be taken back to St Saviour's Remand Home. Penny was determined to stop that happening if it was at all possible.

From his manner she sensed that Ferdinand Bilkie didn't want the police involved either so at least he was on her side as far as that went. On the other hand, she knew that Bryn was anxious to let the police know that Kelly had been found so that they could call off their search.

She tried to intervene in the conversation but both men ignored her. Their argument became more heated and personal.

'I see no reason at all for involving the police,' Ferdinand Bilkie stated, his dark eyes flashing angrily. 'What happened was a mere incident not a full-blown accident.'

'In that case, Mr Bilkie, why are you so concerned about the police being informed? If it is only a mere incident then they will simply make a note of what happened for their records and take the matter no further,' Bryn pointed out.

'You do not understand,' Ferdinand Bilkie said in an exasperated tone. 'When you are running a fairground and circus you try not to become involved with the police because they begin asking all sorts of difficult questions. They inform all sorts of other officials who then send inspectors to make sure that all the safety regulations are being observed. They are also concerned that the animals are well-cared for and—'

'And they ask for details of where all your dancers and acrobats have come from especially when they are very young children,' Bryn interposed. 'By the way, how did Kelly Murphy come to be involved in one of your circus acts?'

Bilkie looked from Bryn to Penny and then back again in a hostile manner. 'What are you trying to imply, Dr Cash? I hope you are not accusing me of kidnapping this little girl?'

'When neither of them answered but continued to stare at him questioningly he shrugged and spread his hands wide in a gesture of despair.

'Very well, I will tell you all. She was brought to me by a youth who for a short time worked for me at the fairground. He was a no-good type of lad, a desperado. He has cheated and stolen from me in the past; but he is also clever. He knew that I have for a long time been looking for someone very small, very appealing and dainty to act as a fairy or angel because he knew that the child who was playing the part at the start of the season became sick and so . . .' he shrugged, leaving the rest of the sentence unfinished.

Bryn's jaw hardened. 'So when this young blackguard brought a scrawny little girl along and said that she wanted to join the circus you thought your luck was in.'

Ferdinand Bilkie shrugged. 'She certainly seemed to be exactly what I was hoping to find,' he agreed.

'You were prepared to shell out the money he was asking for her and ask no questions about her background in return for him saying nothing to anyone about what had taken place between you,' Bryn went on relentlessly.

Ferdinand smiled as though in relief. 'I can see that you are a man of the world Dr Cash; you comprehend perfectly.'

'I understand what you did but I don't approve of your motives,' Bryn Cash told him. 'For one thing, it would seem that you did not make any checks at all about her background or why she was on her own. Did it never occur to you that she might be running away from home?'

'I am well aware that many young children run away from home sometimes because they are unhappy and they usually make for the circus,' Ferdinand said deprecatingly.

'Kelly Murphy didn't run away from home,' Bryn said quietly.

'What do you mean? Are you saying that this boy forced her to do so in some way?'

'Kelly had run away from St Saviour's Remand Home,' Penny said quietly.

Ferdinand Bilkie looked startled. 'Heavens! Do you think the boy knew that?'

'Oh yes! What is more he had promised Kelly that you would take her back to Spain at the end of your season at New Brighton,' Penny told him.

Bilkie looked bemused. 'How do you know all this?' he said, frowning.

'He told me so when he demanded money from me before he would tell me where Kelly was and how to find her.'

'I had no idea at all about any of this!' Ferdinand Bilkie declared firmly. He looked perplexed and shook his head in a gesture of bewilderment.

'Anyway, Kelly must stay here in hospital overnight for observation,' Bryn interrupted. 'We will see how she is tomorrow and then decide what action we must take.'

'Would you like one of us to get in touch in the morning and let you know what is happening?' Penny asked.

'Yes, yes; you must do that,' Ferdinand Bilkie stated forcefully. 'Meanwhile I shall give the matter some serious thought.

'Dr Cash, promise me that you will not report what has happened to the police; not before consulting with me first?' he requested as he moved towards the door.

Penny tensed as they waited for Bryn's answer. She hated the thought of Kelly having to go back to St Saviour's knowing she would be punished for absconding. Yet, at the same time she wondered if it would be an equally fraught future for Kelly if she remained with the circus people and they took her to Spain with them.

She sensed that Bryn was also concerned about Kelly's future but, when he finally replied, he was noncommittal.

'I will contact you in the morning, Mr Bilkie and let you know how Kelly is and what I propose to do,' Bryn said dismissively as Ferdinand opened the door to leave.

There was a long uneasy silence between Penny and Bryn after Ferdinand Bilkie left the consulting room.

Finally, Bryn stopped shuffling the papers on his desk and looked up. Penny saw how exhausted he looked and on impulse suggested that they went for a meal.

Bryn nodded. 'I think it's what we both need. Once we are clear of this place then perhaps we can think more clearly about what is the right thing to do.'

'Can I go along and see Kelly before we leave?'

'There's not much point in doing that. She's been sedated and I don't imagine she will be awake until morning,' Bryn told her as he walked towards the door and waited for her to follow.

Twenty-Five

Penny and Bryn barely spoke, apart from discussing the menu, as they ate their meal. Both of them were immersed in their own thoughts about what had happened that day.

Before they left the restaurant an hour later they'd agreed that perhaps it would be better if they delayed discussing what to do about Kelly's future until the next morning.

'Let's sleep on it, shall we,' Bryn suggested as they reached his flat and he took her into his arms and kissed her goodnight outside her bedroom. 'It may all look better in the morning.'

In that he was very wrong.

Penny tossed and turned most of the night unable to put Kelly and what she had witnessed at the circus out of her mind. Whatever happened now, no matter how much it might anger her father, or even what Bryn might advise was right, she was quite determined to protect Kelly. She would also endeavour to give her a better life.

By the time the first morning light crept round the edges of the curtains she had everything planned out in her mind. She knew what she was going to say as well as what she intended to do.

When she joined Bryn in the kitchen for breakfast she told him of her plans to disappear from Liverpool and take Kelly with her as soon as she came out of hospital.

'I thought if I changed my name and Kelly's so that no one knew who we were and then moved to North Wales you would be able to recommend somewhere where we could stay. I also thought that since your family are living in that area then when you visited them you could check that Kelly was all right.'

'It all sounds quite feasible but will you be able to find a teaching job there?' he questioned as he poured her out a cup of coffee and handed her a slice of toast.

'They have schools there don't they?' she asked in a teasing voice.

'Yes, but the children all speak Welsh; you don't do you?'

Penny shook her head, her face registering her dismay. 'I never thought about that,' she admitted.

'Even if you do find a school that accepts you as a teacher there's also the question of a reference.'

Penny sighed. 'Never mind, I suppose I will have to find some other kind of work.'

'You will have to wait until Kelly is well enough to leave hospital and by then after all the newspaper headlines about Kelly's accident at the circus the police will doubtless have tracked her down.'

'I thought you said that she was only staying in hospital overnight as a precaution so that they could make sure there were no after-effects from her accident.' Penny frowned.

'That was the initial idea but we will have to wait and see what the report on her is today.'

'Then in that case let's get cleared up here and I can come to the hospital with you and find out,' Penny urged picking up her cup and plate and taking them over to the sink where she began to fill a bowl with hot water.

'Not so fast! The paediatrician won't be making his rounds until mid-morning so nothing will be decided until after that. I'll come back for you when I hear his verdict.'

The waiting seemed to be endless to Penny. She tidied the flat and then prepared lunch for them both all ready to serve the moment Bryn came in at midday. When he did, he told her the news was good, Kelly had not suffered any lasting ill effects from her accident.

'The police haven't come looking for her either?'

'Not yet, but we really must tell them, Penny. I know you are anxious to make a better life for Kelly but I'm sure you must realize how impossible your plan to run away with her really is and that I simply cannot condone it.'

'Very well, but let me take her to North Wales first, even if it is only for a few days' holiday. I want to have some time on my own with her so that I can explain why she will have to go back to St Saviour's for a little while but after that she will be able to live with me for as long as she wants to do so.'

★   ★   ★

It was barely two o'clock when they reached the hospital. 'I didn't expect to see you back here again today, Dr Cash,' the ward sister said as she came forward to meet them. 'I trust everything went smoothly,' she said with a smile.

'Everything went smoothly?' Bryn repeated in a puzzled voice. 'What do you mean, sister?' he asked looking at her questioningly.

'With little Kelly.'

'I'm afraid I don't understand. We've come to collect her; since I understand that she is well enough for us to take her home.'

It was the sister's turn to look bemused. 'She has already gone, Dr Cash. She was collected shortly before eleven o'clock by a young woman who said she had been sent by you.'

Bryn and Penny exchanged bewildered glances. 'Surely not the police,' Penny murmured, clutching tightly to Bryn's arm.

Bryn frowned. 'Can you explain what has happened, sister? The arrangement was that Kelly should stay here overnight for observation and that she would be checked over by the paediatrician this morning. If there were no complications then Miss Forshaw would be allowed to take her home.'

'There were no complications and she was ready for discharge from here so when this young lady said she had been sent by you to collect Kelly we let her go.'

'You have her signature?'

The sister shook her head. 'We didn't ask for one. I . . . I thought that it was you,' she said looking at Penny. 'She was the same height and build and about the same age. She had fair hair and was wearing a very smart navy-blue suit and a white blouse under it.'

'Didn't Kelly seemed surprised; didn't she tell you she didn't know this woman?' Bryn asked.

'Well, she did protest at first but the young lady said she was taking her to Spain and that seemed to make Kelly quite happy.'

'Marcia Miller,' Penny said quietly.

'Who on earth is Marcia Miller?' Bryn asked looking even more puzzled. 'What on earth was a stranger doing collecting Kelly?'

'I'll explain later,' Penny said her mouth tightening.

'You think someone from the circus has collected her and taken her back to New Brighton?' Bryn persisted.

'Oh no! It's much more sinister than that,' Penny said, tight-lipped.

'What on earth do you mean?'

'I'll tell you later. I think we should be going,' she added quickly, pulling on Bryn's arm so firmly that he hastily thanked the sister and followed Penny from the ward.

'What was all that about?' he demanded once they were outside the ward.

'Come on, Bryn, we must get to the docks right away if we want to rescue Kelly.'

'Rescue her? What are you talking about; I don't understand.'

'You will,' Penny said grimly.

'Do you mean that this woman is someone from the circus; someone Bilkie has sent?'

'No!' Penny shook her head emphatically. 'I'm pretty sure she's not from the circus. I think from the description the sister gave us that the woman was Marcia Miller, who is Arnold's secretary. I think she's collected Kelly under instructions from Arnold; who in turn has been put up to this scheme by my father.'

'Penny, none of this makes any sense to me,' Bryn protested as she raised a hand to hail a passing taxi and hurried towards it.

'I'll tell you on the way,' she promised as he opened the door and she scrambled inside.

'So where are we going?' the cab driver asked, half turning in his seat and looking at Bryn.

'Watson's Dock,' Penny told him crisply. 'Hurry please, it's urgent.'

'Now do I get an explanation?' Bryn asked, as they settled back in their seats and the cab took off in the direction of the Pier Head.

'Arnold's company have boats that travel regularly to Spain and I think he is going to put Kelly on one of them to get her out of the way.'

'What makes you think that? How could Arnold know, or for that matter care, about Kelly.'

'After what happened at the circus they probably read about it all in the newspaper.'

Bryn frowned. 'I don't understand. I know it said that the

circus people were going to take her with them when they went back to their winter quarters in Spain at the end of the season, but why would Arnold want to take her over there now all on her own.'

'Do you know very much about Spain?' Penny questioned.

'I know it's warm and sunny with some lovely beaches.'

'Ships from the Watson company visit all the main ports there and many of their crew come from Spain,' Penny went on, ignoring what Bryn had said. 'My father took me over to Almeria and showed me the hill villages just outside where most of the crew come from. Many of their homes were caves dug into the sides of the mountain. The poverty and slums in that part of Spain are far worse than what we have here around the Scotland Road area.'

'And you think that is where they are going to take Kelly? To leave her with one of the families over there.'

'Either that or turn her loose and leave her to fend for herself.'

'They couldn't do that; it would be criminal!' Bryn exclaimed in a shocked voice.

'Who would know? They have only to say she ran away when they docked. I remember Arnold once saying that they often get stowaways on board and when they reach Almeria they disappear up into the hills.'

'Surely not children as young as Kelly,' Bryn stated.

'No, that's true. They're usually boys of thirteen or fourteen,' Penny admitted.

Bryn shook his head contemplatively. 'You know, Penny, we should have informed the police the moment we knew where Kelly was and then none of this would have happened.'

'No; she'd have been put straight back into St Saviour's Remand Home.'

'At least she would have been safe in there and if we'd gone through the right channels she may well have been released and back in your care again by now.'

Bryn told the cabbie to wait when they reached Watson's Dock. A cargo ship bearing the Watson insignia was lying at anchor and gangs of stevedores were busy loading it.

Penny and Bryn hurried towards it. As they made their way up the gangplank a burly seaman shouted at them to stop but they ignored him.

The commotion that resulted brought a uniformed man on to the deck and he barred their way.

'We wish to speak to Arnold Watson; we understand he is on board,' Penny stated.

The man hesitated. 'He is with Captain Parker and they cannot be disturbed because we are about to sail . . .'

'I know and we must see him immediately before you leave.'

'I'm afraid that is impossible, miss. The captain has issued an order that they are not to be disturbed.'

As they made to push past him the officer grabbed hold of Bryn's arm but Penny managed to slip by. She had been on the ship before and knew exactly where the captain's quarters were and headed straight for them.

Arnold and Captain Parker were deep in conversation but they broke off abruptly when she burst into the cabin without knocking.

'Why did you take Kelly away from the hospital this morning?' she demanded hotly looking directly at Arnold.

'Well, hello Penny, this is an unexpected pleasure, I had no idea you were on board' Arnold said coolly.

'What are you planning to do with her?' she went on, ignoring his sarcastic greeting.

'I'm arranging for Captain Parker to take her to Spain. As I understood it this was where she was going anyway,' he announced pedantically.

'And once he reaches Almeria I suppose you have told him to abandon her!'

'No! As a matter of fact one of the crew has volunteered to give her a home. I am finalizing the necessary arrangements right now with Captain Parker.'

'How dare you! You have no right to do this,' Penny exploded.

'Saint Penny to the rescue once again,' he mocked. 'So what are you intending to do this time. Are you going to go to Almeria with her and live in a cave?'

'If I have to; if it is the only way of protecting Kelly,' Penny told him, squaring her shoulders and facing him boldly.

He stood up and came over to her and put a hand under her chin, tilting her face up. 'Isn't it time you grew up and stopped trying to be a do-gooder?' he sneered, his grey eyes boring into hers.

'Take your hands off me,' she railed, using both her own hands against his chest to push him away. 'Everything is over between us.'

His eyes hardened. 'Your father has begged me to forgive and forget,' he said softly.

'You might be prepared to do that but I never will,' Penny told him contemptuously.

'Not even for the good of your family? Not even for your father's sake? Perhaps you didn't know,' he went on, 'his future depends on it.'

'What do you mean?' Penny's heart thudded and for a moment her attention was distracted from Kelly's welfare.

Arnold lowered his voice. 'He's in trouble, Penny, extremely serious financial trouble, but you have the power to save him from disgrace.'

Penny raised her brows. 'I have no idea what you are talking about.'

'No, he hasn't told you has he. How do you think he has managed to provide such a beautiful home, run a very expensive motor car, pay for you to attend a private school, buy you your own motor car and to be a member of so many exclusive clubs?'

'You know quite well that my father has always run a very successful business and that he has always had a good income,' she said, her voice full of pride.

Arnold puffed out his cheeks. 'Yes,' he said softly, 'that is where the problem lies.'

'I don't understand what you are inferring.'

'It's come to light that your father has been embezzling money from the company for a good many years.'

'What absolute rubbish! What grounds have you for saying such a thing,' she asked, flustered.

'When he ran into financial trouble my father and I took some shares in his company to help him out. Now he says he is unable to pay any dividend, so as shareholders we have to take a decision about what to do next. The obvious answer is to prosecute and take him to court. Can you imagine the headlines? "Respected magistrate sued for swindling his own company".'

The colour drained from Penny's face. 'Your father wouldn't

do that, surely. You must intervene, Arnold. If you are also a shareholder then surely you have a say in how the matter is handled.'

'Oh, I do,' he agreed. 'What's more, my father will listen to my advice.'

'Then for heaven's sake give my father a chance to explain how it has happened and time to repay you. I am sure there must be some way he can do so.'

Arnold shrugged. 'I need some inducement. He is the one in trouble not me.'

Penny felt the colour creep into her face. 'You mean . . .' She hesitated not knowing how to put it into words.

'I mean that I need to have our wedding plans restored. Once you have fixed a date then his debt to us will be wiped out completely.'

'And what about Kelly?'

'Kelly?' He stared at her for a moment as if he didn't know what she was talking about. 'Oh, you mean the slum kid.' He laughed sneeringly. 'Agree to my terms and you can take her with you; you'll find her in that cabin opposite.'

Twenty-Six

As she pushed open the door of the cabin Arnold had indicated Penny's heart sank as she saw Kelly huddled up on the bunk. She was white-faced and it was obvious from her red eyes that she had been crying. Her face lit up when she saw Penny and she spread her arms in greeting.

'You're here at last, that other woman said you wouldn't come,' she sobbed as Penny hugged her close.

Penny looked across at Arnold who was now standing in the doorway observing what was going on with a cynical expression on his handsome face.

'She's all yours for the moment so take her with you,' he ordered. 'Don't forget about what I've asked you to do,' he added cryptically.

Penny looked at him with loathing in her eyes. 'And if I don't obey your orders?'

'Then remember that your father and the kid will both suffer.'

Bryn, looking very disgruntled as if immersed in an attack of deep Celtic gloom, was waiting on the quayside when Penny and Kelly came down the gangplank.

'They virtually threw me off the boat,' he said angrily as they joined him. 'I was afraid they were going to set sail for Spain at any moment with you two still on board.'

'Well, we are all here now safe and sound,' Penny assured him as she gave him a warning look.

Bryn understood immediately. 'Come on then, let's all go home,' he said taking hold of Kelly's other hand. 'The taxicab's still here waiting.'

As they travelled back to Scotland Road, Penny reported the conversation that had taken place on board between herself and Arnold.

'That's blackmail,' Bryn said in an angry voice,

'I know,' she agreed quietly.

'The best thing you can do is take no notice and ignore

everything Arnold has said,' Bryn told her. 'You've got Kelly back safe and sound so be content to leave it at that.'

'I'd like nothing better than to forget everything Arnold said but can I do that? I'm quite sure he meant it when he said he would take my father to court on a charge of embezzlement if I didn't comply with his wishes.'

'I think you should speak to your father first to find out if there are any grounds for that. He may be making it all up merely to frighten you.'

'I don't think that even Arnold would go that far,' Penny said in a dubious voice.

'Well, it's entirely up to you, of course,' Bryn said stiffly, his square jaw jutting ominously. 'If you want to go ahead with your original plans and marry Arnold Watson then I can't very well stop you.'

Penny stared at him in silence. She wanted to tell him that of course he could stop her. He had only to confirm that he really was in love with her and to tell her that he wanted her to marry him and she would know immediately what was the right course of action.

There was so much she wanted to say but with Kelly clutching tightly at her hand she felt it was wisest to remain silent. She wasn't sure how much Kelly understood. The child had suffered enough for one day. She was afraid that if she started going into details or the two of them began arguing over the matter it might worry Kelly more than was necessary.

Anyway, at the moment Kelly was jabbering away telling them all about the circus.

'Why did you run away like that and give us all such a fright,' Bryn asked her.

'I heard you and Penny arguing about telling the police that you'd found me and that I was with you,' she said in a contrite whisper.

'I see.'

'I was afraid you were going to send me back to St Saviour's.'

'You probably will have to go back,' he told her solemnly, 'but as we keep telling you it will only be for a very short time because we will go to the court and ask for you to come and live with us,' he added quickly.

'You did that before and they took no notice of you,' Kelly said in a sulky voice.

'Yes, I know, but I am quite sure it will be different this time. Now promise you won't worry about it and please don't run away again,' he added firmly. 'If you are found by the police and taken back to St Saviour's by them it will be much harder for us to convince the court that it would be all right for you to come and live with us.'

Although he spoke to Kelly in a very reassuring manner, inwardly Bryn knew that it wasn't going to be that simple to persuade the court to release her.

He also felt that it would be in Kelly's interest as well as their own to notify the police right away that she was with them. In fact, he was puzzled that the police didn't already know about it and had come to find out for themselves. However, he decided to delay discussing the matter with Penny until after Kelly was in bed.

Penny focused her attention on Kelly when they reached Bryn's flat in Scotland Road. Kelly looked almost as bedraggled as when she had first met her, Penny thought. Her dress was dirty and torn and she looked as though she hadn't had a wash or had her hair combed for days.

'Now, what are we going to do first?' Penny asked with a bright smile. 'Would you like a nice warm bath or something to eat?'

'A jam butty and then a bath,' Kelly said after a moment's hesitation.

'Strawberry jam?' Penny asked knowing that this was Kelly's favourite.

Kelly's face brightened. 'Yes, please.'

'Milk or lemonade?'

There was a slight pause as Kelly weighed up the two items on offer. She loved both of them but in the end she settled for the lemonade.

'Can I have them while I am in the bath?' Kelly asked hopefully.

Penny pretended to look shocked but then she agreed and Kelly dashed into the bathroom and started removing her clothes before Penny had time to fill the bath with water.

An hour later, no longer hungry and now clean and towelled dry she contentedly sat on Penny's lap letting her comb the tangles out of her damp hair.

Dressed in clean clothes Kelly looked like a different child and Penny saw the surprise in Bryn's eyes when they sat down to the meal he had prepared for the three of them.

After so many adventures and so much talking Kelly was tired and quite ready to go to bed almost as soon as their meal was over.

When Penny returned to the living room after tucking Kelly in Bryn poured them both a glass of wine.

'Have you had any more thoughts about what Arnold Watson said today?' he asked as she sat down on the settee and took the glass from him.

Penny shook her head and a worried look crossed her face. 'I can't believe that what he said about my father is true,' she said ruefully.

'I'm quite sure it isn't,' Bryn said emphatically as he walked over and sat down in the armchair before taking a drink of his wine.

'Then why did he say such a thing?'

'I think he is trying to blackmail you.'

'Why would he do that?'

'I've no idea but I think there is some underlying reason why he is so anxious to marry you.'

Penny shot him a quick look but he avoided her eyes. Once again she wondered what his feelings for her were and whether she was imagining that only a few days ago he had said that he felt the same about her as she did about him. She wished so much that he would tell her again or even that he had sat beside her on the settee.

When he did speak it was not about Arnold but about Kelly's future. 'We really must inform the police that she is safe,' he told Penny firmly.

'Must we? In all probability they will take her straight back to St Saviour's and I can't bear to think about what will happen to her if they do that. The nuns are bound to punish her severely for running away.'

'I know, but I can't see any way out of it. We can't possibly hide her here forever and your ideas about taking her away some-where are ludicrous. The police would trace you in no time at all. They are still searching for her remember and they would be bound to find out where you both were.'

'If only we could persuade the authorities to let her stay in our care,' Penny said wistfully.

'Don't worry, that is exactly what I intend to do,' Bryn assured her. 'The only thing is it may take some time and if they find out that we are deliberately perverting the course of justice it won't be to our advantage.'

'Would it help if I went to my father and asked him to use his influence as a magistrate?' Penny asked as she took another sip of her wine.

'You tried that before and you know he refused to do so.'

'Yes, but now I have some background information about him and if necessary I will face him with it.'

'You can't do that,' Bryn exclaimed in a shocked voice. 'We have both agreed that what Arnold said can't possibly be true and that he only said it to try and blackmail you.'

'Then in that case it will put Arnold in the wrong and if I threaten to take it further my father might do as I ask in order to keep me from doing so.'

'That sounds very muddled but I think I know what you mean.' Bryn frowned. 'Even so, why would punishing Arnold or putting him in the wrong make your father do what you want him to do over Kelly?'

'To shut me up of course so that I don't do anything that might smear his good name or that of his associates,' Penny explained.

Bryn shook his head. 'I think you are quite wrong and that such scheming is dangerous,' he warned.

Penny felt annoyed. 'Will you let me try and see if it does any good?'

'I can't very well stop you.'

'I know that, but will you give me the chance to speak to my father before you inform the police that we have Kelly here with us?'

Penny could tell from the expression on Bryn's face that he wasn't very happy about agreeing to any sort of delay.

She put down her wine glass and rose from her chair. 'Look, I'll go over to Penkett Road right away. It's the perfect opportunity. I don't want to take Kelly with me and at the moment you are here to keep an eye on her.'

Bryn looked dubious. 'Leave it until tomorrow morning; by then you may have thought of a different way of dealing with things,' he prevaricated.

'No, it's my one chance to go on my own. Tomorrow I would have to take Kelly with me and as I said I don't want her to hear an argument going on between my father and me about her because it will only upset her.'

She left the room before Bryn could answer. As she collected her hat and coat she half hoped he would try and stop her. When she returned to the living room to say she was leaving he merely nodded.

On the ferry boat across the Mersey she tried to plan out what she was going to say to her father. She didn't for one moment think that there was any truth in what Arnold had said, but nevertheless she felt nervous about facing him with such a story. However, if it was a way to make her father do what she wanted him to do then she was prepared to tell him.

What if it is true she asked herself when half an hour later she walked down the drive to her home. Would Arnold take her father to court?

The thought sent a shudder through her. Was she opening up a can of worms and doing something she would later bitterly regret?

If on the other hand there was some sort of truth in Arnold's story then perhaps she was doing the right thing in warning her father of what lay ahead.

Twenty-Seven

Penny's parents were astonished to see her at such a late hour in the evening.

'Penny, my dear, what are you doing out on your own at this time of night? Is something wrong?' her mother asked worriedly as she hugged and kissed her. 'Have you decided to come back home?' she asked hopefully.

'I've come to ask you both for a very big favour,' Penny said, returning her mother's welcoming hug but looking directly at her father.

Captain Forshaw looked up from his newspaper questioningly, his heavy brows drawn together in a questioning frown.

'We have found Kelly but we haven't informed the police yet because we know that as soon as we do they are bound to return her to the remand home.'

'Of course they will!' He rustled his newspaper impatiently. 'Surely you realize that is the right thing to do.'

'I can't bear to think of that happening,' Penny went on, 'so I am begging you to intercede and see if you can persuade the presiding magistrate to remand her into my care.'

'Oh Penny darling, isn't it time you stopped worrying about this child,' Leonora Forshaw said wearily.

'No Mother, I'm afraid I can't do that. We've been through all this before and you know exactly how I feel about my duty to Kelly.'

'And surely you must know how we feel about you being involved with this wretched little slum child,' her mother retorted sharply. She picked up a handbell from the table by her side. 'I'm going to ring for Mary and get her to bring us a pot of coffee and then we can chat about it if you wish.'

Penny didn't answer her but continued to stare hard at her father.

Captain Forshaw cleared his throat. 'This is damned awkward, Penny. In all probability the case will have to go back to the magistrates' court and I don't want it to get into the newspapers that I have spoken to the police or even asked a fellow magistrate to do something like that.'

'Why on earth should it get into the newspaper?' Penny asked in a puzzled voice.

'My dear girl, you are so naive. Things like that are always mildly sensational and invariably there is tittle-tattle. Sooner or later someone leaks it to the press.'

Penny was so incensed by his answer that she let her tongue overrule her better judgement. 'Better they leak that than the terrible accusations that Arnold has made about you,' she blurted out.

Too late she realized what she had done and also that there was no way she could possibly retract what she had said without giving some explanation.

They were all silent as Mary came into the room with a tray of cups, a silver coffee pot and a plate of biscuits.

'Did I hear you say that you are seeing Arnold again?' her mother asked. 'Does that mean you two have made up? Oh that is so wonderful,' she went on in a delighted voice not waiting for Penny to reply.

'No, Mother, we have not made up. I saw Arnold when I had to go on to one of the Watson Line boats to rescue Kelly after he had kidnapped her.'

'Rescue her? What ridiculous nonsense is this?' Captain Forshaw said testily.

'Arnold had sent someone to kidnap Kelly from her hospital bed and then had her taken on board one of their freight ships. When I got there he was arranging with the captain for her to be transported out to Almeria where they were planning to abandon her.'

'What!' There was anger and astonishment in Captain Forshaw's voice. 'Penny, do you know what you are saying? Have you completely taken leave of your senses?'

'No, what I am telling you is the truth. Arnold persuaded his secretary to pretend that she was me and sent her to collect Kelly from the hospital this morning.'

'He must have simply been trying to scare you or something,' Marcus Forshaw blustered. 'Kidnap her! I never heard such damn nonsense in all my life.'

'That's only the half of it,' Penny told him. 'He agreed that I could have Kelly back but only if our engagement was back on again and that I set a date for our wedding.'

'Oh, the poor boy! Can't you see, Penny, that he's so desperately in love with you, my darling, that he will go to any lengths to get you back,' Leonora exclaimed clapping her hands together in approval.

'That was not all,' Penny went on. She bit her lip, undecided about whether to go on or to remain silent about Arnold's other threat.

'Go on!' her father said in a hard voice. 'I can see you are holding something back so tell us the rest.'

'It concerns you, Father,' Penny said hesitantly.

'Concerns me? What the hell could Arnold Watson have to say about me that would have any bearing on the matter we're discussing?'

Penny shook her head desperately wishing she had not brought up the subject at all.

'Go on! What did Arnold have to say about me?' her father insisted.

'He . . . he said that your company had been in financial trouble and that he and his father had lent you money to help you get out of the scrape you were in. When they asked you to pay it back you said you couldn't do so. He said that unless I agreed to marry him he and his father were going to sue you; take you to court over it.'

'The lying young dog!' Marcus Forshaw exclaimed heatedly, his face growing florid with anger.

'Marcus, what is going on? I don't understand what this is all about,' Leonora said, her voice shaking, her face white with shock.

'Mother, don't take on so, please don't upset yourself, we all know it's not true,' Penny said quickly as she placed a protective arm around her mother's shoulders.

'Oh my darling, can't you see that it's only because Arnold is so deeply in love with you and wants you to marry him so much that he's threatening you in this way. I'm sure he's saying and doing all these dreadful things to try and make you change your mind,' Leonora whispered.

'Bryn was quite sure that it was without foundation and, as

he said, simply a form of blackmail,' Penny affirmed, looking at her father.

'Not only without foundation but also a wicked way of saving his own damned skin,' her father stated grimly. His face was almost puce with anger and he looked as if he would explode at any moment.

'I can assure you that if anyone is going to end up in a court of law over embezzlement it is going to be that young blackguard not me,' he went on heatedly.

'Why? What has he done? What is this all about?' Penny asked, her curiosity aroused.

'It doesn't matter, my dear,' her father said tersely. 'I don't wish to discuss it. It's probably far better that you don't know,' he added and picked up his newspaper again.

Penny wanted to know the details but she sensed her father didn't want to talk about it in front of her mother.

'Now if you are not going to stay here with us tonight then you'd better be on your way,' he said suddenly, folding up his newspaper and putting it to one side.

'Yes, I must get back, it is getting rather late,' Penny murmured.

'For heaven's sake don't worry about Arnold Watson's threats,' Marcus Forshaw told her. 'I can assure you that they're absolutely groundless and I will be dealing with him when I see him tomorrow.'

'There is still the question of deciding what is going to happen to Kelly,' Penny murmured tentatively, desperate to talk about the real reason for her visit before she left.

'Kelly?' Marcus Forshaw's brow creased in a frown and for a moment he stared at her vaguely as if unsure what she was talking about.

'Well, as I told you, we have found her again after she ran away to join Bilkie's Circus. She'd had a slight accident and had to be taken to hospital but at the moment she is safe. We know we must inform the police where she is because they are still looking for her.'

'Yes, yes, of course you must let them know where she is. You should have done so in the first place. If you had and they'd taken her back into care she wouldn't have been able to run off and join the circus and none of this silly nonsense would have arisen.'

'You don't understand what I'm saying,' Penny persisted. 'The moment we inform the police that we have found Kelly and that she is with us then they will come and take her back to St Saviour's.'

'Yes, Penny, I do understand, and as I keep telling you that is exactly where she should be,' Marcus Forshaw assured her emphatically.

Penny shook her head. 'How can you say that,' she argued. 'It's a really dreadful place, Father. When I went there to see her they—'

'I know, I know all about that,' he cut her short. 'You've already told me all the details so there's no need to go over it all again.'

'It's not only the drab uniform or the nuns and their strict discipline but the grim surroundings of St Saviour's,' Penny went on, ignoring his interruption.

'It's a remand home not a hotel, remember, so you must expect the conditions to be like that,' her father retorted rather impatiently.

'Please Father, you must speak up for her. If you contact the authorities or your fellow magistrates, they know you and will listen to you. Surely you can persuade them to let Kelly stay with me.'

Marcus Forshaw ran a hand over his chin. 'I can't do anything about it at this time of night but I will think it over,' he prevaricated.

'Yes it is very late,' her mother intervened as Penny stood up to leave. 'Surely it would be better if you stayed here tonight and went back to Liverpool in the morning?'

For one moment Penny was very tempted. The thought of being able to have a hot bath and slip in-between crisp cotton sheets in her own pretty bedroom and all the attached comforts she would be able to enjoy filled her mind. Then, resolutely, she shook her head.

'No, Mother.' She bent and kissed her mother's cheek. 'I must get back.'

'Why, darling? You can leave first thing tomorrow, the moment you've had your breakfast.'

Penny shook her head and kissed her mother on the brow.

'I left Kelly in bed fast asleep and if she wakens and finds I'm not there she will be very frightened. She will think that I have deserted her again,' she explained.

'Please, Penny. I'll be worrying about you all night if you go now.'

'Nonsense. I'll telephone and let you know I'm all right the moment I get to her,' she promised.

Twenty-Eight

Bryn's flat was in darkness except for a light left burning on the landing when Penny arrived back at Scotland Road.

Having removed her shoes, she padded in her stockinged feet towards the bedroom she shared with Kelly hoping that she wouldn't disturb Bryn, because she didn't want to talk about Kelly any more that night.

Although she'd felt relieved that she had managed to persuade her father to think again about intervening over Kelly's future, on reflection she was not a hundred per cent sure that he would do so.

Kelly was sound asleep, one hand beneath her cheek, her dark hair half covering her face. She stirred slightly as Penny got into bed and murmured Penny's name. Then as Penny's arm went round her she snuggled down into sleep again.

Kelly was still sleeping soundly when Penny awoke next morning. Very quietly she slipped out of bed, gathered up her clothes and took them along to the bathroom to get dressed in there.

She hoped Kelly would go on sleeping for a little while longer to give her time to relate to Bryn what had taken place when she'd spoken to her father the previous evening.

'My father was horrified by Arnold's accusation,' she told him. 'He also hinted that the real truth was that there was some misdemeanour that Arnold had committed that was extremely serious.'

'It sounds as though Arnold was trying to inveigle you into committing yourself into marrying him so that your father would never reveal his misdeeds,' Bryn said thoughtfully.

'It seems to be something like that,' Penny agreed, 'but my father didn't go into any details and I thought it was wisest to drop the whole thing. He was extremely annoyed, though, when he heard what Arnold had said about him.'

Bryn looked dubious when Penny went on to say that her father had promised to give the matter of Kelly more thought.

'I have asked him to see if it is possible to arrange things so that Kelly doesn't have to go back to St Saviour's but is put into my care right away,' she explained.

'I still think it is our duty to let the police know that Kelly has been found and that she is safe,' Bryn insisted.

'So we will as soon as I hear from my father,' Penny promised.

'No, I mean now, right away. The police are still actively looking for her and there are posters on every news-stand in Liverpool. If he intervenes and is successful then well and good but—'

'If we tell them before he has a chance to speak to the authorities then the first thing they will do is come here and take Kelly back to St Saviour's,' Penny pointed out.

'Yes, but she will only be there as a temporary measure while the necessary arrangements are being made,' Bryn persisted.

'No —' Penny shook her head emphatically — 'we can't risk it, Bryn. They'll insist on taking Kelly away and she will be distraught.'

'We are breaking the law, Penny, and we could both be accused not only of hiding her but also of hindering the police from doing their job,' Bryn argued.

'Please Bryn, leave it until midday and then come what may whether we have heard from my father or not then I will go along with your idea,' Penny promised.

The moment Kelly appeared they changed the subject well aware that she was listening to every word they said.

'I'm sorry but I'm going to make that call before I see any patients,' Bryn said firmly as he stood up from the breakfast table ready to leave for the hospital.

Penny followed him out on to the landing. 'Please Bryn, leave it until after your clinic is over. It's only a matter of a couple of hours,' she pleaded laying a hand on his arm.

He hesitated and his jaw jutted stubbornly, and for a moment Penny was afraid he was going to refuse. 'Oh, very well,' he said reluctantly.

Penny devoted the morning to entertaining Kelly, who very much wanted to go to the park, but Penny was afraid to risk doing that in case someone recognized her and reported the matter to the police.

'In an attempt to delay Bryn making the dreaded call Penny prepared an early lunch so that the moment he came in it was on the table ready.

They were halfway through their meal when there was a loud imperious knocking on the street door. It was so loud that they exchanged looks of alarm.

'I'll get it.' Bryn pushed back his chair and went down the stairs.

Penny looked startled when a couple of minutes later he ushered Inspector Robinson into the room.

The Inspector was in full uniform and Kelly took one look at him and her face crumpled with fear. She scrambled down from her chair and dashed into the bedroom she was sharing with Penny and slammed the door shut.

'I'm sorry to interrupt your meal,' he told them, looking from one to the other. 'I have been in court all morning dealing with the Kelly Murphy case. I have come to let you know what has been decided about her.'

'Bryn, you told them that she was here,' Penny exclaimed accusingly.

'No I didn't, although I know I should have done so. It was the right thing to do.'

'Yes.' Inspector Robinson looked grave. 'It was a waste of police time looking for her when all the time she was with you.'

'Now you know she is safe, can she stay here with us? We'll take good care of her and make sure she doesn't get into any more trouble,' Penny said earnestly.

'Well, it's not quite that simple,' Inspector Robinson said crisply. 'Her case will be reviewed again shortly. That will mean another appearance before a magistrate.'

'Surely she doesn't have to go back to that dreadful remand home does she?' Penny implored him.

'In the meantime,' Inspector Robinson went on solemnly, 'it has been decided that she may remain in the care of a responsible person.'

'Oh, that's wonderful. So you mean she can stay here with us.'

Inspector Robinson held up a hand. 'No, Miss Forshaw. Captain Forshaw has been designated to be her temporary guardian.'

There was a moment of silence as Bryn and Penny exchanged

surprised glances with each other. 'You mean my father told you where she was and then said he would be responsible for her?' Penny asked in an astonished voice.

'That's what the outcome of this morning's discussion has been.'

'I don't understand.' Penny shook her head in disbelief. 'My parents won't have Kelly inside their house; my mother certainly won't agree to that arrangement.'

'She already has,' Inspector Robinson said crisply. 'The terms agreed are that Kelly Murphy will reside at Captain Forshaw's house in Penkett Road, Wallasey until the case is brought to court.'

'I don't believe it,' Penny gasped. 'There must be some mistake.'

'There is no mistake, Miss Forshaw. Those are the terms. I also understand that during the period she is in their care you will also reside there to help look after the child. If this is not acceptable to you then Kelly Murphy must be returned to St Saviour's Remand Home.'

Penny and Bryn again exchanged bewildered looks.

'Of course I will agree to the terms you have outlined,' Penny said stiffly. 'I will do absolutely anything rather than have Kelly sent back to St Saviour's.'

Inspector Robinson nodded in acknowledgement of her decision.

'When do we have to take Kelly over to Wallasey?' Bryn asked.

'Miss Forshaw and Kelly Murphy must both accompany me there now,' Inspector Robinson told him. 'I have a motor car waiting outside.'

'Must we go right away!' Penny protested. 'I need time to explain to Kelly what is happening and also to pack some clothes for us both.'

Inspector Robinson frowned and looked at his watch. 'I can give you ten minutes, no longer,' he said curtly.

'Take whatever you need at the moment and I will bring the rest of your belongings over tonight,' Bryn told her.

Penny realized that Kelly was still hiding in the bedroom because she was afraid of what was going to happen to her so she went to tell her what had been resolved. She found Kelly was shaking so much with fear that it was difficult to reassure her that everything was going to be all right.

'You've nothing to worry about; we're going to my home in

Wallasey,' she repeated over and over again as she hugged her close and stroked her hair trying to calm her.

'No, I want to stay here,' Kelly sobbed.

'That's not possible,' Penny explained. 'Inspector Robinson is going to take us both back to Wallasey and he has said that you can stay there with me for the time being. If we don't do as he has asked they will take you back to St Saviour's.'

Kelly stopped shaking and there was a look of relief on her tear-stained face. 'You mean you are coming as well?' she asked looking up trustingly into Penny's face.

'Oh yes, of course I am. I will be staying there with you,' Penny promised.

Ten minutes later Penny and a very subdued Kelly had said goodbye to Bryn and were seated in the back of the police car on their way to Wallasey.

It was a dull grey morning with a heavy drizzle making it feel damp and cold. Penny felt almost as nervous as Kelly about what lay ahead of them.

Although she had said very little since Inspector Robinson had stated his terms she was concerned about the sort of reception they would get when they arrived at Penkett Road.

Her father was obviously expecting them. He came out into the hallway to greet them the minute Mary opened the front door to them.

'Come along in, Penny, your mother is waiting in the sitting room,' he said briskly.

He exchanged a few brief words with Inspector Robinson who left almost immediately.

Kelly held back reluctantly as Penny moved towards the sitting room. 'Come on, Kelly, this way.' Penny placed an encouraging hand on Kelly's shoulder and urged her forward. 'You've met my mother before so there's no need to be shy.'

Leonora Forshaw was sitting in an armchair drinking a cup of coffee when they went in. Her rather forbiding look as she greeted them softened to one of concern when she saw that Kelly was shaking.

'Are you cold, child? Come over here by the fire and warm yourself. I'll ask Mary to bring you a hot drink. What would you like?'

Kelly was too nervous to answer. Aware that if she did she would probably ask for lemonade which would not warm her up at all Penny suggested, 'Shall we both have a cup of hot chocolate, Kelly? Mrs Davies makes the very best hot chocolate I have ever tasted. She used to make it for me as a special treat when I was a little girl.'

'Hot chocolate – what's that?' Kelly looked at her in a bemused way.

'Well it's rather like cocoa only very much nicer,' Penny explained.

'You sit down here by the fire and get warm while Penny goes and asks Mrs Davies to make it for you,' Mrs Forshaw said indicating the footstool by her feet.

Penny held her breath wondering if Kelly would comply or not.

'I won't be gone for more than a minute,' she promised, smiling encouragingly at Kelly as she gave her a little push forward.

When she returned Penny was surprised to find that not only was Kelly sitting on the stool but that her mother was talking to her.

'I was telling Kelly how much prettier she is now that she's done her hair so nicely,' Mrs Forshaw explained when Penny looked at her enquiringly. 'She seems to be a changed child since the last time I saw her.'

'Well, that was several months ago,' Penny commented wryly.

Mary arriving with the mugs of hot chocolate fortunately broke the uncomfortable silence that followed.

'Your father has told me about Arnold's accusations,' Leonora Forshaw stated as they sipped their hot drinks. 'He also told me many other things, some of which you do not know about and which I must say have deeply shocked me. By mutual agreement we have decided not to mention them again,' she added cryptically.

The rest of the day passed fairly amicably. When Penny told her mother that Bryn would be coming over later in the day with some of their clothes, and all the other things they'd had to leave behind because she hadn't had time to pack them, her mother insisted that she should telephone Bryn and invite him to have dinner with them.

'I think he was going to try and come early so that he could see Kelly. She will be in bed if he comes as late as that,' Penny demurred.

'Surely not! Is it really necessary for her to go to bed before seven?' Leonora Forshaw asked in a surprised voice. 'I'm sure Kelly can manage to stay awake until we have finished eating dinner. In fact, why not let her join us at table.'

'At dinner!' Penny couldn't keep the surprise out of her voice.

'Yes, that is what I said. You'd most certainly like to stay up and have dinner with us wouldn't you, Kelly?' she asked in a tone that made refusal impossible.

Kelly shot a scared look at Penny and waited for her to say something.

Momentarily Penny felt at a loss for words. Everything was so different this time. She realized that her mother was trying to make amends for how badly she had treated Kelly in the past, so she went along with the idea.

She smiled encouragingly. 'Bryn will be here as well so you will enjoy that won't you, Kelly?'

Nevertheless she was concerned in case Kelly disgraced herself in some way. At Bryn's flat they had always eaten at the same time and there had never been any problem but a more formal dinner with people she was not at ease with was quite another matter.

Twenty-Nine

Penny could hardly believe the change in her parents' attitude and the way they were accepting Kelly's presence in their home.

Her mother was continually fussing over Kelly and making sure that she was being well cared for. There was none of the uncomfortable atmosphere she and Kelly had experienced when she'd brought her home before.

Her mother had even suggested that Kelly should have the guest room but Penny decided that for the first few nights at any rate it would be best for Kelly to sleep in her room.

'She is probably feeling very unsettled and nervous and if she wakes up in the night and finds herself in a strange bedroom she might be frightened,' Penny explained.

'Yes, you are probably right,' her mother agreed. 'Once she has settled down though if you would like Kelly to have a room of her own then let Mary know and she can make the guest room ready for her.'

Penny had a quiet hour with her father in his study the morning after she returned home and he told her in strictest confidence the truth behind Arnold's allegations.

'There has been a case of fraud, or embezzlement, as Arnold described it but it concerned the Watsons' company, not mine,' he told her. 'I won't bore you with the details but Arnold had been wrongfully taking money out of his company and by so doing defrauding the shareholders. He came to me and asked for my help in covering the matter up because he was so worried. It was not only the disgrace it would bring down on their company, but he was also concerned about his father's wrath if he ever found out what had been going on.'

'So you let him have money to help replace what he had taken,' Penny said thoughtfully.

'Yes, but it was the wrong thing to do. At the time, however, I felt I had no option because you two were engaged and planning to be married,' her father told her.

'You shouldn't have let that stand in your way,' Penny said sadly.

'I know but it was a very tricky predicament. I thought you were in love with him and I couldn't bear for your heart to be broken. Nor did I want it to come to light that you were marrying a chap who was such an out and out scoundrel.'

'So if I had gone ahead and married Arnold you would have continued to keep quiet,' Penny said reflectively.

'Of course I would. I hoped that Arnold had learned his lesson and that it was something he'd never do again. I hadn't even told your mother about it until a few days ago and I forbid you to mention it to anybody,' he said firmly, his mouth hardening into a tight line.

'That means that Arnold will get away with his misdeed and at the same time this wretched secret will always give him a hold over you,' Penny mused. 'So what happens about it now?' she asked when her father remained silent. 'You really ought to do something to stop him making accusations about you.'

Her father shrugged. 'I'm not sure. At the moment I'm not going to do anything. I need time to give the matter some deep thought.'

'Surely, since Arnold's father is your oldest friend and a business associate, then you ought to tell him what has been going on.'

'That is the problem,' her father admitted. 'The matter has lain dormant for quite a while so I am not sure if it is wise to disclose all the facts. To do so might upset the harmonious relationship I have at present with William Watson.'

'Can you trust Arnold to remain silent, though? He has already falsely accused you and he may do so publicly if he ever thought that it might be to his advantage to do so.'

'I doubt if he would risk doing that because he would be afraid that I would retaliate by informing his father of the true situation.'

'That's all very well but which of you would William Watson believe; you or Arnold?' Penny frowned. 'Blood is thicker than water you know, especially when it comes to something as serious as that.'

Marcus Forshaw shook his head. 'I don't know, Penny. You are probably right in what you are saying but I wish to leave the matter in abeyance for the moment as there are more important things to deal with.'

Penny's face brightened. 'You mean the problem over Kelly's future?'

Marcus Forshaw sighed deeply. 'Yes; I am not at all sure what the outcome of that will be. To be truthful I think you are going to have to reconcile yourself to the fact that she will have to go back to St Saviour's. Furthermore I think that her sentence will be extended as a punishment because she tried to abscond.'

'Oh no! That would be terrible. You have no idea how badly they treated her when she was in there. I couldn't believe that nuns could be so harsh and cruel.'

'You mustn't believe everything she told you,' he admonished.

'It's not what Kelly has said. As I have already told you I went there and I saw how things were for myself. I also experienced how unfeeling the nuns could be,' she told him hotly. 'I can quite understand why she ran away.'

'Kelly was caught breaking the law and appeared before a magistrate so the nuns no doubt believed that it was necessary for them to be strict with her,' her father murmured.

'You may be right about that and it is why they treated her as they did,' Penny conceded, 'but the whole place was so grim and forbidding.' Penny shuddered at the memory. 'Promise that you really will do all you can to persuade the authorities to let me look after her,' she begged.

'Yes, of course I will but I feel I should warn you that it may not be successful. In all probability they will consider you to be far too young for such a responsibility.'

Penny was grateful that her father was being so cooperative, but she was even more astounded at the change of heart her mother seemed to have about Kelly.

She remembered how antagonistic her mother had been when she'd brought Kelly home immediately after the accident. She had always referred to Kelly as 'that child' or 'the little guttersnipe' and had wanted nothing at all to do with her.

She had even insisted that Kelly took her meals in the morning room, yet now she insisted that she should eat with them. They not only ate breakfast and lunch together but Kelly now had dinner with them except when they had important guests.

On those occasions orders were given to Mrs Davies that a 'special tray' was to be taken up to Kelly after she was in bed.

Kelly responded well to this pampering and sought Mrs Forshaw's company whenever possible. She was eager to sit on a footstool at Leonora's feet or hold her hand as they walked round the garden together.

As she watched them from the window, Penny wondered what they talked about so earnestly on these occasions, but as long as they were enjoying each other's company she thought it wisest not to interfere and so she said nothing.

Kelly was not so reticent. She explained that Mrs Forshaw was teaching her the names of all the flowers growing in the garden and that she was going to let her pick some of them and bring them indoors and then she would show her how to arrange them prettily in a vase.

Mrs Forshaw also schooled Kelly into shutting doors quietly, how to greet people politely when they called and to be helpful in a dozen small ways.

Penny was amused when her mother showed off her little protégé when friends called. Kelly was allowed to hand around the plate of cakes or biscuits to them and even encouraged to entertain them by reciting one of the little poems that Leonora had taught her.

Mrs Forshaw took a great delight in brushing Kelly's hair each day and she bought her a supply of different coloured hair ribbons. Kelly loved them and listened patiently as Mrs Forshaw taught her how to either match or contrast the ribbons with whatever dress she was wearing.

She also insisted on buying her some new clothes and took her shopping herself. They came home with two new dresses, several pairs of socks, some black patent leather shoes and some new pyjamas.

This had not only surprised Penny but saddened her a little. She wondered if her mother was regretting that she had done none of these things with her when she'd been a child. It had been left to Nanny to buy her new clothes, to teach her manners and how to behave in company.

It was five weeks before Captain Forshaw was informed that Kelly's case was due to come to court. Penny and Bryn both assured him that they intended to be there and if possible they wanted to speak on Kelly's behalf.

'I'll do my best to make it possible for you to do so,' he promised, 'though I'm not at all sure that it will do any good.'

The days leading up to the court appearance were fraught for Penny. She thought very carefully about how Kelly ought to be dressed as well as about what she would wear. She even asked her mother's opinion on the matter and was amazed that her mother was so concerned.

'The more sensible and plainly dressed you both are the better,' her mother stated. 'Kelly's such a dainty little thing that you don't need to put her in frills to make her look pretty or to create an impression.'

'That's exactly what I thought,' Penny agreed. 'I thought she would look best in her pink print dress, white socks and the black patent shoes you bought her.'

'No, I think we should buy her a new dress and that it should be dark red and quite plain,' Mrs Forshaw stated after a moment's consideration. 'Dark red with perhaps a little white lace collar sounds quite sensible. Have you decided what you will wear?'

'I'm not too sure. Something tailored. A navy blue dress and matching jacket perhaps.'

'That sounds admirable but we must focus on Kelly. Make sure that her hair is newly washed and shining and that she looks well cared for,' Mrs Forshaw fussed. 'Oh, and make sure that she has a clean handkerchief in case she is reduced to tears,' she added.

'I also think we ought to take her through what might happen when she is taken into court and perhaps try and coach her on how she should behave if the magistrate asks her any questions.'

'What do you mean?' Penny said with a frown.

'Coach her; tell her what she ought to say, for one thing,' Mrs Forshaw said sharply.

'How can we do that? We don't know what sort of questions they will ask her.'

'Your father will have a pretty good idea. Leave it with me and I'll have a word with him.'

'I suppose it might be worth a try,' Penny said hesitantly.

'Of course it is,' Leonora Forshaw said firmly. 'How she answers any questions that are put to her will go a long way to helping them decide what is best for her. If she speaks out clearly they will be more receptive to what she says. If she speaks politely it will also convince them that she is not the sort of child who should be put in a place like St Saviour's Remand Home. They will see that she will benefit far more from the kind of home life we have been able to give her.'

'Yes, Mother, I am quite sure you are right,' Penny agreed fervently.

'In my opinion she is far too young to be put through such an ordeal as having to appear in court,' her mother went on. 'It's enough to scare her out of her wits.'

'I know and I agree with you but I am sure she will cope with it all right. She has been to court before,' Penny reminded her.

'What a tragic life the poor little thing has had,' Leonora Forshaw sighed. 'From what she has been telling me there are so many younger children in the family that even her mother appears to have neglected her dreadfully.'

Penny nodded in agreement but said nothing. Her mother's change of heart and her acceptance of Kelly continued to surprise her.

In view of what her mother had been saying she was tempted to ask her if she could bring Kelly back there if the court gave her custody but the thought that might be pushing things too far restrained her.

It might be better to wait and see what the outcome of the hearing was. If, as her father feared they decided to send Kelly back to St Saviour's then perhaps she could appeal to her mother to intervene and ask her father to speak again to his fellow magistrates.

Now that her mother was so fond of Kelly she might even be able to persuade her to apply for Kelly to be released into her custody. She felt sure that if Captain Forshaw's wife offered to give her a home the court would not only listen but immediately agree to such an arrangement. After all, she reasoned, they had been quite happy for her father to be responsible for Kelly while they waited for the hearing so why not let him have her permanently.

It would mean, of course, that her parents would no doubt expect her to return home and look after Kelly. She quite liked the idea now that things were so different at home but she wondered what Bryn's reaction would be. If only she knew what his feelings about her really were she thought uneasily.

Thirty

Kelly's appearance in the court was a nail-biting time for all of them. Penny was up extra early to make sure that as well as being dressed up in her new clothes Kelly was looking her best in every other respect.

Before they left Penkett Road Mrs Forshaw inspected them both like a sergeant major marshalling troops for battle. Kelly had to hold out her hands so that Leonora could see that her nails were clean and she even checked to make sure that Kelly had a freshly laundered handkerchief in her pocket. Then she hugged her and wished her well.

Captain Forshaw insisted on driving them to Seacombe Ferry and kept reminding Penny how important it was to be at the court in good time. Repeatedly he asked where Bryn was going to meet them and worried about whether he would arrive in good time.

'I sincerely hope he doesn't get held up by some emergency or other at the hospital,' he said loudly, trying to make them hear above the clatter of the gangplank being lowered from the *Royal Daffodil* when it pulled alongside as they reached the terminal.

'Why don't you come with us just in case he does?' Penny invited but her father shook his head. 'I don't want to be seen actively influencing my fellow magistrates,' he mumbled as he bid them goodbye and wished them good luck.

Once they reached the court Penny and Kelly were shown into a side room that was far less intimidating than the main courtroom had been, and it was agreed that Kelly could sit beside her. Bryn, however, was asked to sit in a separate row which made it impossible for them to speak to each other during the hearing.

Penny felt her spirits sinking as the magistrate, a middle-aged man with a bald head, sharp features and gold-rimmed spectacles, took his seat and started shooting question after question first at her and then at Bryn.

His expression was inscrutable but he kept making copious notes on a pad in front of him. It was like being interviewed for a job, Penny thought uneasily. She half turned and glanced sideways at Bryn to see how he was taking the interrogation and saw the puzzled look on his face.

When it came to Kelly's turn to be asked questions by the magistrate Penny's heart sank even more. She gave Kelly's hand a reassuring squeeze because she was so frightened that she was visibly shaking, and she was sniffing and snuffling trying hard to keep back her tears.

Although they had spent a long time coaching Kelly on what to say and telling her to make sure she spoke up clearly, Penny was very aware that her replies were often disjointed or hardly audible.

By the time it came to the summing up Penny felt in a complete turmoil. She was sure the magistrate hadn't understood the case as well as he might despite all their efforts to make him see how much Kelly needed to be with them and how keen they were to do the very best they could for her.

Penny waited in growing trepidation as he looked up from the copious notes he had made on his pad. 'This child is in need of strong supervision and needs to be in a very stable background,' he pronounced solemnly in a hard voice as his stern gaze fixed on Kelly.

'That is exactly why we want you to let us take her into our care,' Bryn stated. 'Miss Forshaw and myself are both very concerned about Kelly's future and we can assure you that we are determined to give her all the support, guidance and love that she needs.'

'How are you proposing that you will be able to do that, Dr Cash?' the magistrate queried, looking at him from over the top of his glasses. 'You are both single people. You live and work in Liverpool and Miss Forshaw's home is in Wallasey. Exactly where will Kelly Murphy be living since, as I have already said, she needs to have a very stable background?'

Bryn paused and took a deep breath. 'For the present Kelly will be living at Penkett Road in Wallasey with Miss Forshaw and her family. I can assure you that there will be no problems of any kind. She will be well looked after and supervised by them and I will be keeping in close touch and visiting them every day.'

When there was no comment at all from the magistrate who was shaking his head as yet again he read through his notes, Bryn cleared his throat and added earnestly, 'There is one other extenuating point that we have not yet mentioned.'

The magistrate looked at him over the top of his glasses. 'Well, go on, Dr Cash what is it?' he asked testily.

'Miss Forshaw and I are planning to be married quite soon so it will only be a matter of a few weeks before Kelly has the permanent home background with us that you feel is so important for her,' he stated. 'In the meantime as I have already said, she will be in Miss Forshaw's care and they will remain living with Captain and Mrs Forshaw in Wallasey.'

'I see! So you and Miss Forshaw are soon to be married? Well, that does put a different complexion on the case,' the magistrate conceded as he made further notes on the pad in front of him. Then he looked directly at Bryn, his brows drawn together in a frown. 'Why didn't you mention any of this sooner, Dr Cash?' he asked with growing impatience.

'I didn't want to embarrass Miss Forshaw by making a public announcement. We haven't completely finalized all our plans,' Bryn said crisply.

'I see.' The magistrate took off his gold-rimmed spectacles and pulled out a large white handkerchief and concentrated on polishing them. 'Well,' he said after he had replaced them, 'in that case my decision must be that Kelly Murphy returns to St Saviour's Remand Home until you have done so and you and Miss Forshaw are married.'

'Kelly is extremely unhappy about being at St Saviour's because some of the older girls there are bullying her,' Bryn persisted. 'Miss Forshaw is so concerned about this, as well as worrying about Kelly's welfare and her future, that she is finding it extremely difficult to concentrate on the preparations for our wedding.'

The magistrate pursed his lips in a silent whistle and once again referred to the copious notes he had made, shaking his head from side to side as if perplexed.

'I did intend to make a ruling right away, but as a result of this additional information I now need to talk the case over with some of my colleagues. You will be informed of my decision in due course. In the meantime Kelly Murphy may remain in the care of Captain and Mrs Forshaw.'

Penny had been very taken aback when Bryn had informed the magistrate they were about to be married, but she said nothing as the three of them left the courtroom. Although she was relieved that they still had Kelly with them she was anxious to sort matters out with Bryn as soon as it was possible to do so. She had been completely stunned by his remark and couldn't put it out of her head.

She wondered if she had heard correctly or perhaps misunderstood exactly what he'd said but decided to wait until the two of them were alone, rather than discuss the matter in front of Kelly.

Kelly was jubilant that she was going back to Penkett Road. She skipped along the pavement between them, holding their hands and chattering away happily. All traces of the nerves she'd been suffering from while she had been in court had vanished. Penny didn't have the heart to point out that once the magistrate had reconsidered the case she still might have to go back to St Saviour's.

Bryn was due at the hospital at midday so Penny decided to take Kelly straight back to Wallasey to let her mother know what had been decided so far. Bryn promised to join them for dinner at Penkett Road that evening after he had finished work.

Leonora was slightly mystified when Penny said that the magistrate was going to consult with colleagues before reaching a decision.

'I never heard anything like it,' she grumbled. 'Your father would have made his mind up and taken the right decision there and then if he'd been the one dealing with it. It is so obvious that she would be better off with us rather than in St Saviour's. That man shouldn't be on the bench if he can't decide the outcome of such a simple case.'

Penny hesitated, wondering whether to tell her the real reason for the magistrate's indecision but then held back. She wanted to have the opportunity talk to Bryn first. She would feel such a fool, she told herself, if she told her mother that she and Bryn were to be married and then found that he had only said that to ensure that Kelly was left with them.

In the afternoon Penny took Kelly to the park at Harrison Drive which was at the other end of the promenade from New Brighton. It was more than a mile away from Bilkie's Circus so there was no fear of Kelly hearing the strident music blaring out from the sideshows to remind her of what had happened so recently.

As they walked home she felt at peace with the world. Kelly was holding her hand and enjoying an ice-cream cornet. As she listened to her happily chattering away Penny thought how wonderful it would be if Kelly was permanently in her care and they could always be like this.

She had grown so attached to Kelly that she couldn't bear to think of being parted from her; certainly not if Kelly had to return to St Saviour's. She was quite prepared to make any sacrifice necessary in order to take care of her and to see her grow up happy.

After they'd finished their evening meal with her parents and Kelly was tucked up in bed, Bryn suggested going for a walk.

'Now, what exactly did you mean by what you said in court?' Penny asked tentatively when they reached New Brighton and headed for the promenade.

Bryn frowned and looked away pretending not to know what she was talking about.

'Why did you make such a statement?' Penny asked bluntly, the colour rising in her cheeks as she ignored his attempt to draw her attention to a huge liner on the other side of the Mersey that was being manoeuvred into position in front of the Liver Buildings by three small tugboats.

'I did get carried away,' Bryn admitted ruefully. 'All I could think about was how desperately you wanted to prevent Kelly having to go back to St Saviour's. I was pretty sure that the one thing that stood in the way of that happening was the magistrate thinking that as a single woman you wouldn't be capable of looking after her properly on your own.'

'I see.' She felt her emotions churning knowing that she had desperately been hoping that he had meant what he'd told the magistrate.

'Well, what you said certainly made him think again,' she

admitted dryly, conscious of the tension between them. 'If they check up on your statement though and find that it's not true then they are bound to take Kelly away immediately and that will be a terrible blow for her.'

Bryn hesitated then guided her towards one of the shelters on the promenade that were strategically placed there to shield people from the keen wind coming off the river. 'They don't have to find out that I was wrong do they?' he asked as he turned her round to face him, his gaze searching her face.

Penny felt her heart flip. 'I . . . I don't know what you mean,' she stuttered.

'Oh yes you do,' he murmured softly. He pulled her closer and looked into her eyes.

Penny's heart thundered. She knew Bryn had told her he loved her and she had dreamed of the day when he would ask her to marry him so that they could spend the rest of their lives together. Now that it was happening she wasn't sure whether he really meant he loved her or whether he was offering to marry her because he knew how much she cared about Kelly.

As his mouth came down and covered hers in a hard demanding kiss all her doubts vanished. As she surrendered willingly to his kiss and felt the pressure of his body against hers and his arms tightening around her she gave a deep sigh of happiness.

'I've been wanting to do this again for a very long time,' he told her softly.

'So have I,' she whispered back.

'What? Wanting to kiss me or waiting for me to kiss you?' he teased.

'Both!'

They laughed, but when he released her from his arms within seconds Penny felt anxious again, and still needed to be convinced even though it took her every vestige of strength to ask him.

'If you really are quite sure that it is what you want to do and that you are not marrying me simply for Kelly's benefit,' she said hesitantly. Even as the words left her lips common sense told her that even if Bryn was doing it for Kelly's sake then it was because he knew how much Kelly meant to her.

Bryn pulled her back into his arms and as his lips once again claimed hers, Penny didn't need any more words to confirm his feelings.

'I think we'd better go and tell your parents our good news before someone else does,' Bryn said when they finally managed to pull apart.

'You mean you are going to formally ask my father for my hand in marriage?' Penny giggled.

Bryn took her into his arms once more and kissed her again.

'No, not exactly because if I do that he may refuse,' he said in a serious voice. 'I think it might be better if I tell him outright that we are planning to get married and hope he approves and is in agreement.'

'What if he forbids it?'

'We'll still go ahead and get married because I have no intention of letting you escape, not now that I am sure you feel the same way about me as I do about you.'

Anyway,' he added as she reached up and kissed him on the cheek, 'It wouldn't be the first time you've gone against his wishes now, would it?'

Thirty-One

Captain Forshaw didn't raise any objection at all when they told him and Mrs Forshaw their news. Indeed, he seemed almost relieved to hear that Bryn and Penny were to be married.

'Let's hope this means that Penny will settle down now and put all thoughts of getting custody of Kelly Murphy right out of her head,' he stated his voice full of relief.

Mrs Forshaw's hand flew to her mouth in a gesture of alarm. She seemed to be about to speak but hesitated as if she was unable to find the right words. Then the expression on her face changed to one of relief and her hand dropped to her side as she heard Bryn say, 'On the contrary, we are hoping that it will mean we can have custody of Kelly; in fact, we are hoping that in due course we will be allowed to adopt her.'

'Surely you don't intend to take a step as serious as that,' Captain Forshaw said in a bemused voice.

'Oh yes we do. It was as a result of telling the magistrate this morning that once we were married we intended to offer Kelly a safe and secure permanent home with us that he decided to reconsider the case. Now we are hoping it will mean that Kelly will be released into our care immediately and that she will not have to go back to St Saviour's again.'

Captain Forshaw frowned. 'I'm not quite clear; surely providing her with a home will have to wait until after you are married; how else will you take care of her?'

Penny promised at the hearing that she and Kelly would remain here with you until we are married. If you don't approve of that,' Bryn hurried on as he saw Captain Forshaw was about to interrupt, 'then they can come across to Liverpool and live with me again like they've been doing.'

'No, no; that would be most improper. Penny certainly can't move in with you permanently until after you are married,' Mrs Forshaw gasped.

'Then unless she stays here she has no alternative but to go back to the room at Mrs Reilly's that she had before,' Bryn stated. 'It worked out quite well the last time. Father O'Flynn has already promised Penny that she can have her teaching job back again and I'm sure that Mrs Reilly will agree to look after Kelly when she comes home from school until Penny finishes work.'

'No, I absolutely forbid it,' Captain Forshaw blustered, angry colour rushing to his cheeks. 'This is Penny's home, so of course she must remain here until you are married.'

'And what about Kelly?'

'We want Kelly to stay here as well, isn't that right Marcus?' Leonora stated firmly.

Penny held her breath waiting for her father's reply. She knew they had already told the magistrate that this was where she and Kelly would be living and she knew that to some extent the decision to let them have custody of Kelly depended on it. She also knew that it was more than likely that her father would be asked to confirm that they were living with him at Penkett Road.

'Yes dear, you are quite right, Kelly will have to live here as well,' Captain Forshaw confirmed directing a look at his wife who was nodding enthusiastically in agreement.

Before Penny could recover from her feeling of relief Bryn had held out his hand to Captain Forshaw to seal the agreement. 'That is most magnanimous of you sir,' he said gravely. 'I can assure you they will only be staying with you for a very short while until we are established in our own home.'

'There is no hurry, no hurry at all,' Captain Forshaw told him pompously as they shook hands.

'We thought a very quiet wedding at a register office with you and Mrs Forshaw as our witnesses.'

'Good heavens no; that will never do!' Marcus Forshaw said firmly. 'I want my daughter to have a traditional white wedding; a grand occasion, not some hole in the wall affair.'

'I was hoping that we could be married before the new school term starts in September,' Penny murmured.

'No my dears that's not possible; the new term is only a week away. Surely you realize that a wedding of this magnitude takes months to organize,' Leonora Forshaw intervened.

'Furthermore, you haven't decided where you are going to live now have you?' Captain Forshaw pointed out.

'I thought we could live at my flat,' Bryn said tentatively.

'No, no. My daughter needs a proper home and I most certainly don't want her living in the Scotland Road area of Liverpool ever again!'

'I see.' Bryn felt slightly crestfallen. He certainly hadn't thought things through, he thought ruefully. Apart from where they would live he had never for one moment considered having a full-scale white wedding. He looked across at Penny hoping for guidance.

'If a white wedding and all the trimmings is in accordance with Penny's wishes then I am happy to go along with it,' he conceded.

'Good! In that case all we need to confer with you two about is the date and then if you let us have a list of your personal guests, Bryn, you can leave the rest of the arrangements entirely to us,' Captain Forshaw stated in a firm voice that brooked no argument.

'Yes, we will arrange absolutely everything down to the last detail,' Leonora beamed. She looked so delighted by the idea of organizing all the wedding arrangements that Penny hid her disappointment that she wasn't going to be able to do things as she wanted them and hugged her mother and followed Bryn's example of thanking them both profusely.

Afterwards though, both she and Bryn agreed that they would have preferred a quiet affair with only their immediate family present.

'It's not to be so I think the best thing we can do is go along with what your parents want and just be thankful that they haven't put up any objections to us getting married,' Bryn said resignedly.

'How could they possibly object to you,' Penny quipped, her eyes shining with love.

'Quite easily,' Bryn told her somberly. 'I'm only a doctor working in a hospital, I live in a rented flat in one of the worst areas of Liverpool and I have no real prospects.'

Penny was so elated by the thought of marrying Bryn, so bursting with happiness about what the future would bring, that for several days she didn't notice how very subdued Kelly was when she was told about the wedding.

When she found Kelly curled up in a ball in one of the armchairs, her body shaking with convulsive sobs, she was concerned.

'What's the matter? Don't you feel very well?' She gathered Kelly into her arms and rocked back and forwards. 'Come on darling, tell me what is wrong; have you got a pain?'

It was several minutes before Kelly could control her sobbing and breathing enough to speak coherently.

'It's about the wedding. What's going to happen to me when you get married?' she asked in a shaky voice as soon as she could speak. 'Will I have to go back to St Saviour's?'

'No, of course you won't have to go back there. You will be living with us,' Penny promised pushing Kelly's hair back from her tear-stained face and kissing her on the brow and then hugging her even closer.

Kelly pulled away and stared up at her wide-eyed and bewildered. 'Do you mean I can stay with you for ever and ever and ever?' she asked cautiously.

'Yes, for as long as you want to do so and that is for ever and ever if you wish.'

'You mean I won't have to go back to live with me ma ever again?'

'Well,' Penny hesitated, 'we'll have to think about that. Surely you will want to see her and your dad and your brothers and sisters?'

Kelly shook her head. 'Not really. I'd sooner live with you.'

'Surely you'd like to be able to go and visit them from time to time?' Penny persisted.

'Maybe.' Kelly shrugged her shoulders. 'P'raps. Not to *live* with them again, though.'

Once she was convinced that Penny had meant it when she had said she could go on living with her, even after she and Bryn were married, Kelly's spirits bubbled up and she began to take a lively interest in all that was going on. She was especially excited when Penny told her that after the wedding they hoped to have a house quite close to Penkett Road.

'Does that mean we can come to see your mam and dad whenever we want to?' she asked, her eyes shining.

'That's right. When you are a little older you will be able to visit them on your own,' Penny promised.

'I'll be eight soon so that's old enough to go out on my own, isn't it?'

'Probably. Wait until we find a house and then we will see if it's possible. It really depends on how busy the roads are between our new house and here.'

'You mean you don't want someone else knocking me down,' Kelly responded with a cheeky grin.

From then on Kelly listened avidly to all the talk about the forthcoming wedding. Her excitement doubled when Penny told her that she was to be a bridesmaid and she immediately ran to see if Mrs Forshaw knew about this.

Kelly held her breath as Leonora confirmed that this was true and that Kelly would be wearing a specially pretty dress for the occasion and would carry a posy of flowers.

Kelly was silent for a moment as if unable to believe what she'd been told, then she began dancing round the room chanting in a sing-song voice, 'I'm going to be a bridesmaid, a bridesmaid,' until they were all putting their hands over their ears and telling her to stop.

Although she stopped her chanting, Kelly was eager to know more about the wedding and bombarded Leonora with questions. Most of them were about the dress she was to wear and what it would be like.

Her exuberance diminished slightly, however, when Captain Forshaw told her that he had arranged for her to attend the private school where Penny was once again going to be a teacher. She thanked him politely but as soon as she was alone with Penny she burst into tears.

'Whatever is wrong, you will love it there,' Penny assured her.

'I won't, I hate going to school. At St Saviour's I was always bullied by the bigger girls when we were in the classroom and the nuns were always punishing me because I made mistakes and didn't do my lessons right,' Kelly sobbed.

'This will be different, I promise you,' Penny assured her. 'Look, we'll be there next week and when you meet them all you'll soon see that what I am telling you is right. You will find the teachers are all kind and understanding and the girls very friendly.'

'They weren't friendly when you took me there before,' Kelly reminded her. 'It was because they pushed me over in the playground that I broke my arm.'

'It really will be different this time, I promise,' Penny assured her.

'I won't be able to do the lessons. I couldn't do them at St Saviour's,' Kelly said in a sulky voice.

'Yes you will, I'll make sure about that so don't worry about it any more. As soon as I find out which class you are going to be in and what the lessons will be like then I will coach you here at home.'

When Bryn asked Penny to fix the date for their wedding, Penny was so concerned about Kelly that she insisted that their wedding must wait until Kelly had settled down at school.

'Until I am sure that she is settled and happy at school I simply can't put my mind to the preparations for our wedding,' she explained.

'How long is that going to take?' Bryn asked, his voice full of disappointment.

'At least a term and that takes us up to Christmas,' Penny sighed. She laid a hand on his arm. 'I do wish we could have done as you suggested and had a quiet wedding at a register office. The trouble is both my parents seem to be setting such a great store by us having a big wedding that I can't bear to disappoint them.'

'In that case it means it had better be a spring wedding,' Bryn mused. 'I'm not sure I can wait that long,' he added with a mock groan. 'Shall we say it will be on April the first?'

'No, that might be tempting fate too much,' Penny said, laughing. 'We'll make it as early in April as possible but certainly not the first.'

Although Bryn had agreed to the delay, her mother was not so easily mollified. She was already busy with preparations for the great day.

'We must decided on what Kelly is to wear,' she persisted. 'She's such a dainty little thing. She will look lovely in the dress I am planning to have made for her but obviously I need your approval before I go ahead.'

'Leave it for a while; at the moment I want Kelly to be able to devote all her energies to her school work,' Penny insisted.

'Oh, very well,' her mother sighed. 'You can still start planning where you will live. It will probably take several months for all the legal details to be settled and you haven't even looked at any houses yet.'

'I'm leaving the house-hunting to Bryn.'

'That's fine of course but you must at least have a look at it before he buys it and make sure it is the sort of house you want.'

'Your mother is quite right and you need to make sure that it has a garden for Kelly to play out in and also a garage for your car.'

'My car!' Penny looked bemused. She hadn't driven since the accident when she'd knocked Kelly down.

'You'd better take it out for a spin now the better weather is here again, not leave it standing there idle and taking up space in my garage,' her father said gruffly.

'Yes, I'll do that,' Penny promised. 'I'm sure Kelly would enjoy having a ride in it.'

The thought of driving her Baby Austin once again pleased her. When her father had first forbidden her to drive again she had missed the convenience of being able to go everywhere in Bluebell. In the months that followed, because she had spent a great deal of time in Liverpool and had so many other things to worry about, she had put driving the car out of her mind. Now she wondered if she had the courage to drive again.

The accident hadn't been in Bluebell but in her father's great big Humber, she reminded herself. If she had been driving Bluebell then she was sure it would never have happened.

Mary O'Donovan the little Irish maid and Martha Davies the housekeeper were also involved in all the wedding preparations. They had both taken Kelly to their hearts and were often called upon to keep an eye on her so that Penny and Bryn could spend time together choosing their new home.

The house they finally decided was right for them was a newly built one in Belgrave Street and only a short distance away from Penkett Road.

'I suppose I'd better bring mother along tomorrow so that she is the first to see it,' Penny said with a smile.

'Yes, do that. Perhaps you should wait until your father is at home and then he can drive her here, it might be too far for her to walk.'

'I can bring her in my car. Yes,' she went on quickly when she saw the surprised look on Bryn's face. 'My father has said I ought to be driving it again and he is quite right.'

'So that is why you were so concerned about making sure that there was a garage,' Bryn said with a laugh. 'What does Kelly think about your car?'

'Oh, she loves it, especially when I told her that it was called Bluebell.'

When she took her mother and Kelly to see the new house the next day Penny was surprised to see a Rolls Royce parked outside.

'My goodness, the estate agent must be doing very well out of all the new property being built,' she commented as she parked behind it.

As they went inside she stopped and gave a gasp of annoyance. Standing in the front room gazing round at the fittings was Arnold.

'What are you doing here?' she asked coldly.

'How nice to see you, and you too, Mrs Forshaw,' he said blandly, extending a hand to Leonora.

'Why are you here without my permission?' Penny demanded.

'I was thinking of buying one and renting it out to one of our workers,' he smirked. 'The builder said this was the only one that was ready for occupation and so I asked if I could have a look round.'

Penny bit down on her bottom lip. She could think of nothing to say except to tell him to get out and she didn't want to do that because she knew it would upset her mother.

'So you are contemplating making this your home when you get married in April are you,' Arnold commented in a supercilious voice. 'Very cosy! I hope you will find it comfortable. I must be off; I don't think it is suitable for any of my staff as it is far too poky.'

He stood in the doorway and raised his brown trilby in Leonora's direction. 'It's so completely different from the sort of house I was planning on buying for Penny,' he said with a disdainful smile. 'We would have lived in Warren Drive, which of course is considered to be the very best address in Wallasey,' he added almost as if she was a stranger to the area.

Thirty-Two

Penny and Bryn's wedding date was set for the fourth of April and although it was some time away Penny found the days were flying by so fast that she was concerned in case everything would not be in place in time.

First and foremost was her concern about Kelly settling at school. It seemed to take her forever to do so even though this time the situation was very different from when she had taken her there before. This time Kelly's attendance at the private school had been arranged by Captain Forshaw and was treated accordingly not only by Miss Grimshaw, the headmistress, but by the rest of the staff as well.

Penny made sure that Kelly was wearing school uniform so that she wouldn't feel out of place but even so Kelly was so nervous on the first day that she could barely answer when spoken to.

The other girls in the class tried to befriend her but it took almost a week before she was relaxed enough to talk to them and confident enough to join in whatever they were doing.

It was much the same with her work in class. For the first week she appeared to be quite hopeless, then, as she became more at ease with the people around her, it seemed that her brain began to function. To Penny's great relief, by the end of the first month she was almost on a par with all the others in the class.

During the half-term holiday period Penny divided her time between coaching Kelly with extra lessons and dealing with her own wedding preparations. She wanted to make sure that her mother was coping well with everything even though April was still a long time away.

Kelly listened avidly to all their talk about the wedding and the part she would be playing. 'It sounds a bit like one of those fairy stories you sometimes read to me at night before I go to sleep,' she told Penny.

Sometimes Penny felt much the same. Bryn was her Prince Charming and once they were married all would be right with their world, she kept telling herself whenever her mother raised some fresh problem about the invitation list, or catering problems, or the hundred and one other details that seemed to crop up as April drew ever nearer.

To her relief Kelly was quite eager for the new half term to start so that she could get back to school and meet up again with the new friends she had made in her class.

She had worked very hard at the extra lessons Penny had given her while they'd been at home and when school restarted both of them were delighted to find that she had managed to catch up with all the others.

Kelly was now looking forward to Christmas because not only did she have a part in the end of term play but she had been invited to a number of parties that had been planned by her new friends.

As soon as the Christmas holiday started Penny insisted that they went over to Liverpool to visit Kelly's family.

'We will take over some Christmas presents for them; you can choose presents for Lily and Brian and the baby; whatever you think they would like,' Penny told her when she pulled a face and said that she would rather not go to see them.

'I don't have to stay there do I?' Kelly asked anxiously as they packed up the toys for the three younger children and Penny added a box of fancy biscuits and some chocolate and sweets for the whole family.

'Not unless you want to do so,' Penny told her.

Kelly shrugged but didn't commit herself. Instead she asked about what she had to wear.

'Well, you don't want to wear your school uniform, so what about a jumper and skirt and your new winter coat with the fur collar? You have a fur hat and gloves to go with it so you will keep nice and warm.'

'I really don't have to stay there do I?' Kelly asked again anxiously.

'I've already told you, not unless you decide you want to do so,' Penny assured her. 'If you would like to spend Christmas Day with your mother and your brothers and sisters then you can and I'll come over and collect you afterwards.'

This time their visit was very different from other occasions.

When Penny knocked on the door a burly middle-aged man with black curly hair and vivid blue eyes opened it.

'Da! You're home.'

'My little darlin'! Sure it does my heart good to see you again,' the huge man greeted Kelly warmly, sweeping her up off her feet and hugging her close and kissing her before directing his attention to Penny.

'I'm Shamus Murphy and you must be this Penny Forshaw I've been hearing so much about,' he said as he held out a massive hand and gave her a hearty handshake.

As they went in Penny was aware that Ellen Murphy seemed to have changed her ways completely. Not only was she tidily dressed and her hair combed but she was no longer clutching the baby to her chest. Indeed, the baby was now a toddler and making its way around the room by moving from one piece of furniture to the next.

The other two children, Lily and Brian and had also grown apace and seemed prepared to talk to her. Brian confided that he had now started school and liked it.

'Sit yourself down now and the wife will be making a pot of tea for us all,' Shamus said cordially, almost as if she was an old family friend.

While Ellen did as he asked, Shamus, his melodic Irish voice laced with gratitude, started to thank Penny profusely for all she had done for Kelly.

'Treated her like one of your own so you have,' he said, his handsome face expanding into a broad smile. 'I was heartbroken when I received a letter from Father O'Flynn to say the poor child had met with an accident. When he said she had broken her leg but you were going to look after her and even taking her into your own home to care for her until she was better my heart was overflowing with relief, so it was.'

'Yes, she is quite better now and attending a school in Wallasey where I am one of the teachers,' Penny told him.

'She looks happy enough,' he murmured as he stroked Kelly's head. 'Are you looking forward to coming home to spend Christmas with us, me darlin'?' he asked, directing his question at Kelly.

Kelly looked uncertainly from her father to Penny and back again. 'I don't know,' she said in a small voice.

'Sure now, but you must be wanting to be here my darlin? You must want to be back with us all, your ma and da and your brothers and sisters?'

Kelly wriggled uncertainly, edging closer to Penny and linking her arm through Penny's.

'Aah, Miss Penny, it's easy to see you've won my child's heart so you have,' Shamus said with a deep sigh. 'Well, I can't say I'm surprised, a lovely lady like you.'

Penny decided that probably there would never be a better moment than now to ask if Kelly could stay with them for good. Taking a deep breath she said, 'I was wondering Mr Murphy how you and Mrs Murphy would feel about letting Kelly come to live with me. I'm getting married quite soon to Dr Bryn Cash and we would both very much like Kelly to come and live with us permanently.'

'Live with you permanently?' He drew in a deep breath that made a whistling sound. 'You're meaning on a steady basis; working as a young skivvy in your grand home is it?'

'No, no, of course not,' Penny said quickly. 'Kelly would live with us as part of our family. In fact, we . . . we would like to adopt her.'

'Adopt her!' Shamus Murphy's vivid blue eyes widened in astonishment and his voice rose high in a mixture of amazement and anger. 'Am I hearing aright? Are you saying that you and this doctor fellow want to adopt my little daughter. Whatever for? You'll be having little ones of your own in next to no time and then what happens to my little darlin' after that? She'll be the cuckoo in the nest so she will: the little drudge who'll be expected to fetch and carry and act as a sort of nursemaid to your little ones while you get on with living the high life.'

There were high spots of colour on Penny's cheeks as she faced him. 'That is most certainly not why we want to adopt Kelly, Mr Murphy. The real reason is that I have grown very fond of Kelly and I feel she deserves a better life than what she can expect to get living here in Cannon Court. For one thing, I will make sure she attends a good school and is properly educated. Kelly is bright and intelligent and she deserves to have the chance to make something of her life.'

They stood there looking at each other for what seemed to

Penny to be eternity. Then running a hand through his thick dark hair Shamus glanced across at his wife who had been listening to every word they said, but remained silent throughout their exchange.

'Well now, Ellen, what would you be thinking about a proposition like that?'

His question hung on the air. Again the silence seemed to be interminable and then Kelly broke the spell that seemed to have rendered them all speechless.

'I want to stay with Penny, I don't never want to come back here ever again.'

'It's not what you want me darlin', there's the rest of your family to think about,' her father told her. 'How do you think your ma is going to manage all on her own?'

'She's managed quite well while Kelly has been in my care and that is well over a year,' Penny reminded him quickly.

'I've had to but only because Kelly's not been here to help me because of her broken leg after you knocked her down with your great big motor car, and then you went and let her break her arm while you was looking after her,' Ellen stated sullenly.

'That's true enough, so it is.' Shamus nodded in agreement. 'There's also the future to think of as well,' he added with a deep sigh. 'I'm not as young as I look. Very soon I'll be too old to go to sea and what's going to happen to us all then?'

'If Kelly is living with me then you will have one less mouth to feed,' Penny said crisply.

'I can see you've got an answer for everything,' Shamus retorted. 'Let me remind you miss that young Kelly is coming up to the age where she's about to be of some value to me; another couple of years and she'll be ready to earn a bob or two, if you get my drift.'

'Kelly is eight years old. She has another seven or eight years at school before you can even think of sending her out to work. If she is living with me then it will be a lot longer because if she continues to progress as she is doing now there is no reason why she shouldn't go to university.'

'University!' Shamus let out a great belly laugh. 'Giving her airs and graces she don't need,' he said in a disparaging voice. 'She won't be needing a university degree to scrub floors and believe me that is what she'll end up doing.'

'Only if she stays here.'

Shamus shook his head in disbelief. 'You don't think for one minute do you that because you've dressed her up like a china doll in a coat with a fur collar and put a fur hat on her head and given her fur gloves to go with it and got her to talk in a lah-di-da voice that you've turned her into a lady?'

'I've certainly shown her that there is more to life than scrubbing floors,' Penny retaliated.

Penny felt her stomach tighten as Shamus looked questioningly at Kelly. Before he could speak Kelly said, 'I want to stay with Penny; I never want to come back here ever again, Da.'

Once again his booming laugh filled the small room. 'Go on take her, the ungrateful little baggage. Bring her up the way you think is right. I've plenty of other kids.'

Penny breathed deeply and tried to keep her voice from trembling. 'For good? There will be papers to sign to make it all legal,' she went on when he didn't reply.

'Send them to Father O'Flynn.'

'You'll have to be the one to sign them.'

'Send them to Father O'Flynn; he'll check them over and then I'll put my name to them if he thinks it's the right thing for me to do so, even though it will break my heart to be losing my precious daughter.'

'And what about what I think about all this?' Ellen butted in.

'Ah hush yourself, woman. You've never had a good word to say for the child since the day she was born.'

Penny sensed that the atmosphere in the room had changed to one of hostility and as soon as she possibly could she took her leave.

Kelly remained silent until they were on the ferry boat and Penny was too concerned sorting out the jumble in her own mind to talk to her. She wondered if she had done the right thing in broaching the matter or whether she should have waited and let their solicitor make the approach.

'Am I really going to live with you for ever and ever?' Kelly asked as they took their seats in one of the inside cabins out of the cold.

'I hope so,' Penny told her, and she put an arm round Kelly and pulled her closer.

'I'll be really good and work hard at school and I'll never run away again.'

Penny's face clouded. Kelly seemed to have forgotten that her case was still under consideration. Would Kelly still feel the same way if she found she had to go back to St Saviour's and finish out her sentence, Penny wondered.

Penny had had so many anxious moments over the past few weeks, ever since Shamus Murphy had agreed that he was willing to let them adopt Kelly. She had been on tenterhooks from the moment he had said he would sign the relevant papers to make Kelly's adoption legal in case he changed his mind.

She couldn't comprehend how any father and mother could willingly part with their own child. Even though Shamus had agreed to the arrangement she was worried that Ellen would try to persuade him to change his mind.

There had also been the question of whether or not Kelly would have to go back to St Saviour's.

Her father had brushed aside her fears and assured her he would deal with that side of things. She'd been dubious though, wondering whether he had sufficient authority to be able to persuade his fellow magistrates that this was permissible and the right thing to do.

She could hardly believe it when he eventually told her that as long as he would assume full responsibility for Kelly's welfare until the adoption papers were finalized there would be no further action taken and she could forget about Kelly ever having to go back to St Saviour's.

It brought such an upsurge of relief that she felt as if a great load had been lifted from her shoulders. The worry that had clouded her mind like a thick grey mist seemed to have cleared almost instantly.

From then on she was able to concentrate on the final preparations for her wedding. Her mother had already organized so much that there was really very little left for her to do but she was anxious to make some last minute changes at the new house they were buying in Belgrave Street. She particularly wanted to be the one to choose the wallpaper for the sitting room and for the bedroom that was to be hers and Bryn's.

Penny also accompanied Bryn when he went to buy their new furniture. He was bringing several major items from his own flat in Liverpool. They would not need to buy dining room furniture but they wanted a new sofa or settee and armchairs for their sitting room. The single bed he'd used at the flat was moved up into the attic room to be used by Dillwyn Jenkins.

Dillwyn Jenkins, a dark haired, dark eyed young girl who was to be the live-in maid was already installed. Mrs Davies had recommended her and since she came from the same Welsh village as Mrs Davies she'd promised to keep an eye on her and explain to her what her duties were.

Dillwyn and Kelly had quickly become good friends; she had won over Kelly when she had shown unbridled delight in Kelly's room and promised never to disturb any of Kelly's precious possessions when she had to clean the room.

There were also curtains, carpets and rugs to be ordered. On her mother's advice she bought only the very basic needs for the kitchen. 'You will get so many things of that kind as well as ornaments and bedlinen as wedding presents,' Leonora told her.

As they checked over the list of guests who'd been invited to the reception, Penny was disconcerted when she saw that Arnold's name as well as that of his parents were on the guest list.

'We couldn't very well ask Mr and Mrs Watson and not include Arnold, now could we,' her mother stated.

'Well, let's hope he doesn't accept. I shall feel very uneasy if I know he is in the church, or at the reception,' Penny muttered.

Kelly was so excited by all that was happening that Penny took her along to Ellison Brothers in Liscard Village so that she could choose the wallpaper for her own bedroom. There were so many pattern books to look through and so many pretty wallpapers that Kelly took a long time to make up her mind. Penny thought she might like one with animals or even fairies on it but Kelly was reluctant. Eventually, with the help of Penny and one of the assistants, she chose one that had sprigs of wild flowers scattered over it.

A week later Penny took her mother to Belgrave Street so that she could see for herself how very different it looked now that the final decorating had been completed and the new furniture installed.

'Its transformed it from a shell into a home,' Mrs Forshaw enthused. 'I'm sure you and Bryn are going to be very happy here,' she added with a warm smile.

'And Kelly as well,' Penny reminded her.

'Yes, of course. I hadn't forgotten about Kelly. You might like to have some time to yourselves, though, so why don't you leave her with us, just for a week or so until you are settled in.'

Before Penny could respond there was a loud knocking on the front door. Penny and her mother looked at each other in surprise.

'Who on earth can that be,' Penny said, frowning.

'I do hope it's not Bryn,' her mother said sharply. 'Its your wedding day tomorrow and it would be most unlucky for him to see—'

Her comment was cut short abruptly as the kitchen door opened and Arnold Watson walked in.

'I was passing and I knew you were here because there was a blue Austin parked in the driveway and I can't think of anyone else who owns such a car,' he said. 'I think it must be fate working for me because I was on my way to Penkett Road with a wedding present for you.'

Ostentatiously he held out a large flat package wrapped in shiny white paper and trimmed with silver ribbon.

Penny hesitated. 'I've already received a very handsome gift from your parents,' she murmured making no attempt to take it from him.

'This is from me; a personal gift. One which I hope will bring back memories,' he added, a strange glint in his eyes as she took it from him.

'How very intriguing, do open it, Penny. I'd love to see what it is,' Mrs Forshaw gushed.

Rather reluctantly Penny began to untie the silver gilt ribbon and then to remove the wrapping. Inside was a large framed picture in a heavy silver frame. As she stared at it the colour rose to her cheeks and there was anger in her eyes as she looked at Arnold.

'What is it, may I see it?' Mrs Forshaw held out her hand and Penny passed the framed picture over to her mother.

'The Kiss,' Mrs Forshaw murmured. 'Why, that's by Gustav Klimt, isn't it? A very famous painting.'

'This is only a print, I'm afraid.' Arnold laughed. 'Even with my wealth I couldn't afford the real thing.'

'It's certainly very colourful, very expressive – and of course he's quite a modern artist. I believe it was painted in 1908 or just earlier, shortly before the war wasn't it?'

She studied the picture more closely. 'A man and woman kissing in a field of flowers. Yes, very pretty.'

'Something I hope Penny will always treasure. I thought it might be rather nice for you to have in your bedroom.' He smiled as he took the picture back from Mrs Forshaw and handed it to Penny. 'I have a replica of it as well and I particularly like the golden halo that surrounds the couple. It brings back such wonderful memories of what used to happen and what might have been.' He smiled again and then looked at his watch. 'I must be off. I have an important business appointment to keep, but when I saw your car outside, Penny, it seemed to be such an admirable opportunity to give you your present and to wish you good luck for your forthcoming wedding.'

Before Penny knew what was happening he had grabbed her by the shoulders and implanted a hard deep kiss on her unresponsive mouth.

She was shaking so much when he released her that the picture she was still holding crashed to the floor and there was the sound of shattering glass as it hit the ground.

'Oh dear, how very symbolic,' Arnold said dryly as he bent down and picked it up. 'Still, it is only the glass that is broken and that can easily be replaced.'

Thirty-Three

To Penny's relief the fourth of April dawned sunny and promised to be quite warm; a perfect spring day. It seemed to her to be a good omen; a sign that, rather like Kelly's adoption, everything was going right.

After a leisurely breakfast, as she began dressing ready for her wedding, Penny's spirits soared. Everything was working out so wonderfully well. She was reconciled with her parents and very soon Kelly would be officially in her care for ever.

Her wedding was the pinnacle of all her dreams, she thought contentedly. She was marrying a man she truly loved; one she trusted and one who loved her and put her happiness and well-being before anything else.

As she slipped the billowing mass of silk and lace over her head, she stood there reflecting on her good fortune as her mother fussed around her, tweaking the material this way and that to make sure every fold was in its right place.

Although, like Bryn, she had initially wanted to have a very quiet wedding, Penny realized that so many people had become involved that the church would be packed. As well as friends and family some of her father's business associates would be there as well as a great many representatives from the various committees that both her parents were on.

Bryn's family, who had travelled from North Wales to Wallasey the previous day were staying at a hotel in New Brighton. Bryn's eldest brother was to be best man and his other brothers would be assisting as ushers.

Mrs Forshaw, wearing a pearl grey outfit and a matching picture hat trimmed with pale cream artificial roses, left Penkett Road for the church with Kelly five minutes before Penny.

Bryn and his best man, both in morning dress, were waiting at the altar steps when Penny arrived. Bryn drew in an audible gasp as Penny, looking slim and lovely in her flowing white lace wedding dress, came down the aisle towards him on the arm of

Captain Forshaw who was resplendent in tails. Kelly, as her bridesmaid, was walking a few steps in front of her and looked very pretty in her pale blue dress that was trimmed with white lace.

'It's like living in a fairytale,' Kelly exclaimed to Leonora Forshaw, her eyes shining, when afterwards they all posed for the wedding photographs, before a cavalcade of motor cars transported them all to the reception at the Grand Hotel in New Brighton.

At the end of the meal Kelly watched in awe as Bryn put his arm around Penny's waist and more photographs were taken when together they cut the impressive three-tiered wedding cake.

'I wish I could come with you,' Kelly sighed dreamily when Penny, who had now changed out of her wedding dress into her going away outfit of a pale blue tweed suit and soft white jumper, rejoined them a little later ready to leave for their honeymoon in Scotland.

'I'm afraid it is not allowed,' Bryn told her gravely. 'You have to be the one to stay here and look after Captain and Mrs Forshaw. We also want you to make sure that Dillwyn has our new home in Belgrave Street all ready for us when we come home.'

'You are going to let me live there with you?' Kelly asked anxiously as Penny hugged her and kissed her goodbye.

'Of course we are; for ever and ever. You have even chosen which room you want and how it was to be decorated,' Penny reminded her.

'Yes, we are all three going to live there happily ever after,' Bryn promised as he kissed the top of Kelly's head.

Kelly's smile returned. She stood on the footpath between Captain and Leonora Forshaw, along with Bryn's family and other friends, waving until Penny and Bryn's car turned the corner and they were lost from view.